LENA WOOD

ELIJAH CREEK & THE ARMOR of GOD

VOL. I

BOOK 1: THE SEVERED HEAD

BOOK 2: THE ANCIENT OMEN

Cover art and map illustrations by Daniel Armstrong

Printed in the United States of America
Published by Braughler Books LLC., Springboro, OH

Second edition, first printing, 2018

ISBN: 978-1-945091-91-9

Library of Congress Control Number: 2018956649

Ordering information: Special discounts are available on quantity purchases by bookstores, corporations, associations, and others. For details, contact the publisher at:

sales@braughlerbooks.com
or at 937-58-BOOKS

For questions or comments about this book, please write to:

info@braughlerbooks.com

Braughler™
Books
braughlerbooks.com

all praise & thanks to

Yahweh, the Greatest Spirit
the Ancient Omen, still speaking

THE SEVERED HEAD

BOOK 1

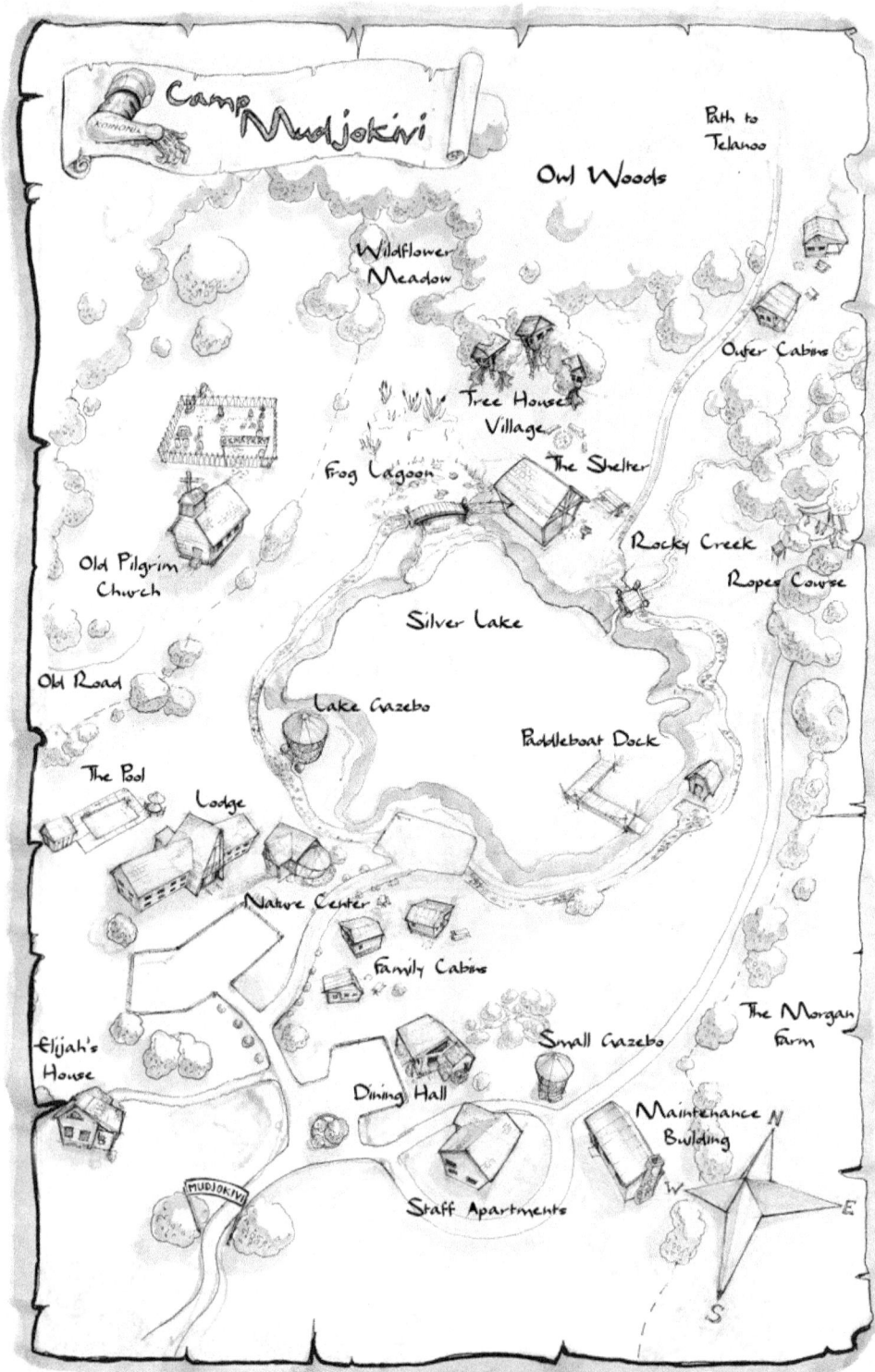

CHAPTER 1

Never—not in my wildest dreams—did I ever imagine that an innocent peek into an old church would change my life forever, turning me into the wild vagabond I am now. But it did.

My name is Elijah Creek, and I descended from the Creek Indians—at least I always hoped so. My dad's family came from southern Georgia where the Creek nation lived. We didn't know where mom came from. She was adopted. But since her hair and eyes are dark, I thought she might be Indian too.

Sometimes I wonder what would have happened if I hadn't volunteered as a stagehand for the junior high play. We were doing *The Adventures of Tom Sawyer.* I wanted to be Injun Joe—I had the dark hair and eyes for the role—but I can't act.

My cousin Robbie…now he could act. We were nothing alike, and I mean nothing. I lived in a log house in Camp Mudjokivi, a nature camp my dad ran. Robbie lived in what everyone in town called The Castle. It was old and drafty and had a tower with mice—or worse—living in the walls. His parents had plans to make it into a bed-and-breakfast, but I hadn't seen much progress. It looked more like Bates Motel from the movie *Psycho.*

Robbie was ready to turn fourteen but could have passed for eleven. I called him Chunk. He called me Rail. He sings an acts; I draw a little. I've always liked the wild outdoors, while he's an indoor person and likes studying history and stuff. So he's not the coolest cube in the tray. But we got along.

That fall, Robbie had roped some of us into helping with costumes, set building, and the dangerous work of hanging lights, curtains, and backdrops. We'd been through our basements and attics, searching for curtains and costumes and backdrops, but with no luck.

Reece Elliston called me after an hour of searching and said, "No luck here. All our curtains are hanging in windows, and we don't have any pioneer-type dresses."

"We're going to have to branch out," I said. "Robbie had an idea that the old church may have some curtains. Want to check it out?"

"Sure. Can Mei come too?"

When Reece did anything, Mei wasn't far behind. They were opposites too. Mei had dark eyes and short dark hair to Reece's long blond hair and blue eyes. Mei was shy while Reece spoke her mind. I think they struck up a friendship because they were a little different from everyone else: Mei's from Japan, and was still working on her English. Reece had this bone condition, and sometimes had to use a cane.

By the time all of us—Robbie and me, Reece and Mei— were done with dinners and homework and had met up on my porch, it was nearly dark. The days were getting shorter already.

The only reason I hadn't explored the church was because it was condemned and Dad said no. But I hadn't asked about it for a long time.

Old Pilgrim Church and the graveyard behind it sat on a grassy hill surrounded by an overgrown meadow and woods, west of Camp Mudjokivi where I lived. The camp hooked up with the Morgan farm to the east. To the north was a big scary hunk of land I named Telanoo, which sounds Indian, and is short for The Land No One Owns. Owl Woods, the camp's nature preserve, bled over into Telanoo.

Mom was upstairs with the twins, so I asked my dad if we could investigate the old church, and first he said no, it could be dangerous. Then right in the middle of our conversation the phone rang and while he was talking I mouthed the words, "I'll be careful," as I backed out of the house. So he nodded and waved me off. I have lots of duties around camp, and Dad pretty much lets me have the run of the place because he knows I'm responsible.

· · · · ·

The old church was locked. But one of the basement windows was broken so it wasn't really like breaking in, though Reece said it was.

I kicked out the rest of the glass and checked for sharp edges where I'd be crawling through. Before going in I turned to Reece. "You don't think God will strike me with lightning, do you?" I liked kidding Reece about her religion.

She grinned. But then she threw in, "You'll probably be okay. Just don't slash an artery on that broken glass."

Reece—for all her sweetness—has an acid streak. And just when you least expect it, she'll get a dig in. She seems fragile because of her looks—she's small and sort of pale—but she's not.

I dropped into the church basement. There was barely enough twilight coming in to see my way up the stairs. I reached out the broken window for Robbie's flashlight. He was chickening out already. I could see it on his face.

"Forget it," I said and sent him and the girls around to the front door. I'd been training myself to see better at night, but on my way through the basement and up the stairs I heard skittering noises from one of the dark corners: big sounds, not so different from the ones Robbie and I hear in the walls at The Castle. I couldn't see what it was. Pretty creepy.

By the time they got to the front door, I'd unbolted it from the inside. We lost most of the natural light in that few minutes, but we went prowling anyway. The girls stayed close to Robbie because he had the flashlight. Reece can't afford to fall and break anything, so I warned them that the floor slanted down to the front stage. There was hardly anything inside except for a few rows of old fold-down seats. The place was musty smelling and a weird kind of cold, even though outside was warm and mellow.

"Usually there would be a velvet curtain in front of the baptistery," whispered Reece, as we crept toward the stage, "and some short curtains in front of the choir loft. The railing is still there, but someone must have taken the curtains when the church closed. Let's check downstairs. Some old churches use curtains as classroom dividers."

We made our way to the stairs. "Don't be afraid if you see a mouse, or a rat," I cautioned. "I heard noises down there."

Reece turned to Mei and whispered, "Mice, maybe. *Daijoubu.*"

"It is all right," Mei said. She and Reece often swapped words. Reece would say it in Japanese, then Mei would say it in English, or vice versa, to learn each other's language.

It's amazing how quick it gets dark, once the sun drops into the woods.

I helped Reece down to the basement where there was nothing more than three squares of gray light coming through the windows—one minus all its glass—and Robbie's flashlight.

"Hold it steady," I told him. "You're going to rattle all the life out of it."

Something scratched at the floor behind us. Reece and Mei sucked in air.

Robbie whispered, "Let's go."

"Why are you whispering, silly?" I asked loudly, kicking at a piece of trash on the floor. "Let's show those rats we're here." I was talking and kicking my way into being the brave one. My mind knew there was nothing to be afraid of, but my heart was thumping. "This was your idea anyway, Robbie. We'll have one quick look around and be done."

In a minute we were stuck together like one person with eight shuffling feet and four heads. Four pairs of eyes bugged out, trying to pick details out of the dark. We followed Robbie's shaky flashlight beam around the room: just cement block walls oozing ground water and three or four doors.

"Classrooms," Reece whispered, nodding toward the doors. I had just said that whispering was dumb. Obviously, she hadn't taken my lead.

"Classrooms, yeah, I know," I said, though as far as churches went, I really didn't know the layout.

There was pretty much nothing downstairs, except for a rusty furnace at the far end, and what looked like a door behind it made of painted planks. Reece spotted the door too.

"Storage," I guessed.

"Probably," she said.

We all moved as a clump in that direction and watched the door for a minute. Robbie's eyes were like glass marbles. I could tell he was more than ready to leave.

"Let's look in there," I said.

"It is okay?" Mei asked.

"It's okay," I said, and shook the others off. "If there are any curtains, I bet they'll be in there."

The door was swollen shut with dampness and age, but a few good yanks and we were suddenly looking into a low, pitch-black room with a dirt floor.

"It's a crawl space," I said.

Robbie moved the beam slowly around the wall. There were no shelves or boxes, only large hooks embedded in the stone walls.

"Hooks," Robbie breathed.

I knew what he was thinking: torture chamber. But they were just for hanging stuff on.

On the left wall was a doorway, or rather a place broken open in the damp stones, big enough for someone to walk through. Robbie's flashlight beam danced on that black hole. None of us wanted to go any farther. What was in there? I just had to know.

"Come on." My voice had dropped into a whisper despite my best effort. We were in a clump again, moving toward the hole…through the hole…into a small, damp room. Robbie's light dipped to the dirt floor. The girls gasped. My heart—which was already thumping at fifty miles a minute—jumped into my throat and lodged there. Along the far wall there was a mound of dirt, human size: rounded at the top, squarish at the bottom.

I could barely even breathe the words: "A grave."

We were all frozen in place for a moment. What happened next would shove my heart back down into my chest and throw every muscle into superhuman speed and strength mode. From somewhere behind us came a sound soft as a whisper…*scuff*…*scuff*…*scuff*….Immediately my mind whirled back to the minute before when I was practically yelling, and suddenly I wished I'd kept my big mouth shut. Somebody was out there and unless they were deaf, they knew exactly where we were: in a makeshift mausoleum with only one way out.

CHAPTER 2

Ideas flipped through my mind like a deck of cards. I grabbed Robbie's hand and turned off the flashlight, throwing us into pitch dark. We could make a run for it, except for Reece, and I'd have to carry her. I'd noticed Mei going stiff as a board as I flipped off the light. *I might have to carry her too.*

There was one more *scuff,* then the sound stopped.

He knows we're here, I thought to myself. I figured he was about halfway across the basement, between us and the stairs.

My eyes adjusted and fixed on the patch of gray that was the doorway. My ears stayed cued. I hoped with every pounding in my chest that a dark shape wouldn't move into that gray doorway. I had no weapon. The flashlight was still in Robbie's hand, and if I grabbed it again, he'd think I was *him* and die right there, or worse, start screaming like a banshee.

Scuff scuff…snt-snt-snt. The sound was getting fainter. He was leaving, tiptoeing up the stairs. I thought, *Maybe he has no right to be here either. Maybe we're no more intruders than him… or it…or whatever.* I'm not a real believer in ghosts, but in a church basement grave in the murky dark, when your knees turn to jelly, so does your brain. But I was in charge, so it was up to me to take the lead.

All quiet.

None of us moved.

"Stay," I whispered. "Give me the flashlight."

I took it from Robbie's hand, crept out into the basement, turned the flashlight on and swept the room. Nothing. "Let's go!" I whispered back to the others.

There was a scuffle behind me, and in a second Robbie was pressed against my back, Mei behind him. I curled my arm around Reece, half carrying her as we flew across the church basement and up the stairs. We were light as feathers on those old planks. Reece's feet hardly touched the floor.

I turned the flashlight off right before we got outside. The moon was just above the trees, in gibbous stage, making the lake a shimmery sheet before us. The light of the moon above and its reflection on water below washed the landscape of the camp in phosphorous magic. I breathed in relief at the sight of it. Scared as I was, we were really only a few hundred yards from home. I peeked around the corners of the old church. No one was running down to the lake, or through the graveyard to the north. And the open meadow with woods beyond on the side farthest from camp—empty. Whoever he was, he had disappeared like mist.

Reece was breathing hard. I took a few gulps of air myself. Mei sniffled and looked at Reece and kept repeating something in Japanese that sounded like tie-hen. I think Robbie was crying, at least on the inside. We were over the fence and on our way to the lake path when he burst out with a flood of questions.

"Who was that?" he asked. "Do you think he knew we were there? There's somebody buried in there, Elijah! What are we gonna do? A murder! I can't believe it! A murderer at Camp Mudj?!"

"Shhh! Come on!" I said. "To the lodge!"

I led the way, since I know every square inch of the camp, every gopher hole and every dip in the trail. I kept looking back, wondering how that man or creature or whatever it was could have vanished like that.

There'd been a staff meeting in the lodge earlier, so the fire was still going, but down to embers. The only other lights were the red exit signs above the doors. We got Reece a pillow and sat on the floor. I tossed a log on the fire.

"We've got to go back," I said.

Mei's eyes got wide and she made an owl-type moan. "Noooooo. Terrible!"

"Taihen!" Reece cried.

"Not tonight," I corrected, "later. Tomorrow. By light of day."

Reece had caught her breath by now. "We were trespassing and we got caught."

"We didn't get caught!" I said.

"We did!" she snapped.

"Whoever he was, he left when he heard us, so he had no business being there either," I defended.

"Somebody's buried in that room!" said Robbie, his eyes glowing orange from the embers.

Costumes and curtains seemed much less important than looking for a church phantom and doing a little digging in that basement. But here was the problem: a full schedule of events at Camp Mudjokivi. It would be risky to get back into the basement without being seen; a hundred squealing kids from New-point and Northwest Elementary schools were scheduled for an overnighter. They'd be swarming the place with leaf books, butterfly nets, and bug boxes. (It's a wonder Camp Mudj hasn't been picked clean by now, with all those bugs getting regularly carted off to their doom.) A church group was coming for a "prayer retreat" at the lodge too. Camp was booked solid.

We stared at the fire. The girls would back out, I figured. But I wasn't going by myself. Robbie might need some arm-twisting. I could see in his eyes that raccoon-stuck-on-the-screen-door look, a "What in the world was I thinking, how did I get myself here?" kind of look. I almost laughed.

"I'll do the digging," I coaxed. "And if I...hit...anything..." I paused. Robbie turned a little green, so I added, "Hey, you know, it could be buried treasure."

"Oh sure," he said sarcastically. "The pirates of Ohio with their gold doubloons and pieces of eight—buried in the shape of a body. Right."

"Other people than pirates bury treasures!" I defended.

"Like who?"

"Rich people who don't trust their relatives. And...and eccentric old women with thirty cats and stuff like that. I'm just saying we don't know what's there until we dig. It just doesn't make sense to bury a body there when there's a cemetery right out the back door."

"Maybe he makes it look like body, so no one touch it," Mei suggested.

"Good thinking," Reece told Mei. "This is dangerous, Elijah."

Mei nodded. "Maybe we should not touch it."

"Well, I'm not digging," Robbie said, crossing his arms.

"And I said you don't have to. You hold the flashlight."

"I may not even watch."

"I don't care."

He slumped a little, like he was giving in. I was ready to do it by myself, if necessary. But I really needed someone to come with me...to hold the light.

CHAPTER 3

It ate at me, wondering what was in that basement, but I finished out the week of school and waited for the elementary kids and the prayer retreat people to leave. Aunt Grace, Uncle Dorian, and Robbie came over for Sunday brunch. My cousin had mustered his courage by then. While they had coffee and dessert, we got ready to go.

Then it poured rain and the lodge roof started leaking again. Dad had us moving buckets around for the rest of the afternoon.

"Did you find what you needed in the old church?" Dad asked out of the blue as we mopped up the last of the leaks and put chairs out in rows.

Robbie kept his head bent to the task of mopping, but shot me a look.

"Nah," I said casually. "Nothing there. It was a bust."

"I don't know what you're looking for…"

"Curtains, backdrops. Big stuff to paint or hang. We have to come up with the play scenery ourselves."

"There's some canvas from that party tent that fell to pieces. It's still in the maintenance building, stored with the lumber."

"Thanks. We'll take a look at it," I said.

"What was in the old church?" he asked curiously.

"Nothing, Dad. Just a few seats. That's all."

"And rats and ghosts," Robbie said with a fake laugh.

"Should be torn down, really. Or burned…dangerous old eyesore," Dad said, surveying the ceiling for drips. "The fire department could use it for practice."

Robbie and I eyed each other and brain-waved *uh-oh*.

· · · · ·

From the window in my room, I'd kept a nightly stakeout on the church with my binoculars for as long as I could stay awake. The gibbous moon had grown to full and gave good light, except when night clouds turned the whole camp to one big shadow.

On Monday after homework and dinner, Robbie and I set out for the old church. Clouds were low and purple and heavy. Heat from the lake had made a fog. Twilight came early.

I couldn't get him past the fence.

We squatted there behind a hedge of Virginia creeper vines, which separated camp from church property—him with the flashlight and a sock cap over his blond hair, me with a shovel—just staring at Old Pilgrim Church while the purple clouds overhead got lower and darker.

Finally, out of frustration, I leaped the vine-covered wire fence and left him hunkered down by himself. I hoped he'd follow, from loneliness if nothing else.

"C'mon. Let's go. If we get in any kind of trouble, I'll take the—" I broke off when a movement up the hill caught my eye.

A hunched, sickly silhouette with a cone of light coming out of his belly moved through the fog. It was an old man creeping from the church with a flashlight in one hand, a sack and a long stick in the other. In a minute I could make out that the stick was actually a shovel. Robbie had stood and reared back to make the leap over the fence, so I jabbed a finger in the direction of the old church. He spotted the old man and froze. I shoved him back down behind the fence.

Stashing myself as far into the Virginia creepers as I could, I was still in plain sight if the man—not a hundred yards away—should look my way.

Don't look, I thought. *Don't look, don't look.*

Fog and clouds had turned Camp Mudjokivi from a fun nature camp into one of those old black-and-white horror movies. The old man made his way through the tombstones and stopped. He put the sack down and started digging. This was going to take a while.

"'Lijah!" Robbie whispered through the fence.

"Can you see him?" I asked.

"Sort of."

"Stay put."

"'Kay."

Time passed. My leg went to sleep, so I poked at it to wake it up. I had to be ready to run, just in case. I pictured myself trying to get away, dragging one leg behind me through the fog like in an old mummy movie, and nearly got tickled, in spite of my predicament. I wasn't really too scared. After all, what could one old man do to me?

He was digging a pretty deep hole, though the sack wasn't big enough for a whole body. I started getting the creeps thinking about what might be in that sack, and hoped Robbie wasn't thinking the same thing.

Don't come calling for me, Mom, I said in a prayer to the air. *I'm okay.*

Finally the old man put his shovel down and started messing with the sack. I fought off getting sick when he pulled out a limp arm and dropped it in the hole. Then he pulled out something round—a head!

He held it in his hands, looking at it for a minute as if to tell it good-bye, and then dropped it in the hole too.

He started shoveling again, more hurriedly and with a lot of scraping noises.

"Did you see?..." came a little mouse voice through the creeper vines.

"Yeah," I whispered back.

"A head!"

"Yeah…"

"And an arm!"

"Shhh!"

"He murdered someone and stuck 'em in the church until—"

"Shhh!" I said again.

Sometimes fog conducts sound. If we could hear every scrape of his shovel, I reckoned he might be able to hear our whispers, even above night sounds from the woods and cars on the road headed toward town. He threw the sack into the grave, shoveled a few more minutes, and wiped his forehead with the back of his hand. He went back through the tombstones just the way he'd come, now dragging the shovel behind him. He stopped once, looked back at the cemetery, and brought his shoulders up, then down, like he was heaving a big sigh.

Then he looked in our direction.

I tried to be invisible by very slowly inching my way even farther under the vines, careful not to snap a twig or crunch a leaf. *Quiet, Robbie,* I kept saying in another air prayer, *don't freak out. He's not looking at us, but above our heads at the lake. That's all. He's done the deed and he's feeling satisfied. Whatever you do, don't throw up!*

Fog glided up from the lake and swallowed the old man just before he went behind the church. I took the opportunity to leap back over the fence…and came down on Robbie's back.

For me it was like landing on a tight, sweaty roll of sleeping bags. For him it must have been like getting showered with an armload of baseball bats. My worst fear at that second was that Robbie would yell and give us away. But even as my knees and elbows punched holes in him, Robbie went facedown into the ground with a quiet "Ghhhfmm." It was admirable.

I rolled off him and landed on one knee, puzzled for a second as to where my other knee was.

Somehow my right foot had gotten stuck in the fence. For a really awkward few seconds I was stuck there, my arms thrown out for balance, one knee lodged in the damp ground, one leg stretched out behind me. I bet I looked ridiculous, like a water fountain statue without the fountain.

I yanked my foot free from the wire fence, and down I hurtled, head over heels. There we were, spread-eagled side by side, him facedown, me faceup on the grass. We didn't move. We listened. I turned my eyes up the hill for any hint of a beam of light coming our way.

"You okay?" I asked.

He panted a couple of times. "Yeah. Did you see that? It's a murder! We've got to call the cops!"

"Hold on. Shhh. He's still in the church. He may be able to—"

"Elijaaah!"

My heart thudded to a stop. Mom's voice rang across all hundred acres of the camp and into the next county.

I was on my feet in half a second, flying down the hill to the lake like I had wings, hoping Robbie was behind me. If Mom could catch sight of me, she'd stop calling; if not, I had about five seconds before her voice would ring out again, loud enough to rattle the windows in Old Pilgrim Church. I hoped the old man didn't hear. He was still in the basement probably, putting the shovel away…or digging up the rest of—

"Elijaaah!"

Drats!

Heart pounding, legs burning, I zipped along the lake path, then cut back up the hill toward home, wishing there was woods or a building between Old Pilgrim Church and me, or that the fog would swallow me. The main part of the camp was a bowl shape. Sound carried. Every morning we'd hear old Mr. Morgan sneeze, regular as a rooster at dawn, from his back porch through the strip of woods way on the other side of camp. Through that broken basement window, I was betting the old grave digger could hear our feet pounding the pavement of the lake path, and Mom yelling my name, clear as a bell.

I glanced back. The church was little more than a black cutout on a gray background, the tombstones little tabs drifting through the creeping fog. Robbie stumbled up the hill behind me, panting and holding his side.

I dashed the last hundred yards of the driveway. Mom was on the porch. I waved and she waved back, happy to see me but annoyed. "Elijah, I forgot about the PTO meeting. We have to leave in five minutes or we'll be ridiculously late," she said, tossing her long hair, digging keys out of her purse. "Change clothes and bring your homework."

"I already did my homework."

She opened the screen for us. "The first PTO meeting of the school year tends to run long. And the play meeting! You didn't tell me about that."

"I'm just a stagehand."

"But I think you're supposed to be there, and Robbie's in the cast. Grace called wondering where he is. She's on her way there now. Didn't you have a note or something about it?

I couldn't get a baby-sitter on such short notice, so if your meeting about the play gets done early, you can watch the girls and do your homework in the back of the commons."

"I already did my—"

"Girls! Time to go!" she called up the steps. "You're muddy, Robbie. Have you boys been wrestling?"

Bounding up to my room, proud of the speed of my long legs, I had changed clothes before Robbie could drag his short self up the stairs.

"You ran off and left me out there!" Robbie wheezed.

"Did not! I had to get to Mom before she gave us away."

"Did he see us?"

"Nah."

He ran a hand over his blond head. "My cap! It's out there!"

"We'll get it later." I shoved a book into my pack and rooted around my desk for a couple of pencils. Mom seemed determined that I still had homework to do. Better to play along.

"What if he saw us?" Robbie asked. "What if he knows that we saw what he did?"

"He doesn't know who we are."

"If he heard your mom call you, then he knows your name."

A chill ran down my spine, but I kept my voice steady. "He'd think I was a camper, one of a hundred."

"We should call the cops," Robbie said, still panting as he scraped mud off his pants leg with his thumbnail.

He was right. I knew that. But I slung my pack over my shoulder and snapped, "We're not leaking a word, not until we've thought this over. Sleep on it, okay. Lock your doors and windows tonight and just sleep on it. Something just doesn't make sense."

We raced down the steps. I made sure the door was locked behind me, though in Magdeline, Ohio, we hardly ever bother.

But this time I locked it, because as we'd dashed past the nature center and the lodge, what I saw—and what I wish I hadn't seen—was the grave digger man standing on the stoop of that old wreck of a building, staring pretty much in my direction.

I couldn't let my imagination run away. There was no way of knowing if he saw us. It was pretty dark. He might have been staring down at the lake, like before, very pleased with himself.

We were probably okay, I said to myself. *Yeah, we're okay.*

CHAPTER 4

Robbie ran up to me in the school hallway the next day. "So!?"

"I don't know yet."

"You said you'd sleep on it. Did you find my cap?"

"I didn't sleep much, and no. It's probably still at the fence." I'd spent a good deal of the night watching out the window, grateful I was safe on the second floor, glad that the house stairs creaked when anyone climbed them.

"Hi."

Reece and Mei were waiting at my locker.

"Hi."

I tried to put on my best face, but it was too late. Reece picks up on people's looks—she can almost tell what they're thinking. It's spooky how good she is at it.

"What's wrong?" she asked.

"Wrong?" I asked innocently. "I'm still looking for costumes, if that's what you mean. No luck yet." Kind of a lie, and the last thing on my mind. But sort of true.

Reece rolled her eyes like I'd insulted her.

Robbie looked at me and I looked back at him. We had to tell them or they'd just keep pecking at us like hens until we did.

"Gather in," I said. We made a huddle in front of my locker. Robbie and I took turns summing up what happened, except for me telling the part about seeing the old man on the church stoop afterwards looking like he saw us, and about losing sleep over what it all meant. That could wait.

"You have to call the police!" Reece said.

"We don't know it was a murder," I defended.

"People who lose a head and an arm usually die," she said sarcastically.

"It was the shape of a head and arm, but we don't know—"

"Buried in a graveyard?! What do you think it is, a bowling ball and a…a…arm-shaped thing!?"

"Okay, okay! Keep your voice down."

The last thing we needed was a bunch of other kids with appetites for treasure or detective work listening in, wanting a piece of the action.

Mei politely warned, "The bell will ring."

Reece nodded Mei on to her class and winced as she turned herself down the hall. She had her cane today. I couldn't help wondering if the escape from the church—me dragging her up the steps and across the camp last week—had been too much of a strain. I suddenly felt guilty, remembering how I'd crossed the camp last night in roughly fourteen seconds—like I had wings. She'd never be able to run like that, free as a bird. I couldn't think about it.

I followed her and whispered in her ear. "Hey, don't say anything about this, okay. Let's all decide together. Whatever we do, Reece, you're a part of it, okay?"

She stopped and smiled. "Thanks, Elijah."

"I value your input."

She laughed. *"Value my input?* Where'd you get that crazy phrase?"

I grinned. "That's what Mom says the president of the PTO says to the parents when they disagree over things."

"I bet they say that when somebody has a stupid idea, and they don't know how to shut 'em up."

Reece gets to the root of things.

"I really mean it," I said. "See you in English."

* * * * *

At lunch Robbie and I sat in the cafeteria and talked in code.

We have to be in "second lunch," which is just a nicey-nice name for: all-the-pizza-and-cookies-are-gone-but-we-still-have-plenty-of-things-like-creamed-corn-and-shepherd's-pie. (The eighth grade pretty much believes that shepherd's pie is either made out of old shepherds, or what old shepherds scrape off their shoes.) The senior highers who have cars skip second lunch and drive to the Whippy Dip for its famous cheeseburgers and raspberry milkshakes.

Over stiff veal parmesan and cold succotash that day, Robbie and I decided our options about the mystery were to *spill* (tell the police), *talk* (tell our parents) or *dig* (check out the grave ourselves). We couldn't spill without talking first, or our parents would explode. So that narrowed our choices to talk or dig. Robbie was for talking. I was for digging. Despite how things looked, I had a nagging feeling in the back of my mind that things weren't what they seemed. Or maybe I just couldn't get my mind around a murder at Camp Mudj. My camp. My home!

"Why would he bury a whole body in a church basement, then move part of it to a cemetery?" I asked. "It's loons."

"Maybe he could only carry parts at a time. And maybe he's moving it because he knows we were there. He's hiding the evidence."

"But why only a few feet away, in a fresh grave that would be easy to find?"

He didn't have an answer.

I don't mind saying I wasn't crazy about getting cornered in that dark hole under the church again. So we worked out a compromise. We'd start digging in the cemetery—better for quick getaway. We'd dig only until we found the sack, no deeper, and decide what to do after that.

"If it is a body," I said, "there'll be evidence on the sack: blood or hair. We can tell the police we saw the old man and thought he was burying treasure. It's a good 'kid answer.' We won't get into trouble."

Robbie was satisfied. Next we had to convince the girls that we should dig. After science, I followed Reece to homeroom. We sat in the back, next to the window.

"It's not exactly true," Reece said, referring to what Robbie and I planned on telling the police if we found a body.

"It's half true."

"Hidden in half-truths are full-blown lies," she said in a preachy tone.

"Is that in the Bible or something?" I snapped. She made a deadpan face, as if I was an idiot.

"We'll just dig down to the sack, no farther," I said.

"It's evidence."

"Not if there's no crime."

I was right and she knew it. Really, honestly, if I had thought we had a real murder on our hands, I would have told Dad. The last thing I'd want was Camp Mudj in the headlines and me on the front page of the paper. Mom would be the first to serve me a sentence—probably baby-sitting my six-year-old twin sisters, Nori and Stacy, twenty years to life.

Reece thought about what I suggested and stared out the window, her eyes darting across the school yard, looking at nothing. Her eyes looked extra light blue and she seemed pale. She was probably in pain.

"I want to be there," she said finally. Then we had to shut up because there were announcements coming over the PA.

I was glad she wanted to be a part of my plan. But...what if we had to make a quick getaway? What if the man should come while we're digging, start shooting at us, or something? How could I...

As the announcements rambled on, she slipped me a note: *I know you think I'll just slow you down.* She'd read my mind.

This was the jam I always got in with Reece. She was a good friend and not giggly and dumb like most other girls. She was interested in Indians too. Pretty much everyone liked her, but no one hung around her much because she couldn't keep up. Some days she'd be fine and others she'd be on crutches. It was hard to know how to treat her. I'd seen adults talk almost baby talk to her when she was on crutches, like having weak bones made you dumb.

Ever since Reece and I became project partners last year and won the regional science fair, we'd stayed friends.

I studied her note a minute and wrote back: *You and Mei can be our lookouts, okay? We'll use Dad's walkie-talkies. They reach as far as the cemetery. You can watch from the lodge and hear what's happening. If something goes wrong, you'll be first to know.*

This idea she liked. She whispered. "And a phone's nearby. In case."

The bell rang, and we gathered our books. "Exactly," I said. "And if something happens, you're safe."

"What about you?" she asked with worry in her voice.

"He couldn't catch me. I'm fast enough to—" There I went again, bragging. "I...I'm fine. I'll be fine."

"It's all right, Elijah. I know I can't run. It's a great idea about the walkie-talkies. We'll do it that way. You're a genius."

CHAPTER 5

Robbie stayed after school to run lines for the play. It was raining out, but I walked home instead of taking the bus so I could clear my head. The afternoon rain darkened the colors of the leaves to deep green and amber and rust. A few cars swished by on the wet street. The air smelled of earth and leaves. Even in town you're never far from nature. Cut from east to west by one main drag with a few blocks of businesses, Magdeline, Ohio, is lopsided: most of the homes are on the south side. On the north, a couple of little alleys lead down behind the businesses to parking lots, but there's not much else in the way of civilization except for camp and the Morgan farm.

Lots of kids in Magdeline wished they lived in a big city, with movie theaters, fancy restaurants, sports arenas, and malls. They have a point. In the restaurant department, we only have the Whippy Dip, two pizza places, and Florence's—also known as The Greasy Cup, because the coffee comes with a free oil slick on it—where no one under eighteen would be caught dead. We have a drive-in theater, one of the few left in the state, but it's closed half the time. If you need clothes, there's just one sad little department store and a Family Bargain Mart down the road in a shopping center not worth diddly-squat. For sports there's just school football, basketball, and some summer leagues. What you see is what you get.

So Magdeline's not the greatest. But I have to tell you, living at a camp has just about every advantage in the world: a log house to live in with a loft and fireplace; the A-frame lodge and cafeteria with an even bigger fireplace; the lake, the pool, the ropes course and trails; a real lagoon and wildflower meadow; our nature center is home to snakes and lizards. And working for my dad is the best.

The disadvantages are the regular truckloads of little kids running around and Dad being on call twenty-four hours a day. Sometimes the phone will ring at midnight, or later, the nurse reporting some kid with screaming nightmares or appendicitis. Or a raccoon topples a trash can at 3:00 in the morning and scares a bunch of little girls. Or a sewage pipe busts and leaks all over the camp. When Dad's out till daybreak, Mom gets upset and tells him to hire more help. He'll say we can't afford it, and they'll get into a tiff.

I was thinking about all the fall activities—hayrides and hot dog roasts, and planning for Halloween: the "Spiders, Bats, and Other Creepy Things Week," and how the play was pressing down on me, not to mention that I potentially had a slasher murder on my hands. I was on the front porch of my house before I realized the walk home hadn't moved me one step closer to peace of mind.

I do my best brainwork when I become Indian. So, with my bow and arrows and canteen, I set out for Owl Woods, thick and quiet, with a stream running through it all the way to Telanoo. Robbie and I used to climb with binoculars and sandwiches to the top of the biggest chinquapin, which we named Great Oak. Swaying in the breeze in the thin top branches, we could see foxes, squirrels, chipmunks, deer, wild turkey, and a slew of small birds. The high places of the camp are visible from there: the lodge roof and my front porch, also the Morgan barn, and even some rooftops from town.

Dad always takes the all-night campers into the woods. He can do owl calls and the owls actually come, which is very cool. I never get tired of seeing a great horned swooshing through the trees with its huge head and wide wings coming right at us.

Beyond the farthest end of Owl Woods, beyond Great Oak, is where I do my serious thinking, at a place that even Robbie doesn't know about: a thick clump of evergreens I named The Cedars. Indians attach importance to cedars, or so I've read. It smells nice, it's quiet in there, and you're completely hidden. The ground is covered with soft needles—it's perfect for small fires and comfortable sleeping. When the wind comes through, you can hardly feel it, but you can hear it: like putting a seashell to your ear, but better. Close your eyes and hear the ocean roar all around you, even above your head.

Maybe Indians like cedars for the same reasons.

I put down my gear and found a dry spot to sit against a tree trunk. I closed my eyes, breathing in mellow cedar and the earthy smell of dying leaves. I stretched out my legs. It was good to be alone and secret and safe. I would listen, and The Cedars would tell me the right thing to do about the severed head and arm.

· · · · ·

When I got back to the school auditorium, work on the play was in full swing. Mei was painting sets. Miss Flewharty, the director, was pushing Reece and Robbie around on the stage. They had lead roles: Reece was Becky Thatcher, Tom Sawyer's girlfriend, and Robbie was Sid, his pesky half-brother. I jumped into helping the construction dads hang the lights and the main backdrop, a huge cloth scrim of green hills and blue sky and clouds. Some of the parents really got into working on the junior high production, even taking time off to help out. The office-type dads loved the manly work, stuff they didn't usually do at home: hammering and sawing and hauling. The set didn't have to be all that good either. Minutes after closing curtain, it'd be in the dumpster.

Dad's canvas came in handy. The construction dads made wood frames and nailed it on, making flats, which Mei paint-ed for the interior scenes, like Aunt Polly's kitchen. A lumber company donated some old planks for the famous whitewashed fence scene.

When most of the cast and crew had gone home, the four of us met backstage. In less than a minute we got into an ar-gument over the digging. Reece had second thoughts. She was still afraid Robbie and I would get shot or something. She came back to the idea of calling the police, or at least telling an adult, or at the very least digging during the day. Mei agreed with everything Reece said. Robbie was just about to jump ship too.

I stood my ground. My original idea still seemed best to me. But had I known what was about to happen, I might have agreed with Reece and saved everyone in Camp Mudj a huge fright.

·   ·   ·   ·   ·

There was an overnighter going on, and I knew the drill: the campers would be in the dining hall until 6:00; then to a scav-enger hunt down by the lake; into Owl Woods from 8:00 to 9:00 for a lesson on nocturnal animals; then back out to the lake for s'mores and songs around the campfire before bunk time. Robbie and I had roughly an hour—from 8:00 until 9:00—to dig a few feet down and get the sack. Easy enough.

We'd managed to haul our gear around back of the lodge and into the cemetery without being seen. We had a shovel, a walk-ie-talkie, two flashlights, and rubber gloves—we didn't want to leave fingerprints on the severed head. But finding the actual site took longer than we thought. Everywhere we stepped, our

feet sunk into humps of loose, crumbly dirt. I knew they were
molehills, but told Robbie in my creepiest voice that dead people had probably been clawing their way out of the ground. He
told me to shut up like he halfway believed me.

I thought we'd never find the grave.

* * * * *

"We're here," I finally whispered into the walkie-talkie. The
girls had been dropped off by Reece's mom and were staked
out in my room. The lodge was too busy for a stakeout, so they
were to tell Mom we were testing the walkie-talkies, if she came
home early from her night class in landscaping.

"The grave wasn't in the cemetery," I told Reece and Mei.
"It's just outside in another little marked-off place next to one
lone tombstone with no writing on it that I can see. It's like a
reject grave."

Over the airwaves Reece said, "It's a good thing the place
isn't in the graveyard, because you know what just struck me?"

"What? Over," I said.

"It's illegal to dig up someone's grave."

"Oh. Yeah. Okay. Well, the fresh hole is beside the reject
grave. So, um…roger, over and out."

"Watch your time," said Reece. "Over and out."

The hole was small, maybe two feet square. We got busy, me
digging, Robbie holding the light and keeping watch for little
flashlight beams to come dancing out of Owl Woods, a sign
that the campers were coming down to the lake.

I worked fast as I could. The ground moved pretty easy.
When I started huffing and puffing, Robbie offered to take
over. I said no. I felt like we were close, and I didn't want him
freaking out if he hit something gross. Sure enough, in another
minute or so, my shovel sliced through damp dirt cleanly and
hit something soft, but resistant.

Deep as the woods are, a big silvery moon on a clear night sheds plenty of light on the path to Owl Woods. A pack of campers were running ahead of the others, without flashlights. We had no warning until we heard a scream. I had just said, "Pay dirt!" knowing I'd hit the sack, when a yelp echoed across the lake, followed by other yelps and full-blown screams. Two things travel well across that lake—sound and light. We heard the campers just as they saw us. I knew what they thought, seeing two guys hunched over a shovel near a cemetery, outlined in moonlight. From across the lake, we looked to them like the old man did to us—grave diggers, or worse: grave *robbers.*

"Duck!" I said, dropping the shovel, grabbing the flashlight, shoving Robbie to the ground, and flattening myself belly down in fresh dirt all at once.

"They saw us!" Robbie said.

I was on the walkie-talkie. "We've been spotted! We're out of here! Over!"

"Who?" came Reece's voice through the static.

"Campers!"

"Go!" she said.

We had maybe a minute before Dad and Bo, our activities and security director, would be out of the woods and around the lake to investigate. My hand went down into that grave—there was no time for rubber gloves—and clawed at dirt until I felt cloth. I grabbed hold and yanked. Out came a mud-caked sack. I didn't have time to process the idea of Dad catching us at grave-robbing, and not believing our treasure-hunting story which, at this particular moment, sounded pretty lame.

"Stay down!" I barked to Robbie.

We belly-crawled for a few yards until we were beyond the church. Bent low, we dashed across the weedy meadow on the far side of the church property and dove under some low branches at the fence line. There we could see but not *be* seen. I turned to Robbie. "We follow this tree line around the back of the property. Stay in the shadows. We'll get into the woods, circle around, and cut behind the kids. We'll cross the creek to dilute our scent, and make it to Great Oak."

"I can't see!" he wheezed.

"Follow me, do what I tell you, and not even bloodhounds can track us."

· · · · ·

Police lights flashed red, a siren wailed. Robbie stayed so close behind me through the thickets of Owl Woods that I kept nicking his shins with my heels. But I knew my way. He didn't. We finally got to Great Oak, scrambled up to the top, and watched from there until the campers had been herded into the lodge and the police lights went off. The uproar had died down when it hit me—Mom.

"Reece!" I spoke into the walkie-talkie. "Are you there?"

"Where are you? The police came!" She was breaking up, and I could barely make out her words.

"I know. We can see 'em from here. Is Mom back?"

"No, but she's supposed to be here any second! The babysitter just brought the twins in. Where are you!?"

"Up a tree. We're safe and hidden. If she asks where I am, tell her I'm at Robbie's."

"I'm not lying to your mom! I'll tell her the truth, that we're testing the walkie-talkies."

"Half-truth," I teased. "We'll be there in fifteen minutes! Over and out."

"Wait! What happened?" she asked.

"We have the sack. That's all. Over."

Robbie had caught his second wind. "What about the sack?" he asked. "What do we do with it?"

We had two choices: stuff it in my shirt and try to sneak it into my room, or wedge it into a fork in the branches of Great Oak. I explained the choices, then asked Robbie, "Stuff or wedge?"

"Wedge," he said. "If your mom sees it, it'll be in the garbage."

"Okay." I wanted to turn on the flashlight and inspect the sack for blood and hair, or flecks of gold. But we couldn't afford to have the top of Great Oak lit up like a lighthouse across the top of Owl Woods. One of the campers would catch sight of us from the lodge, start squalling, and the police would be on us like a dragnet. I rolled the sack tight. On our way down the tree, I stuffed it into a fork in one of the middle branches. "I'll run over here and get it before school tomorrow," I said. "We'll keep it in my locker."

"I want to come back with you," Robbie said excitedly. "Can I stay over?"

"Yeah, man." I pressed a friendly fist to his shoulder. It was good to hear him getting into the spirit of the adventure.

As soon as my feet hit ground, I broke into a run, careful not to leave Robbie too far behind, but straining to watch through the trees for the lights of Mom's car pulling into the camp. I stopped once for Robbie to catch up, and punched on the walkie-talkie. "What's the status?"

"Coast is still clear, but hurry, Elijah. Your dad asked where you are. I said, 'Out testing the walkie-talkies.' Over."

"We're at the edge of the woods. Start coming downstairs, but keep talking to me. Over."

"Okay. Come on, Mei," I heard her say.

We kept up the banter until we saw the girls on the front porch.

I made it sound like Robbie and I had been on the north and east sides of camp the whole time, toward the Morgan farm where I'd lost contact with the girls. Dad came out of the house, and I stomped across the yard, acting like I was mad we'd missed the whole thing.

CHAPTER 6

By the next morning at breakfast, everything had been explained. I said we'd been testing out the walkie-talkies to see how far they'd reach, that the girls had tried to tell us about the big fuss, but that we were out of range in a gully, and they kept breaking up. We didn't know what was going on until we saw the police cars leaving, just as we came out of the woods. Mom and Dad believed me.

But I couldn't help thinking about that Bible verse or whatever it was that Reece had said: hidden in half-truths are full-blown lies. I didn't know anything about grave robbers; that was true. But only sort of true.

We were all around the table—the twins, Robbie, and me. (Robbie had to borrow a shirt for school, because his was caked with dirt where he'd lain on the grave. I said he'd slipped in the gully.)

Stacy plopped a wad of butter on her pancakes and asked, "Did they catch the grave robbers?"

"They weren't grave robbers," Mom answered. "The police concluded they were probably just kids digging for night crawlers, and were scared off by the campers' screams."

"What are night crawlers?" Stacy asked, making a yuck face.

"Big, juicy worms that come slithering out of graves at night!" I said.

"Not at the breakfast table, Elijah!" Mom yelled. Then she turned to the twins and said comfortingly, "They don't come out of graves, girls. Fishermen look for them in good soil because they make very good fishing bait."

"A little late in the year for crawlers," Dad said.

Nori held the syrup high over her bowl and drizzled a long, skinny brown stream on her pancakes. "Look! There's a night crawler in my pancakes."

"That's enough, Nori!" Mom corrected. She gave me the viper look; that's when her head tips down and her forehead juts forward like she's going to strike, and her eyes drill into me until they almost cross. "Now see what you've started, Elijah?"

I'm always getting viped when the twins are around.

Robbie and I didn't have time before school to get the sack. Reece and Mei were waiting at my locker, disappointed that we showed up empty-handed.

"We'll get it," was all I said.

Antsy to get the mysterious grave sack, the four of us fidgeted and drummed our fingers and exchanged impatient looks through every class we shared. If the rest were like me, they were imagining the worst: that a squirrel or a crow would make off with the sack, or that a sudden downpour would wash away all the bloodstains or gold flecks, though there wasn't a cloud in the sky. I was itching to get that sack. But because the girls had been good lookouts, and because I'd promised Reece I'd include her, I rounded up everyon when the bell rang and suggested we all go together. "Call your moms and tell them we're working on the play and we need to go to my house."

Reece gritted her teeth. "I'm not lying to my mom!"

"And we can take the golf cart!" I added.

I'm not old enough to drive, but I am allowed to use the camp's golf cart, to haul gear and take kids with disabilities to the sites.

Reece burst into a big grin. "The golf cart? Awesome!"

· · · · ·

Mom made a snack, and we ate out on the porch. The girls sat in the swing and we guys got the wicker chairs from the set on the other end of the porch. Mom hung around and poured juice. We tried to make small talk while we ate, but it was hard. Our minds were elsewhere, but we couldn't talk about *that* because of Mom.

"Reece and Mei have never been into Owl Woods," I told Mom.

"A nice day for a walk," she said to the girls. She gave me a wide-eyed fake smile that said, *Do you know what you're doing? What about…her?* Her eyes drifted to Reece, then back to me, then to Reece again.

"We're taking the cart," I answered the goggly way she looked at me, "because…um, we all have homework and we don't want to be gone that long."

"Ah, I see," she said and nodded privately to me in approval.

Moms are funny. One minute they put you in charge of the entire world, the next they think you're too stupid to know that your friend—the one who spends half her time on crutches—can't walk across acres of hilly paths.

Reece was onto Mom's goggly look. She turned directly to Mom and smiled sweetly, but there was a definite edge in her voice: "We do have homework, Mrs. Creek, but mostly we have to take the golf cart because I'm crippled, and I can't walk far without keeling over. People are always doing wonderful favors because of my problem and I really appreciate it. But I don't need to be protected from my own life."

It bordered on backtalk, but Mom just turned a little red and nodded, "Oh, yes…sure, hon."

If *I* had talked to Mom like that she'd have viped me, then yelled and sent me out to pull weeds for the next hour.

In the dead silence we all had a minute to understand that Reece had faced up to her disability, and she expected everyone around her to do the same. She'd break a few heads, if she had to.

I changed the subject. "Is Dad around?"

"He's in a meeting with the architect about the next phase of the expansion."

"Cool."

We sipped and munched.

Mom stood behind me, fiddling with my hair and patting me on the shoulders. "Well, Mei, I saw you briefly at the house the other night, but with trying to get the girls settled down after all the confusion—those kids in the graveyard…Elijah, you haven't formally introduced us."

"Sorry. This is Mei Aizawa. She's from Japan. She and Reece hang out."

"Glad to officially meet you. How long have you been in America?"

"Two years. I like it very much."

More munching.

Robbie said, "Boy, how 'bout that pre-algebra homework?"

We ate fast. As we took our plates inside, Mom tugged at my sleeve. "Drive slow," she whispered, "and you be careful with that little girl. She's delicate."

I rolled my eyes and whispered back, "Only on the outside."

· · · · ·

I left a note on the maintenance bulletin board saying I was driving Mei and Reece and Robbie into Owl Woods.

I can't begin to say how I felt when we set out across the camp that sunny fall afternoon. The wind blew as warm as summer, the trees glowed oranges and reds in the afternoon sun, and yellows and greens against the bluest sky I'd ever seen.

It was like beginning an adventure, a quest. I drove carefully, weaving along the path through the woods. Reece leaned her head back and closed her eyes and let the wind blow through her long blond hair.

"Watch the road," she said. How she knew I was looking at her I can't guess. Then she said, "Elijah, about your Mom. She's really nice, and I didn't mean to be snotty, but if I don't make it plain, people don't get it."

Mei loved the cart. "I never did golf in Japan, but we have many small cars, like this one!" In high spirits, we decided someday we'd all visit Japan. Mei said, "Oh, you must come to my home!" At that moment—me behind the wheel with the trees blazing and the warm wind blowing—it seemed possible.

I got uneasy when the paved path ended and we had to cross a gully and go the rest of the way on foot, because—and this I never told Robbie or anyone, having learned it myself only in the last year from a big map of Camp Mudj—Great Oak was not actually in the camp part of Owl Woods, but in Telanoo. Here we were in the land no one owns with the key to buried treasure. Or murder.

The girls watched from the ground as Robbie and I brought down the sack. We took turns handing it off, using our shirt-tails because we'd left the rubber gloves down with the girls. Even after our feet hit ground, Reece kept staring up through the huge limbs of Great Oak, resting her hand on its rough bark.

"What can you see from up there?" she asked me. "Every-thing," I answered.

· · · · ·

We made a circle. Slowly we unrolled the sack, each of us leaning in to be the first to see the blood—or the gold.

The girls turned it over, examined it inside and out. An old muddy gunnysack, that's all it was, with an old rag inside.

"No blood," I said.

Robbie's shoulders drooped. "No gold."

And no clues about the severed head and arm. Reece dropped the sack; we sat back and heaved sighs of disappointment. That's when Mei reached in once more, to the very bottom of the sack, feeling around, then turning it inside out. There, stuck in the seam, were several tiny rings of wire, all interconnected to make a kind of metal cloth. She held it up with two fingertips. We all closed in around it, studying it in silence for a minute or two.

"What is it?" Robbie asked.

"It's something," I said stupidly, as if *that* were a revelation.

"Mesh," said Reece.

She held out her gloved hand. Mei laid the little piece of wire mesh on Reece's palm. Wadded up, it looked like a tiny pile of sand. When Reece spread it out in the middle of her hand, the whole thing wasn't three inches across.

"It looks old," she said.

Mei studied it. "Jewelry maybe?"

"A woman's jewelry," Robbie suggested.

It hadn't struck me that it might be a *woman's* head and arm in the grave. I looked at Reece and she was thinking the same thing. Maybe the old man had killed his wife.

We went around the circle, giving one theory after another:

Maybe it was his wife's jewelry, and he killed her.
Maybe she just died by accident.
No, because why would he cut up a body? Maybe he's loons.
Maybe he's a serial killer. He looks too old and frail.
Maybe he just kills old, frail people.

That's goofy. And buries them in church basements? Come on!
There's only one body; we can't jump to conclusions.
We don't know there even is a body; there's no blood on the sack.
Right. There would have to be blood.
Unless it's an old body. Then the sack would stink.
Yeah, I think it's a piece of a treasure.
Shaped like a head and arm?

We were back to where we started.

I was thinking we had to find out what the mesh meant, when Reece said those very words: "We have to find out what it means."

I smiled at her. She smiled back. "Yeah." She was in it with me, no matter what. In the fall sunshine through gold leaves, she looked really healthy. Her eyes were all sparkly with excitement and adventure. My heart suddenly thumped in my chest.

We knelt there in a huddle, Reece's hand opened out in the middle of us, holding the little piece of mesh, which she kept touching with her fingertip.

Just looking at it gave us a kind of courage. We all sort of glowed.

"It *is* something," I said again, only this time it didn't sound dumb. "The piece of a puzzle. A mystery. Maybe murder, maybe treasure."

"We have to try digging again. At night," Reece said, which surprised me.

"Or dawn," I said. "We'll have enough light to see without flashlights."

"And this time, Elijah, check the camp schedule *and* the cycle of the moon!" Robbie said, jabbing at my shoulder.

I was ready to take a swat at him, when it all came back—us sneaking through the graveyard, sinking in molehills, digging by moonlight, running for our lives from screaming campers, treed like squirrels. It was nothing but funny now.

I sat back and started laughing. Maybe the whole treasure mystery was just too cool for me to hold inside, or maybe it was the hollow thrill of being in forbidden Telanoo, and no one but me aware of it. I laughed until the others thought I was crazy.

"We have no idea what we're getting into," I said, throwing myself back on the ground. Gazing up through the leaves to the blue sky, it seemed like the whole world was opening up. "Is everybody game?"

"I'm game, Elijah," Reece said right away. "Let's seal it."

I sat up. She closed her fingers over the piece of mesh. I put my hand over hers in the middle of the huddle. Robbie put his hand on mine in agreement. "Game."

Mei looked confused, but laid her hand on top and nodded. "Game."

CHAPTER 7

The girls came over the night before the dig. I made it look businesslike. Mei and I talked about backdrops and costumes. Reece and Robbie memorized lines. Then we had popcorn and Mei made origami animals for the twins. Around 10:00 we started watching an old *Tom Sawyer* movie for research. Robbie and I caught the adventure bug and decided to play like Tom Sawyer and camp out in the Tree House Village. Reece was tired, so she and Mei went off to the guest room, but not before we made a deal. They were to sneak out and meet us before 6:00. If they got caught, they'd say they were coming down to scare us awake. Which could be the truth.

After the movie Mom dug out the winter sleeping bags. She whispered that it was gallant of me to be so nice to a girl with a disability and an international student. "You're a good citizen," she gushed as she gave Robbie and me a thermos of hot chocolate and sent us off into the frosty dark.

Dad was building Camp Mudjokivi in stages, and the past summer had been dedicated to getting the tree houses started. It was going to be the coolest: cabins on stilts in a cluster, each connected by rope bridges with a meeting room in the middle. The village was tucked into the woods, so you'd feel like you really lived up in a tree. The platforms were done and the rope bridges too. We camped on the central meeting room floor, which had a roof over it, and talked about the severed head and arm until every sound from the woods seemed like a footstep. It was hard to sleep.

. . . . .

The sky was all red and purple that Saturday when the four of us—dressed in dark clothes and outfitted with penlights, a shovel, and a garden trowel—crept around Old Pilgrim Church and picked our way through the tombstones and molehills to the far side. Everybody at Camp Mudj was still asleep. Predawn would give us a better shot at avoiding suspicion...or coming face-to-face with the old man creeping around. The girls stood watch for good measure.

I was beginning to think that, for some mysterious reason, things go better with the girls involved. Mom seemed to immediately trust me more just because Reece and Mei were around. Mostly girls are too scared or giggly to do things, but Reece was different. And Mei hardly ever said a word without getting majority approval, so she was easy to have along—and much smarter than she let on: straight As to my Bs, even though she's not great with English.

Robbie and I took turns digging. About three feet down Robbie hit something. The shovel went *clank*—as if on metal—and he was up out of that hole like he'd struck a nest of tarantulas.

The sun was almost up, which meant the linen truck would be delivering towels to the lodge. I told everyone to stay low. I grabbed the garden trowel and dropped down in the hole. In archaeologist fashion, I carefully scraped aside handfuls of dirt. Though I'd braced myself for anything, even dead eyes looking up at me, I still jumped back and gasped when I scraped back a layer of dirt, and two empty sockets appeared.

The others gasped too, and for a minute we froze, staring at the empty eyes of a dirt-smeared, severed head.

It wasn't bone, but metal, and not a skull…a helmet. *A treasure!* Wild with relief and excitement, I shoved my fingers under the nosepiece and lifted carefully. It was kind of medieval, or Roman maybe, and battered. It had a gold tint and mysterious symbols carved into the forehead and all around.

Robbie, who I'm sure had expected to see a rotting face and throw up on it, leaned over the hole with such enthusiasm he almost toppled in. "The arm! Get the arm!" he said.

"I'm getting it! Girls, keep watch! We're almost done." Hesitantly I handed over the helmet to Robbie, barely able to let go. I could hardly take my eyes off it.

Dirt flew everywhere as I shoveled deeper, to the left, to the right. The red sun had just popped over the trees. Dad would be out and about soon. My shovel jammed against something soft, which turned out to be wire mesh, like the scrap that had gotten caught on the burlap sack. I carefully eased it out of the dirt. It was the arm, or rather an arm piece from a suit of armor, solid at the shoulder and forearm with mesh in between, and what was left of a leather glove.

"Chain mail," Robbie said mysteriously. Reece and Mei took their eyes off the camp for a second to give the arm a closer glance.

We'd planned our strategies the night before: if it was a body, we were going straight to Dad to tell him we'd been digging for night crawlers where the "grave robbers" had, and stumbled on a corpse. If we found anything else, it was to be our secret, until a unanimous vote said otherwise.

We'd brought the sack and the rag and the piece of wire mesh, so we'd have everything all together, in case this was a crime scene.

We stuffed the pieces in the sack. I jumped out of the hole, and all of us hurriedly shoved dirt until it looked pretty much like before. "Okay," I said. "Robbie, take these to Great Oak and wait for us there. I'll go back to the Tree House Village and get the sleeping bags. You girls go raid the refrigerator at the lodge. Here's the key. We don't want to risk getting the third degree from Mom at the house. Don't give me that look, Reece, it's allowed. I work here a lot, you know. It's not stealing. I'll meet you around back with the golf cart. "Okay, let's go!"

Reece and Mei and I could hardly contain our excitement on our way back through the cemetery.

"It is a treasure?" Mei asked.

"A mysterious treasure," Reece whispered. "But why would an old man bury pieces of armor in a graveyard?"

"Outside a graveyard," I corrected. "And why bury it in the church crawl space first?" I asked. "And is the rest of it still there? That's the next question."

I wanted to break into the basement right then—and probably would have, just to see what was really buried under that human-shaped mound behind the plank door—except Reece and Mei would have gone into fits. And, yeah, I wouldn't want Robbie hanging around in the woods forever, hungry for breakfast with the treasure all to himself. Just holding the helmet in my hands for a minute, there'd been a kind of tingling up my arms. It occurred to me that Robbie shouldn't rub the symbols or try to read them or chant them or anything. Who knew what kind of strange power the words might have? I imagined getting to Great Oak, only to find the helmet and arm lying near the tree trunk, with a sad little Robbie-looking toad nearby crying *ribbit-ribbit*.

The morning air was crisp and the sky like Indian turquoise. As we crossed the wooden bridge over Rocky Creek, it seemed to me again like we were heading into a different life.

· · · · ·

We sat under Great Oak in a tight circle with the burlap in the middle of us again, but now it held the helmet and arm piece. Reece had the scrap of chain mail nestled in the rag at her feet. Mei suggested we dust ourselves off and wash our hands with the canteen water. Good call. She had brought a tiny little notebook and mini colored pencils. She took notes and made some sketches, stopping every few minutes to look at the helmet, shake her head and whisper, *"Sugoi..."* which Reece translated "wow." We felt like archaeologists, elbow deep in an expedition.

The helmet was hard to describe. Robbie, the history buff, couldn't nail it down to a certain time period. "This is mysterious," he said. "Really mysterious."

In one way it was plain: a simple shape, with no big showy points or blades or plumes coming out of the top, like you'd see in old movies about ancient Rome. But it seemed to be made of several kinds of metal. The main part was a tan-gold metal, like bronze. Six strips of dark gray—designed to protect the soldier's head from club or sword—met at the top and curved down to meet a band that circled the head. Narrow lines etched into the metal arched around the helmet and connected every other end of the steel-looking cross braces, so that when you looked at the helmet from the top, it made a kind of flower or star design.

The band was pale gold and silver-colored, engraved with vines and leaves. Short spikes stuck out in different directions from the band. At the end of some of the spikes were little knobs, or rivets, of copper.

Reece was first to notice that the copper was still reddish and not blue-green like copper turns when it tarnishes. We couldn't figure why that was so, if the helmet was so old. The nosepiece came down narrow but heavy between the eyes and ended in a triangle. The sides and back of the helmet came down to protect the neck. It wasn't the kind of helmet that covered the whole face, the kind that looked like it would smother you, but an open type. Strange letters were engraved between the eyeholes.

It had been lined with leather, which had probably connected to a chinstrap, but most of the lining had rotted away.

The arm piece had a solid metal shoulder and forearm mounted on a sleeve of the chain mail, and a leather glove. A mysterious word engraved on the forearm was the same type of alphabet as the word on the helmet.

Reece looked long and hard at the words.

"What is it?" Robbie asked.

She stared way off as if she had some wild idea, her eyes intense and darting around in deep thought. Then she looked at the word again, then off into nowhere again. You could practically hear the gears in her brain grinding.

"What?!" I demanded.

"If this was English, how would you pronounce it?" she asked.

"I don't know…koiv-wa-via?" I said.

"Or kolv-wa-via," Robbie offered. "The third letter looks more like an *L*. Sort of looks Russian to me."

Mei shook her head. "Not Russian."

Reece's mouth dropped open. She knew something.

"What?!" I cried again.

"Could it be…Greek?" Reece asked.

"Greek?" Mei asked thoughtfully, and started to nod. "Greek, maybe…I have been to a Greek restaurant—Kavouris, New York City. Letters like that. Yes."

Reece got the weirdest look: part fear, part excitement, with puzzlement and hope and uncertainty all mixed in.

"Will you please spill whatever you're thinking?" I said again.

"I'm not sure! But…" She touched the word on the helmet, "but…I think I have to bring someone else in."

"No!" Robbie cried. "It's a secret! You promised! No one else can share the treasure!"

"Reece, no," I said evenly. "We made a pact."

"But we need an expert."

"No adults!" Robbie cried.

"Oh, he's one of us," she said cryptically. "We can trust him."

Mei leaned in. "Who, Reece?"

"The only kid I know who might understand what this means."

CHAPTER 8

I moved my desk in front of my bedroom window so I could do homework and keep half an eye on the church and the edge of the cemetery.

On Monday morning Reece and I had a stare-down at her locker. Her eyes begged at me. We had to get a second opinion about the helmet sooner or later, she said. True, but I still didn't like the idea. It was hard to say no to her. Robbie showed up and had the idea to copy the letters off on paper and have the "expert" decipher them. But for reasons she wouldn't explain, Reece insisted the expert had to see the pieces. She argued again that he was just like us and would swear to secrecy. Then Mei showed up. The four of us were deadlocked. Reece wouldn't break her promise about keeping our secret, but she wouldn't budge about wanting this person in. I had a sneaking suspicion she already *had* been talking to whoever it was.

Robbie agreed with me. Mei refused to have an opinion but nodded at everything Reece said. I called for a powwow at camp when the coast cleared.

· · · · · ·

A lot was going on at Camp Mudj with a Ladies Fall Craft Fair and a Sleepaway Weekend coming up: seventy third-graders from Cleveland schools. I knew from experience that at all hours of the weekend, parents would be driving in to get their whiny, homesick city kids. I personally think Sleepaway Weekend is a bad idea and have told Dad so, but he says we need to take every group that will book us to "stay afloat." Mom calls it Sleepless Weekend. She turns into a grouch and I have to watch the twins while she goes out to drink coffee with her friends.

Play rehearsals were in full swing, but I was determined to get back into the church before the powwow, to get the rest of what was buried in the crawl space—by myself, if necessary.

Then, one night at dinner I heard faint hammering echo across the camp. No one else in my family heard it. It was too late for staff to be working on the Tree House Village. I excused myself, ran to my room, and looked out the window. Somebody had just boarded up the windows and doors of Old Pilgrim Church!

The old man! I hissed to myself. *Drats!*

I ran to the lodge, cut through the assembly room, and pressed my face to the back window for a better look at the church. Sure enough—it was nailed tight. *Rotten luck!* I stomped around the lodge for a good minute, not caring if anyone came in and saw my tirade. I even surprised myself at how miffed I was. *We waited too long! Getting the rest of the treasure is going to be harder now!*

I cooled off and tried to look on the bright side. My guess was he'd closed up the church to protect his secret. The basement grave had been shaped like a whole man, proof enough to me that there had to be more there, probably a whole suit of armor. *Well,* I said to myself, peering out the window again, *at least it's safe. At least it's close by.*

Did he know we'd dug up the helmet and arm piece, which were now hanging in a plastic bag in the upper branches of Great Oak? I hoped like everything that he didn't. I called everyone with an update. Reece pressed me about her expert. In the end I caved. But I decided to plan an initiation at the powwow. I wasn't going to make this easy.

* * * * *

Reece's expert turned out to be Marcus Skidmore, aka Skid. He was pretty new to Magdeline. At our first class meeting last year, he'd stood up and greeted everyone and described himself as half white, half black, and half Latino. Which of course meant he was a hundred and fifty percent of a person, while the rest of us were only a hundred percent. I knew right away he had a big ego. The girls all thought he had a kind of mystique because he was dark skinned like a black person, but with short wavy hair and light green eyes. He was an army brat and had lived all over the world. Skid was always using foreign words and flashing around photos of himself standing in front of the Louvre in Paris and the Coliseum in Rome and the Great Wall of China. He must have been a real annoyance for show-and-tell in preschool.

If I'd known Skid was Reece's expert, I never would have agreed to it. I was especially miffed when she invited him to the powwow before I'd told the others about my decision, before we could plan his initiation trials.

I situated us on the far side of the lake near the trees, which sort of shielded us from the rest of the camp. I built a small fire to take the chill off the late afternoon. The meeting was just underway when—and this was the icing on the cake, as far as I was concerned—Skid made his grand entrance by whizzing in on his skateboard, all the way down the lake path. He was wearing dark jeans and a jacket, a black T-shirt and high-tops—fake-looking street gang getup.

Mei and Reece thought his entrance was just super. Robbie and I rolled our eyes at each other. *That's all we need,* I grumbled to myself, *a show-off, when our secret treasure has to be kept under wraps!* Reece already had sworn him to secrecy, but I made him swear again.

I tossed around some bags of chips and made small talk about the camp just to make him wait, test him out.

As the sun sank behind the trees, Robbie reluctantly pulled the helmet and arm piece out of the sack, and I don't mind saying I was shocked at how quick that suave, world traveler Marcus Skidmore lost his cool.

"Whoa…wow…oh wow, Reece," he whispered, kneeling to touch the pieces reverently. I made him put on rubber gloves. He rubbed his hand over the letters on the helmet like it was a crystal ball. He looked at Reece and smiled. "You were right. It's ancient Greek."

How does Reece know ancient Greek?

We all closed in around the circle. I kept an eye out for camp staff.

"Is the helmet old?" Robbie asked excitedly.

"I don't know, but the words are," Skid said.

"You don't know?!" I carped. "I thought you were the expert!"

Reece showed him the scrap of mesh wrapped in the piece of rag. "Can we have this dated?"

"Possibly," Skid said. He studied the intertwined rings for a minute, then wrapped it up in the rag and put it in his pocket.

"Where are you taking that?" I asked. I could just see him forgetting he had it and blowing his nose on that rag and ruining good evidence.

"I'm going to Chicago with my dad next weekend. He knows a scientist there."

"You can't tell your dad!" Robbie cried.

"I'm not telling anyone anything," Skid said shortly. "But we need answers, like how old is the armor? What's it made from? Where's the rest of it?"

"Proceed with caution," Mei said, quoting a road sign she'd seen, I guess.

Reece agreed. "We have to move quickly, but carefully. And we have to trust each other." Her eyes slid over to me.

Skid pulled a huge book out of his backpack and began flipping through it, but his words were directed at me. "I don't want a cut of the treasure money, if that's what anyone's thinking."

I struck a casual pose. "I didn't say anything."

He gave me a dry look, then went back to his book, a Greek lexicon, and within a minute he'd found both words: "The word on the helmet—*soterion*—means 'salvation.' On the arm piece...*koinonia* means 'fellowship.'" He showed us the pages.

I was a little disappointed with the translation. In the back of my mind, I'd hoped for a real zinger like "Millennium Key" or "Dark Knight" or "Curse of Death." I threw another log on the fire and sent Robbie and Mei to get sticks to roast hot dogs.

"What's the significance of that?" I asked, but Reece and Skid were head-to-head, studying the decorations and markings. "And why Greek?" I mumbled. "Does that mean the armor is Greek? Doesn't look Greek to me." I might as well have been a cricket for all the attention they paid to my questions. I kept myself company doing owl calls while I stoked the fire.

"...and the rest of it may be in the church up there," she told him quietly.

Skid eyed the boarded-up church on the ridge behind the Virginia creeper hedge. "How do we get in?"

"We broke in the first time," Reece answered.

I objected, "We did not, but we'll do it again if we have to, and only if I say so."

I knew right away that made no sense, so I covered with, "The group decides everything. Four votes."

He smirked. "So...only if you say so. The church belongs to you, I guess."

"No, but it borders my camp."

"*Your* camp?" Skid said, leveling his eyes at me. "I'm impressed. Quite the businessman you are." He looked around and nodded. "Quite a spread. What's the name again—Camp Mud-in-your-skivvies?"

Reece burst into giggles.

"Cute," I said, being a good sport. But I couldn't keep the smile going for long.

Robbie and Mei came back with sticks and started the hot dogs. Reece came around the fire to me. She put a hand on my arm to steady herself. "Elijah, don't be mad. We're in this together."

"I'm fine," I said.

"You don't look fine."

"Well, I am fine!" I insisted.

A few days ago I had reassured her that she'd be included in our quest. Suddenly it felt like the tables were turned. Now it was me on the fringe, her telling me that she and Skid wouldn't leave me out. I can't even describe how that tore me up inside.

"He's here to help us." She squeezed my arm and smiled. "We're going to solve it, Elijah, and it may be a much greater treasure than we first thought."

. . . . .

I had defrosted my attitude a little by the time the food was ready. There's nothing that helps the world make sense like wolfing down a three-fourths-charred hot dog with mustard and a mug of hot cider while crickets chirp and fire crackles and night clouds float past the moon. We stashed the armor pieces behind the trees in case anyone like Dad or Bo came upon us in the dark. The fire was down to coals, and the sun had gone down a half hour ago; we huddled closer and decided to get back into the church, but only if it didn't involve breaking glass or any kind of vandalism. Reece insisted. *Drat that old man with his hammer and pocket full of nails! He made a mountain of work out of a molehill. Doggone him!*

The other three took turns telling Skid how they'd seen the old man burying what we thought was a severed head, how the mists had crept up from the lake, how the girls were lookouts with the walkie-talkies. I still wasn't sure he could be trusted. I was steering the conversation to how molehills in a graveyard look like dead people are clawing their way up—all kinds of good scary campfire stuff—when Robbie's face suddenly went slack. He was across the fire from me, facing the woods. I heard a scuffling noise behind me, where the armor pieces were hidden. We hushed. Everyone's eyes turned to the trees behind me. Mei choked back a scream. Nobody offered a clue as to what was happening. From the terror-stricken look on their faces—even Skid's—it took every ounce of willpower I had to turn around and see for myself.

A pair of eyes glowed above the bag of armor pieces. Then two pairs, then four, then more coming out of the darkness, encircling us…five pairs of eyes, seven pairs of glowing eyes…

CHAPTER 9

I can't say which idea came into my head first because they were all there at once: that all that touching the helmet and reciting of the words on it had conjured up evil spirits; that stomping through graves then laughing about it had awakened the dead. But one idea stayed because it made the most sense—after I got a grip on myself. I whispered it to the others as I turned ever so slowly back to the fire: "Skunks. Don't move."

I nudged another log into the fire with my toe, hoping the sparks going up would make them back away.

"Stay put," I said quietly. "The heat drew them out. No sudden moves." Figuring the word *skunks* was not in Mei's vocabulary, and seeing the terror in her eyes, I slowly pinched my nose and said, "Smell bad animal." She got it. We just sat there hoping the family of skunks wouldn't leave a deposit on our treasure or worse: on us. It had happened to a camper once before. He was a rotten kid and maybe deserved it. But the stink and the gross tomato juice bath and being dubbed "Reeking Roland" and "Stench Boy" the whole week...I wouldn't wish it on a dog.

Robbie ever so gently laid a paper bag and some napkins on the fire. Flames flared. The skunks backed away and ambled off into the dark, leaving a souvenir in the air around us. After that the powwow was pretty much over.

Mom smelled me coming and wouldn't let me inside the house until she'd tossed out a robe and made me change behind a bush. When I got into the kitchen, there on the table was a large can of tomato juice, with instructions.

In my room that night, propped up in bed in the quiet dark, with my eyes on the old church and my mind on the powwow, I understood why it bothered me so much that Skid was now in the mix. As I said before, I may be part Creek Indian. So I've done a little study of their ways. They come from a larger group called the Muskogees, who lay claim to the power of the Sacred Fire. People who come together to dance or sing or whatever are people of the same fire, a clan. I just wasn't sure Skid was of the same fire as Robbie, Reece, Mei, and me. As different as the four of us were, we fit together good.

But there was something else too: the legend of the Four Teachers, the People of the Light. No one knows where they came from, but it's said that the first came from the north, the second from the east, the third from the south, and the fourth from the west. The Four Teachers brought the medicine ways to the Indians—arts of healing with nature and ceremonies to keep themselves wise and powerful.

Maybe, in the back of my mind, I believed that four was the best number, like a number of power.

But there were five of us now, and we didn't dance or sing around the fire that night. We almost got into a tiff over the armor, ate too many hot dogs, and came away smelling like Stench Boy.

· · · · ·

"There is a connection! I believe it," Reece whispered to Skid in pre-algebra the next day.

His head bobbed in agreement. The two of them had come up with this wild tale that the dismembered armor had something to do with the closing of Old Pilgrim Church. I could not have cared less about that. The old church had been standing there rotting for as long as I'd been alive and obviously a lot longer. But when I overheard the words *ancient warfare* and *demonic powers,* I perked up. Just as I asked what they were talking about, Mr. Ridenour started handing out the quiz, and for the next hour we were plunged into the cold, murky waters of pre-algebra. (Which I'd already figured out was just plain algebra. They were trying to sneak the hard stuff in on us a year early.)

Over the next week—while Skid was waiting for the test results from his scientist friend on the piece of mesh, and while the other four of us were approaching the final rehearsals of *Tom Sawyer*—I lost interest in their mumbo jumbo. Personally, I came to believe that, if we could find the rest of the old relic, we could get a pretty penny for it. Robbie was half hoping it wasn't worth anything so he could have it for the school's costume closet, and be the first one to wear it if they ever did *King Arthur.* Mei thought we should turn it over to authorities or to a museum. As she put it, "American children act very independent of the families. Not good."

But something boiled up in me the day I found Reece and Skid sitting close in study hall, swapping secrets. I went over and dumped my backpack on their table.

· · · · ·

"What's up?" I said as cool as I could, pulling out a chair.

"Hey, Creek, have a seat."

I plopped down. "I got one already."

Reece leaned across the table. I got a whiff of strawberry shampoo. "Elijah, we were just talking about the—you know, and we were wondering about the best place to keep it. Somewhere we all could get at it easily to study it. But someplace safe."

"The safest place is where it is now," I grumped. "Great Oak."

"But, Elijah, the rest of us…well, it's so far from the rest of us."

"You got a better idea?" I eyed Skid coldly.

He was leaning back, his arm laid around the back of Reece's chair. For the life of me, I couldn't stop the slow burn creeping up my face.

He started a list, with reasons for each one. Under his bed. Because, except for a step-brother in another state, Skid was an only child. He had no little kids at home to snoop around like I had. Or the storage closet in his condo, which was always under lock and key. Or a secret stashing place in the ceiling of his closet. Reece nodded at every suggestion. He started to go on. I stood.

Reece said, "I'd keep it myself, Elijah, but there's no place at my apartment. Mom would find it for sure. Skid just thought—"

"I have to get to class," I said, scooping up my books.

I skulked off with echoes in my head: *Skid said, Skid just thought, Skid this, Skid that. He was a worm, worming his way in, smooth and slimy, taking over the whole operation.* "Snake!" I fumed under my breath. "Night crawler!"

I needed to think. So…rain, snow, or sleet—didn't matter—tonight I'd be at The Cedars. They were calling me.

. . . . .

Skid appeared at the front door of my house a half hour after I got back from play rehearsal.

"I just got a call," he said. "He wants to know where we got it."

I looked at him through the screen. His skateboard was lying out in the yard. He always wore dark colors, which made his dark skin even darker and his light eyes even lighter and a little strange. "Who?" I asked.

"Dr. Stallard," he said coolly. "He called from Chicago."

"It's none of his business," I growled. My head shot around to make sure the twins weren't nearby. I stepped out onto the porch and pulled the door shut. The screen slammed behind me.

"I know that, Creek" he said. "But the truth is we're going to have trouble keeping this quiet."

"Oh, that's a news flash!" I said sarcastically. "See, that's why I didn't want you flying off to Chicago with—"

"It's a thousand years old," he said matter-of-factly.

I was speechless. There was a gleam of satisfaction in his eyes.

"'Roughly' is what Dr. Stallard said, roughly eight hundred to a thousand years old. He knew it was chain mail. And here's what I told him…" Skid's eyebrows went up and his voice got a snooty, parental tone, "I told him that it was secret where we got it, and that it was *in good hands.* He's just worried that we'll ruin the piece, you know, wash all the clues off or lose it or break it. He gave me instructions on how to keep the rest of it safe. He knows we have an archaeological find, that's all. He promised to help."

I didn't trust Skid, but what he said was making some sense. "Well, as long as you keep checking back with me before you talk with him. Every time. And as long as he won't follow you here."

Skid laughed. "He's in Chicago."

"How can you be sure?" I defended.

Skid shoved his hands into his pockets and got quiet. He looked down at the porch floor a minute, then shifted his weight toward me as if to tell a secret, eyes still down. "Listen,

Elijah. I'm not the enemy. I keep my word. You can count on that. I make no claim on the helmet, or the arm piece." Then he looked up and his green eyes drilled into me. "Or Reece."

I wanted to slug him. I wanted to say, "Shut up! She has nothing to do with anything!" But that would have looked like I really did like Reece and was embarrassed to have anyone know it.

He extended his hand for me to shake. "We're on the same side. Deal?"

I hated him and admired him all at the same time, acting like a big shot, trying to smooth things out and be mature, making me feel like a kid. If only I had extended my hand first. If only I'd said something right back about Reece like, "Reece and I've been friends for over a year and nothing or no one will ever change that."

Instead I got hot behind the eyeballs.

"Deal. Sure," I said. "Just be careful, that's all I'm saying."

I shook hands, kind of grudgingly.

"We have the same goal," he said. "We both want to find out the truth."

"I'm curious, though," I said coolly. "Why did you have to see it for yourself? Why couldn't you just translate the words?"

"The words are only part of the puzzle. Reece thinks the symbols could have deep meaning." He didn't really answer the question.

"Well, Skid, you've got your mysterious symbols and deep meaning and all that rot—and then there's the question of big money." I grinned knowingly. "The helmet may be worth a fortune."

His eyes narrowed at me.

"Hey," I defended, *"I'm* not sending it off to the highest bidder. I wouldn't do that. The group decides everything. I'm just saying…" I trailed off.

He knew I had sway over the others and that, if I pressed hard enough, they'd probably go with whatever I decided, no matter what he and his Dr. Stallard said.

"I gotta go in," I said. "You keep everything under wraps until I say so." As the screen slammed behind me, I felt his eyes still drilling into me. What was his problem anyway?

I went to the living room window and watched him sail out the driveway to the entrance road. Smooth and swift, he disappeared into the darkness like a snake.

A few things about Marcus Skidmore: he'd never cheated on a test that I'd seen or heard of, and he didn't lie to the teachers. And though he didn't play up to them like some kids, he was one of their favorites. Whether they liked him because he was one of the few ethnic kids in our school and they were taking care not to discriminate, or because his street gang look made him a little scary and teachers wanted to stay on his good side, I couldn't figure. He'd probably be picked Student of the Year. But the thing was, he didn't do the usual Student of the Year stuff: no save-the-children food drives, or top test scores or extra credit projects, no fancy Christmas presents for all the teachers. He wasn't all that impressive. (Okay, the skateboard stunt down the lake path was sort of spectacular.) Most people thought he was super for no real reason.

Maybe Skid was a con artist and I was the only one in Magdeline who could see it. I hadn't given him the Indian test of character yet, where you close your eyes and listen to a person talk, tuning in for the honesty and integrity in his voice. I tucked that idea in the back of my mind for later and took off for The Cedars.

· · · · · ·

I sat in the cold, velvety, moonless quiet for a long time. Out-side my tent of evergreens, a few snowflakes drifted down. Fall-ing, blowing leaves made dry, papery sounds. Not far off to my right came a clicking sound, like someone tapping a tree limb. A signal. It unnerved me a little. Probably a buck rubbing the felt off his antlers.

I decided that the five of us treasure hunters should make a pact, a serious one—maybe a blood pact—and think up a code word for the armor pieces, like *the costume,* so people would think we were talking about the play. That'd be perfectly natu-ral, asking each other about *the costume.* And Reece was right, we needed a safer place for the helmet. Strung up in a plastic bag out in the woods—that was no place for a treasure. I could see it swinging in the wind from where I sat. Leaves were fall-ing fast, the woods getting barer by the day. Sure this place was remote, even with the golf cart. But once the leaves fell, the possibility of the sack being discovered or of me being spotted by staff or campers was approaching a hundred percent. I could check on it only after hours, but who wants to be in Telanoo, even on the fringes, in the middle of the night?

We needed a place that was near, but seemed far. Clean and dry. Strangely, Old Pilgrim Church came to mind. But, of course, we couldn't go there. The old man was probably gone, though I'd slacked off watching for him from my window, and couldn't say for sure.

I went back to Great Oak, retrieved the sack, and stashed it in the branches of the thickest cedar. *There. You're safe for now. Even if Reece tells Skid where you are, even if he comes looking, he'll never find you.*

CHAPTER 10

The weather turned colder, but "the heat was on," according to Miss Flewharty, our slave-driving director. Miss Flew, as we called her, was very skinny and tall and kind of hunched. She always wore old-fashioned print dresses. Her hair was flat on top and flared out to a dry, frizzy triangle around her chin. She walked loose-kneed with long strides, like she was tired all the time but still had a long way to go. She had us kids do most of the production work ourselves, so we could "learn the ropes," a theatrical term directed mostly at me, I figured. It was my job to keep straight which ropes pull which curtains for which scene changes.

Most after-school rehearsals lasted until…"until I say so!" she screeched at the first person to remind her that, according to the printed schedule, we should have been finished an hour ago. She held off mob scenes only by ordering pizzas and chocolate cookies, so we could work straight through. She let a few more cuss words slip every day. According to last year's cast, she'd be cussing like a sailor by opening night, catching herself only when parents were around. Rumor had it she took up smoking too, from the time scripts came in until the stage crew had stored the last prop. The cast and crew worried more about Miss Flew going mental or getting cancer than about getting the lines and cues right.

Somehow, though, we five treasure hunters managed to cram in a powwow during crunch time. It was cold and dark.

To keep us from freezing, I built a small fire in the same spot as last time: behind the lake. I brought the makings for campfire pies. Nothing was going on at the camp except a model car club meeting up at the lodge, but the woods seemed a safer place. I'd retrieved the armor pieces from The Cedars before the others came.

I showed everybody how to make the pies using bread and canned pie filling. Reece wasn't hungry. She stared into the fire, her face strangely serious, her hair shiny and gold against her navy sweater. She had on jeans and leather boots and had hardly limped at all down the path to the lake. To say she looked "almost normal" would be shortchanging her. Skid had passed my loyalty test: he'd kept the age of the chain mail a secret from the others. When I broke the news, Robbie whooped, "A thousand years old!? We have ourselves a treasure!" His voice echoed across the lake into Owl Woods. He stared at the helmet resting at Reece's feet in its burlap nest.

"The piece of chain mail is that old," Skid said. "We don't know about the rest."

"A treasure," Reece whispered. "But what kind of treasure?" She locked eyes with Skid across the fire and gave him a drop-dead smile. He winked back. I was so steamed, I almost sacrificed my apple pie to the fires of Camp Mudj.

"Will you guys cut the drama and say what you're thinking?" I demanded.

Reece pulled a Bible out of her knapsack and turned to a place she'd marked.

"This is part of a letter to the ancient people of Ephesus. It was originally written in Greek. It says: 'Therefore put on the full armor of God, so that when the day of evil comes, you may be able to stand your ground, and after you have done everything, to stand. Stand firm then, with the belt of truth buckled around your waist, with the breastplate of righteousness in place, and with your feet fitted with the readiness that comes from the gospel of peace. In addition to all this, take up the shield of faith, with which you can extinguish all the flaming arrows of the evil one.'" She paused, "And here's the part I want you to hear: 'Take the helmet of salvation.'"

She looked up from reading, dead serious. "The armor of God."

I paused for a minute before I laughed out loud. "God's armor? I didn't know he needed armor. I thought he was all-powerful or something."

She gave me that you-poor-idiot look. So I picked up the helmet, stared it in the face, and wise-cracked, "A little outdated, don't you think? Shouldn't this be a bio-mask?" Then I held the helmet up beside my own face, looking out at the others. "Looks like God and I are about the same size."

It was like some creep had taken over my vocal cords.

Mei nibbled at her pie and stared at the fire. Skid shook his head. Even Robbie scowled, and he always laughs at my jokes.

Reece went on as if I hadn't said anything. "God provides armor for his warriors, for protection in battle."

"Battle? What battle?" I asked.

"Spiritual warfare."

"Oh yeah," I pretended to know what she meant. "So how did you know they were Greek letters?"

"Every now and then my Bible study teacher shows pictures of archaeology stuff from Bible times. I remembered that some of the Greek letters looked like English. Also, my mom belonged to a sorority in college, and they use Greek letters."

Skid threw in his two cents worth. "Reece is suggesting that the helmet and arm piece are not just relics."

Robbie seemed to get it. "Otherwise they would be in a big museum, not buried behind a graveyard in Magdeline."

"Exactly," said Skid. "It's more about what they mean."

"Hold it," I said. "That letter in the Bible didn't say anything about an arm piece."

"We're on it," Skid said, pulling a gold-colored high-tech gizmo out of his jacket pocket. It was about an inch thick and small as an index card, but it flipped open to three times that size. He punched in something, and read: "'James, Peter and John, those reputed to be pillars, gave me and Barnabas the right hand of fellowship when they recognized the grace given to me.' That was from the letter to the people of Galatia, second chapter, ninth verse."

He closed the little gizmo. I wondered what it was but didn't want to ask.

He knelt on the ground and spread the arm piece out, very carefully. "See," he said. "It's for the right arm."

"So, what do they mean: the helmet of salvation and the right hand of fellowship?" Robbie asked.

Reece looked down at her Bible. "We don't know…yet."

We all got thoughtful. Reece went back to reading the Bible. Mei pondered, "One thousand years?…"

Robbie and I stared into the fire. He asked me quietly, "Do you think it has some kind of power?"

I shrugged. Reece had closed her Bible and was looking up the hill toward Old Pilgrim Church. "Maybe," she answered.

"So what do we do?" I asked, practically.

"We get the rest of it," she said.

I stared at the bronze pieces, engraved with *soterion* and *koinonia*. Firelight danced around on them, making them shimmer and move.

CHAPTER 11

Reece and Mei were real particular that we not "vandalize" anything, so Robbie carefully pried loose the nails of the boards over the front door and basement window of Old Pilgrim Church, and I did a repeat performance of the first time, crawling into the basement and letting the others in. It was early morning when a heavy fog often lay around the lake. Good cover for us. And this time—once we all got inside—I kept my voice toned down and my ears perked up. We had two flashlights, not one, and a shovel. I had insisted that Skid didn't need to come with us—the fewer, the better. In a surprise move, he agreed; and this time I extended my hand first. When we shook hands, it felt like we were even.

The four of us made a beeline for the furnace and behind it to the plank door, which also had been nailed shut. Someone really didn't want us poking around. No one spoke, but I could see it in their faces. We all were hoping that grave in the crawl space held the rest of the armor, intact after a thousand years and priceless. In the back of my mind, I'd already started a list of things I'd buy with my cut of the money: a new, bigger bow and arrow, some high-powered binoculars, and maybe even my own golf cart, dark green with Indian designs.

Still, when Robbie yanked out the last nail, something came over us. Questions.

What if we were digging into a real grave, which was a crime?
What if the helmet had come from somewhere else?

What if some curse was at work here, and we better not disturb it, or else?

I wondered what Reece and Skid had been whispering about at the campfire. Were we mixed up in something holy?

Not that I was concerned about that kind of stuff, or believed it. Church was for old people, and people who needed stuff, like Reece who needed to think that God could heal her. If I were to choose a belief, it would be the medicine ways of the Creeks. How did a guy get to be a medicine man? What powers could you have? I knew this much: medicine powers came from vision quests. Someday—maybe next summer—I'd figure a way to get away from home for a few days and go into Telanoo on a vision quest. I'm not ashamed to say the whole idea was pretty scary—no food or water for days, all alone in The Land No One Owns, seeking a guardian spirit. But to learn the medicine ways would be worth it. I would do it...someday.

One look in the crawl space yanked me back to the present. The grave was empty!

"It is gone!" whispered Mei. Her voice in the half-dark sounded so disappointed. It was the first time she'd acted like she was really into our quest, that she'd gotten over being scared.

We gathered around the fresh hole. Robbie and Mei pointed their flashlights at it. The hole was about three feet deep, with dirt flung out from it across the small room—a rush job.

Reece, who'd been strangely quiet up to this point, said sadly, "It was all here. The whole armor. And he took it. He tore it apart." She sounded like she was going to cry.

"We'll find it," I said.

"No, we won't! Don't you see? He took it apart and buried pieces of it all over. Or..." she gasped in air, panicked. "Or he knows we dug up the helmet and he's destroyed the rest, so we'll never find it!"

"He wouldn't do that," I said. "It's valuable. It may be worth millions. If he does know we have it, if he saw us—" I broke off, but it was too late. Everyone knew what I was thinking.

Robbie gasped at me, "He'll come after us, to get it back!"

We stood there looking at each other, our flashlights casting eerie upward shadows on our faces. I was just beginning to understand what Reece and Skid were hinting at. Maybe the armor had fallen into our hands not by accident, but for some purpose. I didn't have the heart to tell them that the old man probably had seen me the night Robbie and I had watched him bury the helmet and arm piece. If he knew we had part of his precious armor—if he went back and checked that hole beside the reject grave—what would he do to get it all back?

Reece looked up at me, and her sadness really got to me. "What do we do next, Elijah?"

Mei spoke up, and I couldn't believe what she said: "Next step. We find the grandpa."

· · · · ·

Reece had Skid absolutely plastered against her locker the next day, practically touching noses with him. I came up quiet, hoping to overhear before they saw me, but all I got was something about "keep it from him."

Keep what? A secret? The helmet?

"Hey, guys," I said with a thin smile.

"Hey, Elijah," Reece greeted me back with a big grin. It looked real, but who can tell with girls? They'll show teeth if they like you, or if they're dragging your name through the mud, or if they want a huge favor.

I wasn't as sure of Reece as I had been a week ago.

"I was asking Skid if he could help us find the old man," she said.

"You said, 'keep it from him.' What did you mean by that?"

She gave me an odd look. "Yeah. We were talking about how we can get him to lead us to the rest of the armor, while keeping it from him that we have two pieces."

Reece saw in my eyes that I was ready to hit the ceiling. "Wait, Elijah," she said, grabbing my arm. "I know what I'm doing. Skid's not part of the inner circle, are you, Skid? He's just helping out. So he can ask around more easily, arouse less suspicion. If any questions are asked, see, he's never been in the church and can say honestly he had nothing to do with the discovery. All he's done is ask a scientist about some old scrap of metal someone found. He can help us lay low."

Miranda Varner walked by and flashed her emerald greens at Skid. She flipped her hair at him and gushed, "Hi, Marcus."

His back went all straight, he jerked his head with a, "Hey, Mandy," and watched her until she disappeared in the crowd down the hall.

Boy, I hope he likes her, I thought. *I hope he's crazy over her.*

The bell rang and we scattered like roaches when the lights go on. As Mr. Ridenour went through our assignment, I fumed over why Reece didn't check with me first. After all, it's my camp that borders the graveyard, my tools we've used, my hiding places. So it just follows that any decision about the treasure should be my decision.

Robbie and I got to be in first lunch, thanks to a senior high field trip. I was hoping to have a three-minute powwow with Reece. I got stuck in line while she and Skid snagged a corner table and pored over the Bible, like they had some great secret all to themselves. When Reece would look up to see where I was in line and smile at me, Skid would make goo-goo eyes at Mandy at the next table, then be nose to nose with Reece again.

Boy, talk about having your cake and eating it too. Talk about playing the field! Talk about worming your way into the inner circle—night crawler!

Enough was enough. I had to get control of things.

Okay, I wondered, *say the armor does have power. So do medicine ways. What if I mix them both in a vision quest?* I walked home from school after a stop at the town library to get a book on Indian culture. I made a lame excuse to Robbie that I had to work for Dad and not to call me (which made him suspicious, but too bad). I made an excuse to Mom that I had a project with Robbie and that we'd be at the library (so she wouldn't call Robbie's house), and that I'd stay overnight at The Castle. I packed my gear behind locked doors so the twins wouldn't snoop. Dad's map of the area would help me find a shortcut from Telanoo to school in the morning. I sort of knew the way already: follow Rocky Creek until it branched, follow the east branch up the ridge, then across a couple of hills through the Morgan farm. If I stayed on course, and didn't get charged by one of their Black Angus bulls, I'd come out by Old Railroad Lake across from school.

Geared up—and with a brief stop at The Cedars to get the helmet and arm piece—I hiked deep into Telanoo.

The air was clear and crisp, the trees aflame in late afternoon sun. There was the threat of heavy frost, but I couldn't worry about that. I was on a vision quest, which involved discipline and pain. Besides, this questor knew how to make a fire. I'd thought about taking one of the walkie-talkies, but was pretty sure I'd be out of range. I wanted to leave a note for Mom, just in case, but couldn't risk the twins finding it. I had left a note in my school locker, in case I disappeared.

Telanoo is so different from Camp Mudj, it's like another country. The landscape gets suddenly ragged, where sharp rocks push up through thorny scrub brush. There are no paths and only a few animal tracks. Old creeks have cut deep ravines in the rock. Some have said there are caves. I haven't found any, but some parts of Telanoo I've never explored. Without a compass or the sun or the North Star, you could get lost. Not that you'd wander for miles and die and they'd find your bones years later, not that extreme. But I don't mind saying I kept an eye on the terrain before me, because if I should fall and break a leg, it could be bad. The crunch of my steps and the cold cloud of breath around my face kept me company.

Twilight fell. The trees in Telanoo became sparse and bare, as if I had walked through autumn and into winter in an hour. Then there was nothing but a whole sky of deep red and a straight black horizon, except for one dense grove of tall evergreens to the west, which looked like someone had punched a black hole in the sunset. Like my cedars near Owl Woods, this dense cluster was a good place—shelter from wind and frost, with nice dry tinder for a fire.

I set up camp on a level spot, made a ring of stones, cleared a place for the fire, and gathered wood. When the fire took off, I read the Indian book. Come to find out, I wasn't too young for a vision quest. Crazy Horse was thirteen when he had his, though he hadn't purified himself in the sweat lodge or fasted to connect himself to the sacred powers. But his vision had led him through great battles.

What does it mean to prepare for a vision quest? I wondered. *What magic comes from not eating for three days, and sweating for hours?* I felt silly. *How is this supposed to work?* I unwrapped the armor pieces and laid them before the fire. *Soterion*—salvation. *Koinonia*—fellowship.

Indians believe nature and the spirit world work together, the book said. *Are these old pieces of metal connected to another dimension too? Is that what Reece thinks? I picked up the helmet and looked into its empty face. "Who made you? Who wore you? Did he fight? Did he win, or did he die? Was there more than one who wore you?"*

The fire crackled. I was thirsty. I emptied the canteen on the ground instead of drinking it.

I went back over the past weeks, how it all began: from our search for costumes and curtains, to grave-robbing and screaming campers and narrow escapes, to secret meetings about ancient treasure. I poked at the fire. Fire fairies went up into the cedars and disappeared. I was glad it had rained a few days before. Dry boughs above the fire with all these sparks could have put me in a situation.

Maybe the armor is here to teach me something, like how to take control of the group, how to win. I wasn't going to give up the armor until I knew its meaning.

I began to think I should hide it even farther from Great Oak until we decided as a group, as a clan of the same fire, what to do. I just wasn't sure I could trust Skid. With Reece getting friendlier with him, how would I know when she'd be more loyal to his ideas than to mine?

I thought about everything as I looked into the empty face of the armor. I thought of Mom's cooking. It was chicken night; the twins would fight over the wishbone. Dad would probably get a call or two while they ate and have to run and get his clipboard to check on something.

I thought about the shoes I was wearing and which wood makes the best fire. I wondered if I'd forgotten a homework assignment for tomorrow. I thought about what I'd have to kill and eat if I ever had to live out here like a real Indian.

At what exact moment I sensed that I was being watched I don't know. It came in a kind of slow rush, a crawly feeling from head to toe. At first I thought it was the fire dying down, the cold and darkness getting to my back. Then it was in my head, a knowing that I was not alone.

Terror swept through me, then confusion. No one lived in Telanoo, no one crossed it, there were no roads or paths because it led nowhere. *Have I looked too long into the helmet's empty eyes. Am I imagining it's alive? Or is this how visions begin, with sensations of other beings lurking about?* Slowly I looked around. I remembered the skunks and willed myself to be brave in case glowing eyes should come floating in from the darkness. *Has Robbie followed me? Has Skid?*

For a long time nothing happened. *Should I run?* Not a good idea. Even with good night vision, I'd likely break my leg in the dark, trip on a rock, twist my ankle in a crevice, or fall off one of the jagged cliffs. Mom and Dad would never find me. No one would ever come out here.

I stayed put and tried to open my mind to a vision. Nothing happened, but I was still sure someone was out there.

Courage suddenly seized me. I stood and yelled, "Hey, I know you're there!"

Then…above my head…a sweep of air—

The flap of giant wings swooped over my head, their span as wide as an eagle's.

My heart died with one *thud,* then started up again, pounding.

A great horned! It was only an owl.

I sat down hard and gulped cold air to calm myself. I read more in the Indian book and studied the helmet.

Though the owl was gone, the feeling of being watched stayed.

And stayed.

But this was a vision quest. Sure, I was scared and I hadn't really prepared for it by fasting and sweating, but I wasn't going to be a coward and leave.

Sometime past midnight, I put the helmet on, then the arm piece. We'd carefully brushed the dirt off, but they still smelled like a hole in the ground. With the ragged leather glove I took up a rock, turning it over, feeling its weight and coldness. *A caveman's weapon.* With my left hand I kept the fire going. And so I sat most of the night.

By dawn, I'd done something I'd live to regret for a year.

CHAPTER 12

"What happened to you?!" Reece asked the next morning, passing me in the hall.

I was half-frozen, half-starved, and had terminal bed head. Not to mention I'd run a rugged two miles to school and stood outside sweating and shivering until the school janitor opened the doors. I probably smelled, but with my nose hairs frozen it was hard to tell.

"Nothing," I snapped, and hurried on to class. It wasn't so much how I looked; I just couldn't face her knowing what I'd done. I'd hidden the armor pieces where no one but me could find them. And sitting there in class in a brain fog, I began to wonder if even I'd be able to find them again. I'd stashed them under one of the two million nondescript rocks near one of the half-dozen dry creeks way beyond Owl Woods in the wilds of Telanoo.

I convinced myself this was best, to guarantee that no one was going to do anything with that armor until I approved it. I felt like the armor wanted me to win.

· · · · ·

Over the next week, my world unraveled like an old sweater. Reece refused a blood pact because she said it felt like making light of the blood of Jesus—whatever that meant. So I told her—and Robbie later—that the helmet was in my sole possession until we all agreed on the next step.

They all ganged up on me backstage after school. Even Skid was there, and he had nothing to do with the play. Probably Reece had asked him.

"You don't own it!" Robbie snapped. "We all own it!"

"No one *owns* it!" Reece countered, and I was surprised by her anger. "It's...it's...un-own-able!"

"Owns what?" Miss Flewharty came through the backstage curtains, smelling of smoke. We all froze.

"The costume," Reece blurted out, and bit her lip nervously.

"Yeah," I said, and this is weird, but I really didn't want Reece to have to lie, because I know how she feels about it. So I jumped in. "We were arguing over who gets one of the costumes when the play is over, but I guess it has to stay here in the drama closet."

"Which costume is that?"

"The...the coolest costume in...the world," I stammered. My mind was a blank. All I could think of were armor pieces glowing in firelight.

Robbie jumped in as if to rescue me, but he was kind of smirking at me when he said, "Elijah wanted to have it for himself. He's kind of—" he made quotes with his fingers "—*in charge* of that costume, so he thinks he has the final say."

Miss Flewharty turned to me, "Injun Joe's costume? It is neat, isn't it, all that leather and beadwork?"

"But nobody's just allowed to *take* costumes, are they, Miss Flewharty?" Robbie said, snubbing his nose at me.

"Of course not. Costumes are school property. Elijah, if you ever need to borrow something—if your parents are doing a reenactment at the camp, for instance—you might check with me or Mrs. Coyle. We could make arrangements."

"Otherwise it would be—" and Robbie did the quote thing with his fingers again, "*stealing,* wouldn't it, Miss Flewharty, to take something that wasn't yours?"

Right before our eyes, he'd become Sid, the low-down, sniveling brother of Tom Sawyer.

"Oh brother," I said under my breath.

Reece gathered her books like she was leaving. "Well, thanks for clearing that up, Miss Flewharty. I'm really excited about the play. I think it will be great."

"Yes, oh yes," she said, then slid back into director mode. "Now! We have a total of twelve hours—*twelve hours!*—over the next week-and-a-half to whip this show into shape." She turned to Skid. "You'll excuse us." She ousted him off the stage with a nod, told us to find our places, and headed behind the curtain for another smoke.

Robbie and Reece stood there glaring at me. Even Mei, who'd never shown a temper, stood there with her lips tight, her neck stiff, staring hard at the floor.

"We want it back," Robbie hissed. "You get it tonight, or I'm telling!"

"I won't get home until dark!" I hissed right back.

"Use a flashlight," Reece said.

"I don't know if I can find it in the dark!"

Reece put the pieces together quickly and blew a gasket. "You don't mean...you didn't...you hid it...in *Telanoo!?*"

I didn't answer.

"You hid it way out there in the dark..." she said in as unfriendly a tone as I ever heard her use. "That's where you were that night. Why you came to school all messed up. You hid the armor from us, where we could never find it!"

All of a sudden it hit me that it was the most hidden from her. The other kids could go on their own and snoop around for it, but the treasure was absolutely out of her reach.

Her face went all sad and she groaned my name. "Elijah… you lied to us."

"I didn't."

Her sadness and anger and disappointment unnerved me more than those invisible eyes watching me from the dark. Her look felt like everything was over.

CHAPTER 13

For the next few days, they wouldn't even look at me. At lunch I sat by Justin Brill, who was playing Injun Joe. I pretended that I had to ask him about his performance, like if the red and blue spotlights on him in the cave scene were good and scary… shop talk, so no one would wonder why I wasn't sitting with Robbie.

I guess I'd made my point. Maybe they'd all be a little more careful about who was telling who about our secret, or about who was deciding what about a potentially priceless treasure.

Or maybe I'd just lost all my friends.

Losing friends, it's like…well, it's not like anything I can describe. It's not like your heart is broken, because a break you can put a cast on, take a strong pill for, and then go to sleep and feel better. It's more like your heart has the worst case of flu. It aches all over. There's ringing in your ears, the voices of your friends yelling at you. You can't concentrate, your eyes can't see, but your legs still work on automatic pilot and carry you down the hall and in and out of the right classrooms.

I couldn't tell the others my vision quest had fizzled and turned into a helmet-hiding quest. They didn't know anything about vision quests. I was beginning to think that neither did I.

I put a note on their lockers: *My house, then to Tel. for costume. Saturday 2:00.* Anyone else reading those notes in the halls of Magdeline Independent Schools would think the costume people were gathering to make telephone calls. Only the five of us knew what *Tel.* meant.

Saturday afternoon, after I'd done a bunch of work for Dad, Robbie showed up at the lodge, and Mei came too. Skid had left a note on my locker that he'd be out of town.

Reece didn't come. I figured it was because she wouldn't be able to help us search Telanoo.

We got to my vision quest camp easy enough after an hour of hiking. I had intended to draw a map to chart my way out of Telanoo, but it had slipped my mind in the cold and sleeplessness and fear of that night. I'd buried the helmet and arm piece near an *S*-shaped dry creek with a little island of dead grass in it. But in daylight with the sun casting long, cold shadows, everything looked different.

The dry streams each had several *S* curves, and lots of little islands with dead grass. Every flat, fossily rock looked like the one I'd buried the armor pieces under.

We looked all afternoon. I played calm, but panic was creeping in more every minute. We backtracked to the camp and set out again. After another hour of searching, Mei and Robbie were tired and hungry. Me too, but I didn't let on.

Finally—finally!—we found the spot: at a sharp *S* curve in a dry creek—above it on the bank where a flat, fossily rock angled up against another to make a little stash cave. "Here it is! I found it!" I cried. The other two came running, excited. Our hard work had paid off.

I knelt and heaved the rock away, but the armor was gone! I stood there staring at the hole.

"Wrong again!" Robbie whined. "Elijah, why didn't you draw a map or mark it better? What a dumb idea, to hide it under a rock that looks like all the other rocks in—" he spread his hands wide and made a dumb face, "Rock County, U.S.A.!"

"This is the place," I said flatly. "It was here." They both looked at me, stunned.

"You are sure?" Mei asked, sounding scared.

I looked around, spotted the twin trees landmark I'd missed before—the Nori and Stacy trees I'd named that night and had forgotten about until I saw them again—and the *S* curve in the creek with a tiny, distinct island of tall wild grass. My heart sank. "I'm sure."

Robbie became Sid again. "Do you think we're stupid? Do you expect us to believe it just walked away?"

"I don't know! I don't know! Maybe Skid followed me," I said, grasping at straws. "I had the feeling that night that I was being watched. Maybe he—"

"Oh, come off it! I can't believe you led us on this wild goose chase."

"I'm telling you the truth!"

"Like you did that night, when you were—" Robbie made another face, screwing up his features until he looked like a rubber-faced, snarling lunatic, "working for your daaad!"

I came up on my feet and made stiff fists down at my sides. "Hey, you know what, they picked you right for the part of Sid, because you are some big pest! And if you were so suspicious of me that night, maybe you followed me! You wanted it for yourself, so you could dress up like King Arthur!"

"I'm telling your dad! Everything!" he said.

The argument was heading toward a kindergarten fight with us bloodying each other's noses.

Then Mei stepped up. "Who else?" she piped in frantically. "Who would follow?"

"Nobody!" I said, then added desperately, "I don't know… Skid, maybe, or Dr. Stallard. The twins follow me sometimes."

I was scraping the bottom of the barrel by suggesting two six-year-olds would stalk me like ninjas through the woods at midnight. Ridiculous. I was hoping Robbie hadn't caught what I said, when he said with a huff, "The twins wouldn't stay out all night in the cold! What a dumb idea. C'mon, Mei. Let's go and leave Mr. Liar and Thief out here to rot!"

"When did you bury it?" Mei asked quietly.

"Just before sunrise. I'd been up all night, feeling someone was watching me. I…I didn't mean for this to happen."

I watched them jumping across the brambles from rock to rock, negotiating the tangled underbrush. When they were out of sight, I sat down on a log and stared at the empty hole where I'd last seen our priceless treasure.

Where is it!? I screamed inside. *And what have I done?*

CHAPTER 14

"Final Five" was in full swing, the last five days of touching up the sets and working out lighting cues for *The Adventures of Tom Sawyer.*

The whole school was buzzed about the play. No one was even talking much about sports or anything else. Miss Flewharty was a great director—in spite of her strange ways. She probably could have made it on Broadway, or at least some bigger place, like Columbus. The county newspaper had come to take pictures and put the stars on the first page. It was big stuff for little Magdeline, Ohio, where hot news is the furniture store closing for a week while they bump out a wall to expand.

I was at my post—stage left—during dress rehearsal for Act One when one of the back braces came loose from the un-whitewashed fence. The whole thing toppled backwards against the scrim. The splintery wood caught on the materi-al. For a few seconds the curtain tracks above us swayed and creaked. It looked as if the whole stage was going down. Girls started screaming as the weight of the fence ripped the scrim right down the middle and crashed to the floor. A couple of kids working backstage almost got whacked. Miss Flewharty went into a tirade, and called for a break "NOW!" while we "blankety-blank, half-baked carpenters" repaired it. Three of us stage guys and Injun Joe—who's as tall as me but has fifty pound more muscle—hauled it off in a hurry and started ham-mering, bickering as to whose fault it was. We decided that

Tom Sawyer had pretend-painted on it too hard and pushed it over. We sent a guy up to check the curtain tracks and chains.

The crew set the fence up again and waited, but Miss Flewharty didn't show up. Several minutes passed, and we got a little worried. We all really did like her, even though she could act like a cat thrown in the bathtub when she got mad—all frayed and wild-eyed and snarling.

The assistant director, our student teacher Miss Shiloh, gave us another ten-minute break so she could find Miss Flew. Everyone was wandering off to the drink machines, when Reece strode up to me backstage, and stopped with a little gasp of pain.

"How could you do this!?" she snapped.

She wasn't talking about the un-whitewashed fence falling. Mei must have told her about the search in Telanoo and its lousy end.

"Somebody stole it!" I said. I wondered if I should mention that the old man might have seen me before.

"*You* took it first, without telling us."

I'd never seen her so furious, which threw me off guard, so what I said next came out more accusing than I intended. "Well, *you guys* were doing things without telling *me!*"

"Nothing that would risk the safety of the…" Her voice fell to a whisper, she glanced around, *"the costume."*

"You can't know that, Reece. You don't know that Dr. Stallard guy, what he might do if he got his hands on it."

"Oh, for Heaven's sake, Elijah! He can't do *anything* with it now. It's gone!" She winced and closed her eyes and wobbled for a second. I was ready to reach out and steady her, but figured she'd slug me if I tried. "You don't know how important it was to me. You can't know!"

"You think it's magic, or something, with miraculous powers in it. I've heard you talk." I wondered if she believed it could heal her.

"It's not the metal, Elijah, it's the message—the Word—that's powerful."

I kept on defending myself. "But you wouldn't make a pact, so we'd know that everyone would keep their word."

"No, especially not with blood," she preached. "But besides that, the Bible says to let your yes be yes and your no be no."

I threw up my hands. "What does *that* mean?"

"It means to be a person of your word, one who doesn't have to make vows and sign papers in blood. Everyone just naturally trusts a person of integrity."

I whirled to stomp away, but turned back. "You don't trust me now?"

"Deliver the…the costume and I might consider it," she shot back sarcastically.

"I'm telling you, someone followed me into Telanoo and took it."

"Who would do that?"

"I don't know…Skid…or that Dr. Stallard guy. Or the old man."

By this time she was right in my face, her finger nearly pointing up my nose. "You are being paranoid, Elijah Creek. That scientist doesn't know you, or where you live, and doesn't care. The old man never saw us. He may have heard us in the basement, but he didn't see us—" she paused and dropped her finger and huffed.

"We can't know that for sure," I said, wondering if I should tell her what I was afraid of: that he *had* seen me, first when Robbie and I were running from the Virginia creeper fence and again that night I spent alone in Telanoo. Before I could decide, she exploded.

"And Skid?! You're accusing Skid of stalking you into the woods? He would never, ever steal, especially—" she gritted her teeth and hissed, "the armor." Then so everyone in the commons could hear, she bellowed, *"Skid is honest!!"*

The mention of pure, almighty Skid just set me off. I shot back, "Yeah, well, at least *you're* in the clear, because *you* couldn't even walk that far!"

Reece reeled back a step, like I'd hit her. The air around us backstage seemed like it was made of glass and I'd just thrown a rock through it. I turned and stormed off so I wouldn't see the look on her face, but just as I turned the corner to the back hallway and almost tripped over a pile of props, I heard her say my name, soft and sad, "Elijah…"

The next thing I knew I was outside behind the school. The ancient treasure pieces—and my hopes of a new golf cart and other cool stuff—didn't mean a thing now. Nothing. Zero. Reece was the real reason I'd wanted that cart, anyway, so she could run without legs, so we could go tearing around the lake and through Owl Woods with the wind blowing in our faces.

Finding treasure was great, but not as great as having my own clan of the same fire, with a huge mystery that was our own and no one else's. What had started as an awesome adventure had collapsed in on itself like a burned-out star.

I threw myself back against the cold brick wall and tried to swallow. The armor was a curse. My vision quest was a bust. I'd lost a priceless treasure.

My friends.

Reece.

Everything.

Who am I now? Just a rotten creep who'd let his smart mouth get way, way out of line. Who is Elijah Creek? A nobody. Less than that. Elijah Creep.

I stood there in the corner where they keep the kitchen garbage cans, breathing the stench of old school lunch garbage, feeling like garbage.

CHAPTER 15

The rest of rehearsal that night was misery. Miss Flewharty yelled at me for leaving my post. I stayed in the shadows, my face burning, and bolted right after they ran the curtain call. I caught a glimpse of Reece as she limped weakly up to her place center stage, and my first hateful thought was, *she's faking it.* But the real me knew better. More likely, she tried to run to the restroom after I insulted her, to cry in private so no one would ask why, and she pushed herself too hard or tripped along the way.

She had trouble with her lines after the argument too, and Robbie was overacting, playing Sid so snotty that Miss Flewharty cussed at him and told him to tone it down, or the audience would be throwing rotten eggs at him.

Standing alone in the dark backstage watching the play from behind Tom's rickety, un-whitewashed fence, I wondered if the junior high drama department's claim to fame was coming apart at the seams. And if that too was all my fault.

The next morning I faked a stomach ache so I could skip school, even though the cast and crew weren't allowed to cut. I swore to myself this would be the last time I'd lie to Mom. But I had to get back to Telanoo for one more search.

Nori and Stacy were off to school. Mom had to go to Chillicothe, and Dad was up to his eyeballs in eighty middle school kids from Hillsboro learning about pioneer days. I left a note in case he should happen to look in on me: *Dad, I'm feeling better so I went to Owl Woods to find something I lost. I'll be back before the girls get home. And if anyone calls, I'll be at the play tonight. No prob. E—*

· · · · ·

The sky was a sickly white with no sun to gauge time or direction. Since I never used a compass, relying on my wits instead, I got my bearings by the wind and a general sense of the area. I headed due north before swinging around toward the creek where I'd buried the armor pieces. Once there, I looked in the hole again, as if the helmet might magically reappear and stare up at me. What a welcome, creepy sight that would have been! But there was nothing.

The words kept pushing into my mind, echoing what I'd said to Reece: *you couldn't even walk that far, couldn't even walk…*

She loved the armor more than any of us did. Those words carved into it seemed so important to her: *salvation* and *fellowship*. Standing there over that hole with my hands shoved in my pockets to keep them warm, it made perfect sense to me why she'd ask Skid, Mr. World Traveler, to help us with translation. He'd been to Greece, plus he knew Bible stuff.

Much as I tried to justify my actions, everything Reece had done made sense. And everything I had done, didn't. What kind of a person was I, to tear her down and be jealous and mean? How could I ever face her again?

On top of the knoll above the dry creek, I stood on the rock which had once hidden the armor. There wasn't a drop of water in the stream, hardly a shred of life anywhere. The grass had died in the first frost, I guessed. *Frost. Winter coming.* I hadn't noticed how fall was rushing past. Fallen leaves, brown and brittle, rattled across the ground. The last of them were falling now, swirling around my face. Tree limbs above waved in slow motion, dry and black. I felt like I was drying up too, drying and falling. Disappearing into the land. There was no one to help me.

I looked up at the dull sky and whispered for help in an air prayer: *What do I do now?*

I decided right then and there—right out of the blue—to catch the last half day of school. I could snag a ride with one of the maintenance guys making a hardware store run, or walk if I had to. I'd sign myself in and tell Miss Tessa, the school office manager, that Mom would be by later with a note. Which would be true, because I'd leave a note for Mom telling her I felt better and needed to pick up my assignments. All true.

If there was any magic to the armor, it must be black magic. Even though the quest had started out as the coolest thing so far in my life, it had ended up being like the first leg of a roller coaster ride—up, up, up toward wide open sky, then all of a sudden it's good-bye, stomach, and don't forget to write.

So the quest is over. Big deal.

Things would get better again. I just needed to get out of Telanoo. It was too depressing. From my rocky perch, I surveyed the wasteland one last time and spotted something we'd missed before: a faint trail of flattened grass heading away from Camp Mudj, away from the Morgan farm, toward nowhere. Had Robbie and Mei and I made that path while looking for the hiding place? I didn't think so. Actually, I was sure we hadn't.

But someone had. *Someone has been here and left a trail.*

Mustering all my tracking skills, I followed the disappearing trail over rocks and through scrub bushes. I must have looked like a hound on a rabbit's trail, nosing here and there, back and forth across the terrain. At one point the trail disappeared for almost an hour. I crisscrossed the creek and scoured the landscape for trampled grass or broken twigs, anything, when… eureka! A medium smooth-soled mud print on a slab of

soapstone in a low swampy spot between two ridges. A foot-
print. A man's shoe—size nine or ten. Measuring the direction
the shoe pointed against the sharp west wind, he had to be
heading—as the crow flies—toward the old church.

*Who else would follow me into Telanoo and stalk me all night
to watch what I'd do with his armor? The old man.*

Maybe I should have been worried, but I wasn't. Maybe I
shouldn't have felt a burst of hope, but suddenly I did. After all,
was it just coincidence that we four kids had checked that crawl
space in the first place? Was it just coincidence that Robbie and
I had gone spying on the church just in time to see the old man
bury the armor pieces behind the cemetery?

We'd found the armor once—twice, actually—and we could
do it again.

Providing he didn't melt it down into ashtrays first.

Finders keepers! I thought with resolve. *You may have found
it, but we're going to keep it. You buried it, we dug it up; we buried
it, you dug it up. It's our turn now.*

I set out in a dead run, nose still on the trail. It was lunchtime. I had to get back home, then to school.

The trail came and went like a ghost. It split off a couple of
times into what looked like old trails, rutted from the weight
of heavy, hoofed animals like deer or cows. Maybe I'd been
wrong. Maybe people did wander Telanoo in the recent past.

I ended up just where I thought, at the foot of the ridge
below Old Pilgrim Church.

My legs carried me in a blur past the graveyard and behind
the church. I saw something I'd missed before, and stopped
dead. On the side of the church facing away from camp, cut
into the wood siding so it hardly could be seen, was a narrow
door with no doorknob. It stood a little ajar. I remembered
that first night when the four of us came up out of the church

basement to find the intruder had vanished. He'd hidden in there. *Could be a tool closet,* I thought, *a good hiding place.* I went up to it cautiously, trying to get a look inside before I got too close. I put my hand on the door and eased it open. Maybe this was where he hid the treasure. Or maybe he was in there. I braced myself and eased it open.

The closet was about two by three feet, and empty except for a shovel and a scythe, the kind the Grim Reaper carries. In the dirt floor were a few more of those same footprints.

He hides in here.

You'd think I'd be relieved that the toolshed was empty, or disappointed that there was no treasure there. But all of a sudden I was more scared than if a raccoon had jumped out at me, because of what that tool closet told me about the old man.

Old men I know are mostly very nice. My grandpa painted houses and fished a lot before he died. Others I see around town work part-time at the hardware store or sit in Florence's Greasy Cup and drink coffee.

I'd never heard of an old man who hid in abandoned tool closets and followed kids into the woods and spied on them all night in the freezing dark. I never knew an old man who buried things by the light of the moon. We were dealing with a strange, unpredictable person, one who was breathing down the neck of Camp Mudj.

My adrenaline got pumping and I took off, sailing past the back of the lodge where the Hillsboro kids were having lunch. I got to the house, skipped all five steps and flew up to the porch, landing with a *thud.* Once inside, I scribbled off a note to my mom explaining I'd gone to school. I propped it against the saltshaker on the table.

I tore off another piece of paper and wrote a note to stick on Skid's locker. It said, *Skid, I need your help. E—*

CHAPTER 16

Skid tracked me down after school, acting like everything was fine, and asked what I needed. Maybe Reece hadn't told him what slime I was. Which was hard to believe, that she wouldn't call him up and tell him every single word right away. But as I said before, Reece was different. I explained that I had reason to believe the old man might know something about the armor pieces I'd lost in Telanoo. And since Skid had no part in the play, he'd be free to try and locate him. My description of the old man was pretty sketchy: medium height, thin and hunched, sort of frail-looking. Small head, thin hair.

Skid looked at the note, looked at me and said, "I'm on it." He saluted me with his index finger and sauntered off.

I didn't say anything about the trail I'd found, or the shoe print. Just that finding the old man was our last hope.

The four of us weren't speaking, which was a good thing, since Miss Flew demanded absolute silence backstage during the performances. I don't mind saying that we wowed Magdeline and a herd of incoming relatives on opening night with our acting, costumes, lighting, and sets. They responded with flowers and hugs for the girl actors, whoops for the boy actors, and a standing ovation for the rest of us.

Amazingly, between Friday's and Saturday's shows, Skid got the low-down on the old man, quick as greased lightning. He taped a sealed envelope with my name on it to the backstage fuse box on Saturday night. The note said: *Stanford (Stan)*

Dowland, age 78, 26 Jewett Drive, Newpoint. Retired, widower, does part-time bookkeeping. Skid didn't say how he knew this was the guy, only: *He's your man.*

I wanted to tell Robbie I had a lead on the armor thief and ask him to go to Newpoint with me to check it out. A bike trip might help patch things up with him. But since I'd messed things up, and by rights should be the one to fix them, and since I didn't want to be accused of another wild goose chase, I set out alone that cold Sunday morning on the four miles of back road to 26 Jewett Drive.

Stashing my bike in some bushes down the street, I strolled past the house half a dozen times. It was a plain white ranch house at the corner of Jewett and a narrow side street called Crayford, which went up a shrub-lined hill to the left of the house. The blinds were closed. I didn't see lights in any windows.

The attached garage was on the right with the door on the side, and an *L*-shaped driveway leading into it. No sign of a basement, no ground-level windows. The most likely place for pieces of ancient treasure in burlap sacks, then, might be the garage.

What should I do? I wondered. *Stroll up to the front door and announce my presence? Peek in a window? Was it breaking and entering if I didn't break anything, and if I sort of entered by easing the garage door up about eight inches and squeezing under?*

Traffic was sparse in Newpoint early on a Sunday morning. I crossed the street, walked up the driveway, and angled across the backyard like I was heading onto Crayford Avenue. Crossing yards isn't frowned on in my area. Kids do it all the time in Magdeline, coming and going from each others' houses after school.

Three-fourths of the way up the slant of Mr. Dowland's long, narrow yard, I glanced back. I couldn't believe my luck. There was a back door on the garage, and it was standing wide open. I stopped at the edge of his yard under a black locust tree and looked around. *Where is he?* I watched and waited a while. *Why's the door open?*

I ruled out yard work. *Is he out walking a dog? Had the door just blown open? Maybe he's at a neighbor's, having coffee. The longer you wait, Creek, the worse your chances.*

I made a big deal of scratching my head and looking confused, as if I were lost, in case a mom in the neighborhood was washing breakfast dishes at the kitchen sink and spotted me out her window. I cut back across the yard again, curving my path toward the garage. Then I peeked in.

Almost as I'd pictured it, there was a pile of burlap sacks in the corner with a shovel. A dusty blue car hogged most of the space in the garage. I slipped just inside the doorway and pressed myself against the bare stud wall, my heart jack-hammering my ribs.

The car's here. He must be home. Probably asleep. The door must have blown open.

I argued with myself about what to do next. Oddly, I thought about what Reece would do. *Well, she wouldn't go rummaging around in someone's garage without asking, that's for sure. This is a hard call. Mr. Stan Dowland had stolen back the armor, which I had first taken from him and buried in a place that no one owned. And though we had taken it from him first, we hadn't stolen it actually, but found it, and not in a legal church graveyard, but just outside the graveyard, in the dirt next to a reject grave with a blank headstone. So who had rights to it?*

I needed a lawyer.

I was all tied in knots about what to do next when I heard the most horrible, bloodcurdling barking imaginable coming from the yawning doorway. My eyes shot around the corner and landed on a huge, woolly, black malamute tearing across the backyard, his fangs bared, eyes blazing, coming right at me at ferocious speed. At the very instant he bounded through the door, I was up on the roof of the car, half standing, not breathing.

His wild barks cut through the stale air of the little garage. His toenails clawed at the bumper, his weight rocked the car. He wanted at me. If he hadn't been so bulky, and the car hadn't been so slick, he'd have made it up on the hood the first try. I would have been dog food.

I was actually relieved when the old man rushed in and started yelling. I must have looked terrified. He commanded, "Salem! Get down!" When it refused to obey, he grabbed the beast by the collar. Then he started yelling at me.

"What do you think you're doing!?"

"I...I...came for the helmet...sir." It's what Reece would have said: the blunt, unvarnished truth—but with respect.

His thin face went from alarm to pale confusion to flat recognition. He knew who I was: a church-vandal-turned-scared-Indian-boy in the woods, now a burglar surfing on his car roof, trapped. The way he recognized me told me for absolute sure that he'd been the one watching me.

"You! Get out!" he ordered.

"You threw it away...sir. Why can't I have it?"

He seethed. "Thrown away and buried are two different things!"

He had a point, but I was stuck on the car for the time being, so I might as well keep pressing. "It's for my friend. She can't walk. She thinks it has power."

"Oh, the armor has power, all right. But not the kind you could handle. No good will come of it." He kind of laughed, but it was a downright unpleasant laugh.

"Then why can't we have it?"

The malamute was yanking at his arm, teeth still bared at me, snarling and drooling. Mr. Dowland took a minute to hoist the dog up the two steps into his house and shut the door. He turned back to me.

"Let it go. You don't know what you're dealing with."

Why I got so bold, I'll never know. He could have let his black beast loose on me with one turn of a doorknob. But I pressed on, "I didn't break in here. The door was open. I'm sorry. And…but, I can't let it go, sir, not without knowing the story. For the sake of my friend." Cautiously I slithered off the top of the car to the trunk, my knees still rubbery. I glanced at the sacks in the corner. They looked empty. My feet slid to the floor.

"Give it up," he said, "and get out."

"I'll get out," I said, easing toward the door. The malamute was still barking. I could hear snarling, his claws scraping the paint off the door, his body pressing against the wood, trying its strength. I was pretty terrified, but I thought of Reece and the others, and was just frustrated enough not to care what happened to me. "I'll get out…but I can't give that armor up."

"You won't find it."

"I found *you*, didn't I?"

Quickly I calculated the distance between him and the door to his house, and the distance between me and my bike down the street. Gauging my speed against his and his dog's, I could probably just get to it and be off before that fanged creature called Salem could tear me to shreds. I kept one eye on Mr. Dowland's hand.

"I have nothing to say, boy."

But I had something to say to *him*, which just might set him off.

He was facing me, the light from the back door falling on his face. I seriously looked at him for the first time. His eyes were pale blue, but not like Reece's clear sky blues. His were cloudy and not quite focused. His face was very thin and dry, scruffy because he hadn't shaved yet, and carved with deep lines. It struck me that, if Telanoo could be human, its face would look just like his. He hardly had lips, just a thin slit of a mouth, turned down into a frown. He had on a threadbare, green and gray flannel shirt, gray work pants, and beat-up tan tennis shoes. His hair was thin, gray, and greasy, his chin rough and dimply.

Sure enough, Stan Dowland was Telanoo in the flesh.

It was made clear to me looking into that face: he was hiding more than the armor—a secret, deep and dark.

Dark secrets come to the light if you talk to enough people. Someone else besides him had to know the story. I gulped and extended my hand, like Skid had done to me. The right hand of fellowship. Maybe the *upper* hand, if I played my cards right. I flexed the rubber out of my legs.

"My name's Elijah Creek. My dad runs Camp Mudjokivi. And, I'm sorry, sir, but that helmet and arm piece are very, very important to my friend. So, with all due respect, sir…if I have to—and what I mean is, if you can't give me a very, very good reason not to—I'll have to start door-to-door, first with 24 Jewett, then 22 Jewett, and so on down the street, asking questions until I know something about why that armor was buried in Old Pilgrim Church." I gulped and took a step back toward the open door. "I'm not giving up, Mr. Dowland. I'm not."

A gray cloud washed over him. His dull eyes settled on me. "It's not worth anything."

"That's okay. All the better."

Right at that moment, nothing mattered to me but having the scary, shining, empty-faced helmet in my hands...and someday soon, looking across my campfire to see the faces of Reece and Robbie and Mei smiling back at me.

Even Skid's face would be welcome.

CHAPTER 17

Gloomy and put out, Mr. Dowland saw that the only way to get me out of his hair was to tell the story. The last thing he wanted was a door-to-door survey of all his neighbors in New-point. It was brilliant, I'll admit. But it wasn't really my idea. It just dropped right into my head out of nowhere.

We stood out in his backyard while he told his story of all that went wrong at Old Pilgrim Church, starting fifty years back. I was freezing, but I didn't let on. It was clear to me that he was hungry for someone to talk to. He rambled a lot, and in places the story was boring. On other parts of the story he'd pause to stare off in the distance. When he'd come back from wherever he'd been, his eyes would be half out of focus, looking at me and through me at the same time.

All the while, his black beast of a dog whimpered and groaned at the door, still wanting at me. Mr. Dowland wasn't fazed by the cold. I looked over his shoulder and into the ga-rage at the burlap sacks piled in the corner with the shovel…as if…as if he hadn't buried the other pieces yet. *Could they be in his house? Maybe the whole thing is propped up in the corner of his living room. Somehow I had to soften him up.*

"Sir," I said when Mr. Dowland took a long break from telling the story. "We were only looking for old costumes or curtains for the school play. We didn't mean any harm."

He nodded, but said with determination, "That armor will be buried where it should have been all along."

"But you dug it up and moved it."

He looked across his yard and across time. His face clouded over, his chin going all stiff. "Yes, I did."

There was another long pause.

"Whatever happened at that church must have been awful," I said with sympathy and even half meant it.

"Rest in peace…" he whispered. "With pieces of the past… all the dear ones…and the others…tragedies and truth, a piece with a piece, buried…yes, now they will all rest…piece by piece they will rest in peace."

Chills on top of chills went down my already frozen back. He went on telling his story as if talking to someone else.

"See, it wasn't right before, but I have it right now. Piece by piece…they will rest in peace. Like the ones in the ground," he muttered and then just sort of drifted back into his garage and shut the door.

I retrieved my bike out of the bushes and pedaled full throttle all the way home, even down the hills. It was wide open road. As I struggled in my mind to figure out what to do next, I remembered Mei's words: proceed with caution.

As soon as I got home I wrote out his story as best I could. I still didn't have any hint where the treasure was, but two things were clear: Mr. Stanford Dowland was stranger than a two-story outhouse; and getting the gang together—what I'd hoped for before my trip to Newpoint—had lost all its appeal.

* * * * *

"Now! All quiet on the set!" barked Miss Flewharty.

It was the last performance and we cast and crew members were getting a little loopy. Robbie outdid himself as Sid. The makeup crew plastered his hair down except for a cowlick on top, which stood straight up. He had extra rouge on his cheeks. With the ridiculous knickers and blousy top, he was a crack-up.

He sneered and scrunched his nose right on cue. When Tom—played by Greg Moline—teased him to distraction, he burst into girlish wails and the audience fell on the floor laughing.

Reece had everyone on the edge of their seats. Pale and smiling through pain, she played Becky Thatcher mostly sitting down or standing in one spot, leaning on something. In the scene where she had to walk across the stage, they'd rigged up a walker to look like she was pushing a baby doll carriage. She stayed in character—sweet and fragile Becky Thatcher to a tee. I kept beating myself up over her relapse. It was my stupid insult that did it; either that, or by digging up the armor I'd reactivated a curse.

The lights went down to set up for the next scene. I wheeled the props off stage left, and then came Skid out of nowhere to help Reece stage right. I didn't know it was possible for someone as cool as Skid to ooze all over a girl, but that's just what he did. He sauntered onto that darkened stage, dressed all in black and carrying a cane. He oozed all over her like a big blob of tar, and she melted right back at him. They whispered and held onto each other while she limped off behind the curtain. I stood there watching across the stage with an armload of chairs for the next scene. *Did he sneak backstage under the eagle eye of Miss Flew? Did he join the stage crew at the last minute to be close to Reece?*

All I could do was hope Miranda Varner was in the audience and would miraculously see them in the dark.

I tried to reassure myself that a smooth operator like Skid wouldn't want a girl who may never walk right, no matter how sweet and smart and pretty she was. But a taunt echoed in my head, *Wouldn't be the first time you've been wrong in the past few weeks, Creek. Wouldn't be the first time....*

I had every reason to be depressed. No friends, no armor, no help from old Mr. Dowland. I was itching to watch his house night and day to see where he went and what he did, but I'd have to skip school and camp out in a stranger's yard, not to mention the problem of Salem. Pretty impossible. On top of all that, wintry weather was setting in. This time of year, when the lake freezes and the snow starts falling, I'm always glad we live differently than the Indians in the old days. I'm just spoiled enough to want a roof and a bed, a fireplace, and mom's home-made dinners. Despite the weather, Mr. Dowland's story about the whole armor gave me the courage to try again at what I'd failed at before: a vision quest.

· · · · ·

Mei had the sketches of the armor pieces, but she wasn't speaking to me. So I drew my own from memory. They weren't as good as hers, but they'd have to do. I packed them along with another Indian book from the library and my camping gear. I didn't fast and sweat like the Indians usually do before a vision quest, but I did take a long, hot shower with lots of soap, and put on clean clothes. I packed nothing to eat or drink. I told Mom I'd be at Robbie's—so I lied again. But this really was the last time, and before I left, I ran by Dad's office and told him the truth, or sort of—that I'd planned to go to Robbie's (not true) but changed my mind and needed to "go into my cave" (true). It's what Dad says when he needs to be alone. I told him I was going to Owl Woods (also true). But I didn't mention that I was going beyond there into Telanoo.

He gave me a curious look, asked me if there was anything I wanted to talk about. He wasn't prying, because when Dad "goes into his cave" he doesn't want the third degree, so he didn't push it with me either. I'd keep a fire going, I said, and I'd be careful. He told me to take the heavy-duty sleeping bag and the walkie-talkie, which I did, even though the reception breaks up just as you get into Telanoo.

By nightfall my camp was set up beneath Great Oak, due east of its big trunk to fend off a snowy west wind. My tent and sleeping bag would do the rest in the way of protection from the elements. "Shelter is always the first priority," Dad tells the campers in his survival lessons. "Shelter may be a tent, a wool poncho, even forest debris. You can survive several days without food and water. But when it's cold, a person can die in one night without shelter."

I'd picked up a lot of wilderness skills living at Camp Mudj: how to soak up dew in a bandanna and wring it into a cup, how to spot edible plants, how to make a splint. I'd been working on traveling barefoot, so I took off my shoes and socks while I gathered wood and leaves to build a small fire. The ground was like ice. But vision quests aren't about being comfortable.

Ready to begin, I put the Indian book on one knee and read a couple of paragraphs about how the Indians used an eagle-bone whistle in their powwows to call the Great Spirit. Then I looked at the sketches of the helmet and arm piece. If there were a connection between the armor pieces and the spirit world, this was the only way I knew to find it.

I'd forgotten most of the Bible verses Reece had read, but one phrase kept coming to me like an echo in my head, not in her voice, another voice: *Put on the full armor of God. Put on the full armor of God.*

How am I supposed to put it on if I don't have it? Thoughts danced around. The campfire flamed and flickered in the night wind. But nothing special came. Reading the Bible seemed to give Reece and Skid a kind of confidence. But I just didn't get it. Sure, there were cool stories like global floods and man-eating fish and even a witch and visions of seven-headed dragons and all that, according to Reece. But so what?

I'd forgotten what happens when somebody puts on the armor. Reece had explained it, but sometimes when she goes long talking about church things, I drift off.

The wind picked up, whispering through The Cedars just north of my campsite. The "tall brothers" as the Creek Indians call them, thick and black against the dark blue sky, breathed cold messages to me. I slowly rose to my feet. I listened, but couldn't understand anything. That phrase came again inside my head. *Put on the full armor of God.*

I kept watching that dark grove of evergreens, half expecting a great horned to come swooping out, or the shiny-eyed skunks, or even Mr. Dowland to come forth. I braced myself for a scene like the one from the old movie *The Screaming Skull,* where this big skull the size of a hot air balloon comes floating out of the dark.

Someone was in those trees, sure as I was standing there barefoot and alone. Slowly I tucked the sketches in the book and laid it down on the ground. I put more wood on the fire. I walked barefoot away from the camp directly toward The Cedars.

I know you're in there, I thought.

The fire to my back cast my phantom shadow ahead.

I know you're in there.

Strangely calm, I parted the branches and weaved through the trees until I was in the center of darkness. I couldn't see my hand before my face. I couldn't speak. If it was Dowland, I would have heard his feet, even on the soft, dead needles, even over the moan of the night wind.

Someone had been there. I felt him. I turned and looked back at my campsite, to see what he'd seen as he watched me:

a little fire, no more than a mesh of glowing light through the thick cedar branches; a little tent, nestled up against the gigantic trunk of Great Oak; and me sitting there reading. That's how he'd seen me.

Great Spirit, I thought suddenly. *Master of Breath.*

Was it him, was it really him, and was he trying to tell me something?

All of my senses concentrated. Every cell felt alive. Suddenly I could see that I was small and alone. My tall brothers, the trees, were bigger and older and stronger, but they were alive to help me. My fire burned a tiny spot in a dark, cold night, but it was enough for me. I was going to be okay.

And I knew—with no one saying the words—that even when I'm alone, I'm not alone.

The wind suddenly died and there was no sound, none at all. I knew someone was there. A calm like nothing I'd ever felt came over me. I'm not a crier, but I don't mind saying my throat tightened and my eyes watered.

No glowing eyes came, no screaming skull—just the quietest quiet in the universe.

It was like the Master of Breath was holding his breath for my benefit, so I could hear things…like my own heart, and the ocean roaring a thousand miles away.

I heard the trees settling in for the winter.

I heard starlight fall.

Time passed.

At long last, I got the nerve to speak.

"How can I put on the armor, if I don't have it?" I asked, terrified of hearing a voice from the night.

Nothing came, so I asked again. Still nothing, so once more I asked. To my mind came the picture of that forked path through Telanoo. I had taken the path up the hill to Old

Pilgrim Church. But the other path—grassy and trampled—where did it lead?

A voice inside my head, which sounded like myself only more confident, said: *Get it.*

CHAPTER 18

It was the hardest thing I'd ever done, calling a meeting of everyone—Robbie and Reece and Mei and Skid—to spill my guts all over the place and apologize. But I knew that I had to do it. Yeah, it was hard, but in another way it was easy, like bush hogging with Dad when we pull out stumps and thorns to make new paths through the camp. Or like when he and I built the road to the maintenance garage last year, just him and me, arranging bedrock, raking gravel all day long in July heat. It was hard work but good work. Every day I see that road and know what I can do with Dad and me working together. I looked at this meeting like building a new road.

What had really happened to me at Great Oak? I didn't see anything or hear anything other than my own thoughts and that one verse from the Bible. But whatever it was had changed me. Not a whole lot, but enough for me to notice. And enough for me to realize that I needed to come clean.

Before school I wrote out the invitations to the meeting with a big *Please!* at the end. I tucked a wild bird feather and an Indian bead on a leather string in each envelope: red for Robbie, yellow for Mei, black for Skid, and white for Reece. I wasn't trying to bribe them to come; it was more like a peace offering.

I planned to apologize to Reece first, since that was most important. I was afraid she wouldn't come—and with good reason. Really, honestly, I had no excuse for saying that horrible thing to her; it was just me being a punk.

I built a fire in the lodge and began to gather a tray full of stuff—another benefit of living at Camp Mudj. There were stashes of drinks and snacks all over—at the house, in the lodge and cafeteria. I grabbed cocoa and cider packets, trail mix and granola bars, and little pop-open cans of fruit, and beans and franks. I had a banquet ready.

The fire burned strong, casting gold flickers on the vaulted, knotty pine ceiling. No need for lights.

Robbie came in first. "Hey," was all he said. I asked him to help me scoot the couch and recliners close around the fireplace. He got the water going for the drink mixes. Skid came in next, sauntered to the couch without a word, plopped down, and stretched his feet out toward the hearth.

"Hey," I said. "Thanks for coming."

He eyed me coolly.

When Mei came in alone, my stomach sank. She was always Reece's shadow, and you can't have a shadow without the real thing, but there she was. She sat down and folded her hands in her lap and looked at them. I wanted to ask if anyone had seen Reece, but the words wouldn't come.

"Help yourself," I said, spreading my hand to the food lined up on the hearth, as if I was the headwaiter at a fancy restaurant and here was my elegant spread. Skid must have made that same comparison, because one corner of his mouth curled in what could only be called a smirk.

This was going to be hard, and Skid's superior attitude—arms folded, staring at the fire, not getting so much as a drink—made it harder. Whether he'd heard about what I said to Reece, or whether he just hated my guts for being myself, was hard to say.

There was nothing but three lonely sounds in the lodge: Robbie tearing open a drink packet, the pouring of water, and the crackling of the fire. I sat cross-legged on the floor and cleared my throat. "If everyone has what they want to eat, I want to begin by apologizing. Um…I was…kind of hoping that…uh…that we could all be here for this."

Dead silence followed. If they knew where Reece was, no one was willing to say. I'd stepped in quicksand and nobody had so much as a twig to reach to me. Not even Robbie.

Then the door opened. My heart went *thump*.

A gust of cold air rushed across the floor, and Reece came around the corner of the entryway and stopped, holding onto the wall for support. Across the room in shadowy firelight with her blond hair, white sweater and corduroys, she could have been a ghost or an angel. Robbie and Mei turned. Skid kept his eyes on the fire with that half-smile on his face. The door slammed shut. She started across the room haltingly. I stood to go help her, but her hand went up and fire flashed in her eyes, her jaw clenched in determination. Every step hurt her, but she kept coming without her cane. She was saying to me, *I can walk, you idiot, you despicable creep. See, I can get that far.* She stomped on me with every step and I deserved it.

I turned to the fire and made a big project of fixing her a cup of hot cider, her favorite, until she got seated. I presented it. She looked blandly into the cup. "I'd prefer something else."

"Hot chocolate?"

She nodded.

"Sure, no prob," I said.

Mei asked Reece how she was. She said fine.

Skid smiled at her and said, *"Maranatha,"* and she grinned back.

So now they have secret code words? It doesn't matter. I'll say my piece and be done, apologize to Reece for saying the cruelest words in the world, apologize to the group for losing our priceless trea-sure, then they'll go home and I'll go run blindfolded and barefoot through Telanoo and off some cliff.

(Not really, but that's how I felt at the time.)

I gave her the mug of cocoa and bag of marshmallows—so she could get as many she wanted—then I sat cross-legged by the fire again. They say if you encounter a pack of hungry wolves, drop your eyes and get in a lower position to show you don't want to fight.

"The first thing I have to say is to Reece," I began. My throat clogged. I swallowed, coughed, took a breath. "I'm sorry. I don't know what happened to me. I was crazy and mean to talk to you that way."

I would have gone on and told her the big reason I wanted to sell the helmet was so I could have my own golf cart and take her for rides, because I wished for her more than walking; I wished she could fly—

"It's all right, Elijah," Reece said.

"No," I objected. "It's not all right."

"Okay. I just mean you're forgiven."

"Oh." I sat there like a knot on a log. What in the world do you say when someone forgives you? What does it mean? Darned if I knew. Do you say thanks or cool or wow or *sugoi*?

I looked up at her. She smiled and shrugged like it was no big deal. She took a sip of her hot chocolate. Just like that I'd come up out of the quicksand and stood clean on solid ground. Just like that. I couldn't believe I was so off the hook. "Great... thanks. I'm really sorry."

Skid chuckled low, which just fried me.

"And?" she asked.

"And I'm sorry about trying to push the blood oath."

"No, I mean what else are we here to discuss? You don't have to keep apologizing, Elijah."

"I know, but in your religion blood's holy or something, and I knew that."

"I don't believe it's holy, just that 'the blood is the life,'" she said simply. I knew it was from the Bible because when she quotes verses, her voice changes; it gets quiet, but strong.

Everyone was looking at me. "And I'm sorry to you all about the armor. Since it was me who got us into the church, since it all happened on my turf, I thought I had more claim than the rest of you. And I was suspicious of bringing Skid into the group." I glanced at him. "I'm sorry about that too."

Skid's eyes drifted to the fire, and for a minute I thought that was it. He'd written me off. Then his eyes slid back to me. "You can trust me, Elijah Creek. Skidmore men keep their word. We didn't used to...but we do now."

"Thanks."

Having felt lower than a snail trail a few minutes ago, I could hardly believe how clearing the air could lift a man's spirits. All of a sudden I was happy, and starved. I reached for a can of beans and franks, popped it open, and started stabbing in it with a plastic fork.

"Elijah?" Mei asked. "The armor? It is really lost?"

How could I forget the other half of my agenda? "Oh, yeah. Good news, bad news. It's a long story so get comfortable," I answered.

CHAPTER 19

The wind picked up and whistled down the chimney flue. Skid finally got something to eat, and even said the banquet was a good idea. We all gathered in around the fireplace—me on the floor with my back to the heat and everyone else scooted up close, faces aglow. The rest of the lodge was dark except for red exit signs over the doors. The smell of wood smoke mingled with hot spiced cider.

Reece grilled me on details about the church as I laid out Mr. Dowland's story about how he'd come to Magdeline fifty years ago to a church that was already a century old.

"Dowland said they were a close-knit bunch, mostly friends and relatives, and always had a big choir for the cantatas at Christmas and Easter. Old Pilgrim was known for its fellowship dinners, I guess, because the old guy smiled and looked proud when he said, 'Oh, the feasts those women could spread in that basement! People had to eat standing up sometimes on those occasions!'"

Robbie shivered. "Big dinners? In that creepy, rat-infested old hole?"

"I'm sure it was nicer then," defended Reece. "Go on, Elijah, and don't leave anything out."

"Still the church didn't grow. They only added numbers when babies were born, and lost when people moved away or died. The minister wasn't happy with the slow growth, but the church people were content with themselves. One summer, the minister took his family to Europe to trace the family roots. When they got to Ireland, he bought a suit of armor from a gift shop in an old castle. The armor wasn't a real relic, you see, because an appraiser in the village had said it was pieced and patched, and had the marks of unknown armorers, meaning that each piece was made at a different time and place. There wasn't any record of the armor being used in a battle, even though it showed some wear. It wasn't fancy enough for royal processions, and the words engraved on it devalued the whole thing even more. The armor was just an oddity, the appraiser had said, a big trinket and not worth much."

"Not worth much!?" Robbie asked, as if I'd offended him. "Didn't they know a piece of it is a thousand years old?"

"You mean the chain mail?" I shrugged. "How should I know? But here's where I caught a clue, guys. When Mr. Dowland was talking about the minister's ancestral home in Ireland, once or twice he almost said 'my' instead of 'his.' I think the preacher was Stan Dowland himself, though he tried to make him sound like someone else."

"Reaallly?" Reece was hanging on my every word.

"When I told him I knew what the Greek words meant, he stared at me so hard I got really spooked. Anyway, as the story went, the minister started preaching sermons on the armor of God, to get the people fired up. That's when strange things began to occur."

"What strange things?" Robbie asked.

"I'll get to that. He said the trouble started in the thirteenth year and—"

"Thirteen's bad luck!" Robbie broke in.

"No such thing," Reece snapped. "What began to happen, Elijah?"

At that moment a door opened and a big whoosh of air rushed across the floor. The fire sputtered and almost went out. Mei gasped.

"It's just Bo, doing security," I reassured her, and went on after I'd poked the fire back to life. "The minister thought some strong sermons about being in the service of the king would wake people up. So he propped the armor up beside the Christian flag and they all sang 'Onward Christian Soldiers.' After that I kind of lost track. But for the important details, here's the rest, close to the way he told it: The congregation slowly disintegrated. Tragedies and mishaps came in a steady stream. One of the factories in town closed down, then another. Some people moved away, some died, some drifted. The nursery had a dry spell when there were no babies. Dowland's face went gray when he said, 'Just when we thought the misfortunes were over, another terrible thing swept through the church, a thing that can't be explained by common sense, a thing no family should ever have to go through.' He focused in on me at that point, and practically snarled."

"What was the terrible thing?" Mei asked.

"He wouldn't say, but he blamed the armor. I asked him if he thought it was a curse."

When no one laughed at me, I went on, cautious of sounding too weird. "To be honest, that very thing had been in the back of my mind."

They seemed to be taking me seriously. I looked at Reece. "Especially since you and Skid mentioned something about demon powers. Or I wondered if maybe the church was built on sacred Indian burial ground." I laughed. "My own life has been pretty wrecked since that first twilight when we broke into the church. Dowland himself said, 'See for yourself, boy. The church closed down, locked its doors forever.'"

"The minister buried the armor of God?" Reece said seriously.

"I asked Dowland how he knew where it was. He claimed the minister was his friend and had told him, but nobody else."

"Very convenient," Robbie said in a Sherlock Holmes voice.

"When I asked Dowland where the minister was, he said in a low, quivery voice, 'He's dead.' Chills went through me."

Reece's eyes were wide. "You think he's talking about himself?"

"He is," Skid murmured.

We all looked at Skid, who peered at us like a sleepy cat with his eyes half closed. "I did a little more digging in *The Magdeline Messenger* archives," he said. "It's just as you said, Creek."

Turns out Skid had been busy with a little sleuthing. *He is sort of useful after all,* I told myself.

Skid went around behind me and put another log on the fire before flopping back on the couch. I could tell Robbie wanted to yell at him for keeping that juicy piece of information to himself the whole time, but didn't have the nerve.

I went on with the story. "Then Dowland and I got into a big argument. I said to him, 'So, if the armor was left by the minister and he's dead and I found it, that means you stole it from me!'"

"You didn't!" Reece said, shocked but grinning.

Mei and Robbie were hanging on my every word. Even Skid's eyes were fixed solidly on me. Spurred on by their excitement, I reenacted the next conversation, mocking Dowland's gravelly voice, then using my own—pitched higher for contrast:

"'I didn't steal the armor from you, boy. It's not yours!'"

"'But Mr. Dowland, sir, it's not yours, either; it's the minister's, and he's dead!'"

"'That's right, boy! He's dead!'"

"'And why did you wait all night in the freezing cold to get it back from me—a cursed thing everyone was glad to be rid of? It doesn't make sense.'"

Reece's mouth hung open in amazement. "What'd he say to that?"

"Oh, he was madder by the minute, but I didn't back down; I faced right up to him. He just stared off into space and said, 'I did it for the minister.'"

Robbie said in a tone of eerie wonder. "So it was Stan Dowland who bought the armor, cursed the church, and made it close down."

"The church didn't close down," Reece said flatly.

"Hel-l-lo!" Robbie replied in singsong disbelief. "Didn't close?! Where have you been?"

"Pipe down," I told him, detecting a little of Sid still left in him from the play.

"The church never closes down," Reece insisted.

"But the doors and windows are all boarded up," Robbie pressed.

"The church is the people who believe in God. It's not the building where they meet. The church never stops, no matter what. The building over there is ruined and abandoned, but the church goes on."

I thought about it a minute. "The church is...people?"

"Yes," said Reece.

"Weird. I always thought it was...maybe I didn't think much about it."

Mei had been sitting quietly on the floor, warming her hands around her cup of cider. "How long did all these things happen to Mr. Dowland?"

"He didn't say."

"Fifty minus thirteen?" she figured. "The armor came thirty-seven years ago. It caused the trouble. He buried it. We found it. He moved it, buried it again?"

"Looks that way," I answered. "Or he's in the process."

"Where?" Mei asked.

I shrugged. "There's no way of knowing. At the end of his story, he started drifting off, muttering a riddle about a piece of the past with each piece. Then he said, 'Piece by piece they will rest in peace,' and something about 'pieces of the past.' That was his phrase. I'm telling you he doesn't want the armor found. But for some bizarre reason, he still wants control of it. Why else would he follow me into Telanoo, watch all night in the cold, and follow me the next morning to see where I put it?"

Frightened, Mei asked, "Why would an old man do that, hide and watch?"

"I don't know. But I do know one thing: he's not at all happy about our quest."

"He's daft," said Robbie.

"What is daft?" she asked.

Robbie crossed his eyes and drew circles around his ear. It must be the international symbol for crazy, because Mei understood.

Skid propped up on one elbow. "So, Creek, what's the good news and what's the bad?"

"The good news is that it looks like he's still got the armor. I saw burlap bags in his garage, which may mean it's in his house. The bad news is that he's not about to let us have it."

"Why did he not throw it away in the garbage, if it is cursed?" Mei asked.

There was a long, thinking pause. Three ideas were put forth, and we ended up thinking all three might be true: that

Mr. Dowland thought the armor had powerful magic, and destroying it would cause him harm; that "pieces of the past" meant that there was something sentimental attached to each piece and he just couldn't bring himself to destroy it; and that despite how strong he talked, he left open the idea of retrieving the armor sometime in the future.

"For what reason?" I wondered out loud.

Skid and Reece eyed each other mysteriously.

"What?" I asked them.

Robbie perked up, "You know, he could be lying about the whole curse, just to keep us away, to scare us."

"But we're not scared," said Reece.

"I believe his story," I said firmly. "He started getting really sad at the end. Old men don't choke up and go cosmic on you if they're making up tales."

Skid said, "If he'd wanted to scare us off his treasure, he would have done a better job of storytelling, making up tales of people strangled in their sleep by the arm, and eyes glowing red from the helmet."

Robbie jumped in, "Yeah! Or whoever possesses it bursts into flame. Good stuff."

I agreed. "A lot of his story was boring. I left out the details about whose mother came down with what ailment after so-and-so was laid up because of which freak accident just before this person and that person went bankrupt. There's no way I could keep it straight, especially with all that snarling and clawing at the door the whole time."

"What snarling and clawing?!" Reece asked.

"His demon dog Salem. It had my hair standing on end," I said with drama. "I came this close to being dog chow. You should have seen the fangs!"

"Demon dog?" Robbie's eyes popped.

They were on the edge of their seats. So I told that part of it. Skid slowly sat up on the couch. Feet on the floor, arms folded and resting on his knees, he studied me. When I finished the dog part of the story, he said, "Whoa…you're the man, Creek. You are the man." There was actual admiration in his voice. He reached forward and high-fived me.

Reece shuddered. "You can never, ever go to his house again! Not for the treasure, not for anything!"

"Salem…" Robbie said thoughtfully. "That's where those witch trials were, in the 1600s. He named his dog after a witch town!"

The coals had been dying down for a while, but the crackling of the fire had been getting strangely louder. Mei was the first to say something about it. We all perked up and suddenly noticed that, though the fire was low, there was a bright glow on the ceiling. It wasn't coming from the fireplace, but from the high windows at the back of the lodge. A red glow…

"What is *that?*" Mei asked fearfully.

We guys were past the kitchen and at the back door in a flash. Skid pushed it open and our mouths dropped.

Robbie screamed, "The church is on fire!!"

CHAPTER 20

The fire horns blared. Police sirens wailed. It was the second time that fall Camp Mudj had brought out the local forces.

Fire shot out the church windows and through the roof heavenward. I never knew until that moment the nature of fire when it devours a building. The fire knows it has won when the building starts groaning and falling. The fire gets angrier for a short while, when it realizes there will soon be nothing left for it to consume. Its rage becomes the roars of a dying animal, then everything collapses to smoke and ashes. I came away from that night with a new respect for the power and destruction of fire.

The five of us huddled in the back doorway of the lodge with our coats wrapped around us, watching in disbelief until the old steeple tottered and fell. Its huge, forgotten bell crashed into the flames. One hollow *gong* rang out through the roar and echoed across the camp.

In a pitiful few minutes, the old building was a smoldering wreck.

It was an amazing thing to see. Even sort of cool. But when the firemen came over to the lodge, and I saw the look on Dad's face, reality set in. He was afraid sparks could still make it to the lodge, if the wind should whip south.

Since I was the one to call it in, the police came into the lodge and questioned us. The five of us had the name Dowland in the front of our minds, but a secret understanding passed between us. We couldn't accuse a sad old man, not without proof behind it.

With a lump in my throat, I wondered what they'd find in the ashes.

· · · · ·

The fire was big news around town. Nobody knew how it started. I figured it had to be arson, unless those basement rats had taken up smoking. I worried most that it was an omen, or a warning, directed at me.

· · · · ·

The mid-term test schedule put the five of us in second lunch. The chicken and noodles were all gone and we were left with—

"What is it?" Robbie asked, lagging at the end of the line.

"It's called corned beef hash," Skid said, curling his lip in disgust. "I brought lunch."

One look at pink meat and white chunks swimming in grease, and Robbie whined, "Corned beef *trash!*"

There were green beans with fake ham cubes—not too bad—and bread and butter. We all passed on the rock hard, slimy pears, except for Mei. We took our trays to the far table and sat. Skid had a couple of steak fajitas.

"Okay, Elijah," Reece said, "tell us again what Mr. Dowland said about burying the armor—his exact words." She wasn't about to give up.

"He said it would be buried where it should be, where it should have been all along. That was right before he started going weird on me." I pulled my notes from my jeans pocket and unfolded them on the table. "'With pieces of the past…all the dear ones…and the others…tragedies and truth, a piece with a piece, buried…yes, now they will all rest.' Then he said, 'See, it wasn't right before, but I have it right now. Piece by piece they will rest in peace. Like the ones in the ground.'"

Reece grabbed the paper and read it to herself, again and again.

With a mouthful of corned beef trash, Robbie asked, "By the way, Skid, how'd you find him?"

"Microfiche and grandpeople."

"What is that?" Mei asked, cutting her pear with a knife and fork.

"Old library files of newspapers, stored on microfilm. And grandparents—they may not be able to remember your name, but they don't miss a lick about every detail from decades back. I went into Florence's on Saturday morning, got a cup of coffee, and sat down with the Romeo Club."

"Romeo?" asked Mei.

"It's code for Really Old Men Eating Out," I said.

None of us could believe that Skid had gone there by himself and sat with a table of old men in broad daylight.

Kids hung out at the Whippy Dip, never ever at Florence's. It was social suicide.

Robbie said to Skid, "You are loons, man!"

Mei said, *"Sugoi!"*

I said, "You're the man, Skidmore."

Even Reece said, "You're kidding!" and looked up from the paper finally. "We need to make copies of this. Study it and see what we come up with. I think it means there are other graves where things are buried."

"Or will be," said Skid cryptically.

"He means each piece in its own grave?" Robbie asked me, as if I should know. "Or is he talking about us?"

Skid shook his head. "'A piece with a piece' means two pieces together. We found two pieces."

"But what does it mean, 'with pieces of the past'?" Reece asked. "Could there be a mystery buried with each piece? A clue, a memento of the terrible thing that happened?"

"If that were true," Skid said, "there would have been a memento with the helmet."

"There was nothing extra in the sack but an old dirty piece of cloth."

Mei had been fishing potato chunks out of the hash on her plate. Thoughtfully, she sucked air between her teeth, which some Japanese people do when they're puzzled.

"The cloth," she said. "It was piece of blanket."

"That was just to keep the chain mail from falling apart," I said.

"Maybe not," said Reece.

This set us off in a new direction. We speculated over the cloth until second lunch was about over, when Robbie piped up, "You know, guys, I wanted this as much as anybody. A piece of armor would be cool to have. But this is a lot of trouble for what the old guy himself called a trinket."

We stopped and thought. Sad to say, Robbie had a point. Our chances of ever finding the whole thing were slim to none. But his words were like a hammer to my chest.

"Give up? That's crazy! *You're* loons!" I blurted out. "Do what you want, but I can't stop. I have to find the whole armor, I have to find it and put it on, like I was told: 'Put on the full armor of God'!"

Everyone gaped at me. I'd said the words like Reece had said them, strong and ringing with authority. Even I was surprised.

Reece shot a glance at Skid.

I got uneasy. "What? What was that look for?"

"Something happened to you, didn't it?" she asked.

Skid had a sneaky half-smile and a downright friendly gleam in his eye.

So I told them as quick as I could about the night at Great Oak, the presence in The Cedars, and the words that came into my mind from nowhere.

Robbie said, "Well, you can't wear what you can't find."

"Yeah, that's what I thought—"

Skid broke in, "If he tells you to wear it, he will help you find it."

Reece grinned from ear to ear.

"Who? What?" I asked them. "What are you guys thinking?"

"He spoke to you," Skid said. "Who?"

"God," said Reece.

I'd thought as much myself, but still couldn't believe it in the light of a new day. I pushed back from the table and shook my head. "Nuh…nah, I remembered a verse you read, that's all."

"That's how he does it sometimes," Skid said.

"Many times, that's how he does it—through his Word," Reece insisted.

"Why would…God talk to me?"

"He wants to use you!" Reece said excitedly.

I didn't like the sound of that. To me *used* meant "used up," like the year before when I sort of liked Pamela Welch, and she found out, and invited me on a picnic with her family, but just to make her boyfriend jealous. When he wanted her back, she dropped me like a hot potato. Nobody likes to be used, but the way Reece sounded, God using you was the coolest thing in the world.

She bubbled over. "It's not lost forever!"

"Hold on!" I objected. "Suddenly I feel like this is all on my shoulders."

"It is, bud," Skid said in friendly fashion. "You got the call."

"How could I get a call from God when I'm not sure I believe in him?"

"He must believe in you."

I looked at Robbie to see if he was getting any of this—him being the brains of the family—but he was busy poking his fork into Mei's cup of petrified pears. *What was I supposed to do?*

CHAPTER 21

The cause of the fire was ruled inconclusive, mostly because nobody cared much to do any deep investigating. Dad and the rest of the town were plain glad to be shed of an eyesore and a nuisance. I went over just once when no one was around and looked into the charred hole, feeling the faintest twinge of hope that I'd see something metallic. I doubted even the hardest metal could survive that inferno.

The eerie newspaper headline read "Old Pilgrim Burns," and only gave a couple of short paragraphs about when it was built and how many ministers it had. Doing a little math showed me that once the armor came, the church had lasted only seven years.

I couldn't help being morbidly curious about where Dowland was at that moment, if he'd set the fire himself, or if he'd died in it. I wondered who'd feed his dog if he never returned. I, for one, wouldn't be offering to break into that house to check if poor old Salem needed something to gnaw on.

A blue haze drifted up from the ashes, and all of Camp Mudjokivi smelled like smoke for the next few days. Plans were discussed to fill the hole of the ruin before the ground froze.

There was no school the next day because of parent-teacher conferences, and since the gang was all passing, and pretty much behaving ourselves, it was a free day. We decided on another all-nighter to plan our next move, maybe scout around the camp for more clues. The parents actually said okay. Bo was pulling more late security duty since the fire, doing stuff in the upstairs lodge office in between rounds; so we'd be semi-chaperoned. Besides that, every living, breathing soul on the planet trusted Reece and Mei. Robbie, Skid, and I were innocent of any possible mischief just by association.

I pulled our five best sleeping bags out of storage, and made the lodge furniture into a tight, cushy semicircle around the fireplace. Mom sprung for pizzas for us.

Everyone had gotten together and decided to wear the beads on leather strings I'd given them, which was very cool. I'd have to make one for myself, a green one. *Maybe,* I thought, *just maybe the five of us could be a clan of the same fire.*

I told them how I'd pictured the forked path in my mind at The Cedars, how curious it all was, a path in Telanoo. No one but me had seen *The Screaming Skull,* so we watched that and had a good laugh. There were some scary parts all right, but the acting was so bad, you could hardly feel sorry about what happened to the victims.

We were all warm and cozy in that otherwise big dark room. As the night wound down, Robbie burrowed into his bag in front of the fire, like a hibernating bunny with just his eyes peeking out. Reece wrapped herself in a recliner, so Mei followed suit in the other recliner. Skid stretched out flat on the couch in between and folded his arms and closed his eyes like he was dead. I was on the floor, propped against Mei's recliner facing Reece, and looking up Skid's nostrils.

Occasionally a door opened and a draft crept across the floor as Bo came in and out on his rounds. The five of us took turns keeping the fire stoked. Even Reece did. It took her longer and she could lift only the small logs, but no one said, "Here, you rest. I'll do that for you." Being included was important to her.

"Nice fire," I said.

"Yeah," she said back.

Mei fell asleep sitting up, and was slumped over, rubber-spined.

"She'll break her neck," I whispered to Reece.

"The Japanese learn to sleep on the buses and trains," Skid muttered. "They can sleep standing up." His eyelids drooped.

The long, thinking pauses got longer and kind of nice as the night wore on to wee hours. Reece wanted to know in detail about my "call." I told her everything, even the creepy-but-cool feeling that I heard the trees settling in for the winter and starlight falling. She thought that was a beautiful thing.

"It's your turn now," I said to Reece. "Explain again about the power."

Reece reached her hand out of her sleeping bag and curled her finger at me.

I scooted in front of the fire next to her chair and propped my arm on the end table beside it.

"The power's in the message, not in the metal," she reminded me in a whisper.

"Oh yeah, that's right. Then…what *is* the message of a helmet and arm torn off an old patched suit of armor?"

"I think it has to do with the church."

That sounded kind of boring to me, but I didn't say so. The last thing I was *ever* going to do was hurt Reece's feelings again.

"Why here, though?" I asked. "What's so special about our town that *the very* armor of God—if that's what it is—would end up here?"

"The actual very armor of God is invisible, and anyone can have it. But why we have this, this—"

"Show-and-tell version?"

She thought a moment. "Yeah. That's a good way to put it. It's a real mystery, I'm beginning to see. Maybe a huge mystery, one that affects the whole world."

"Huh?"

"I just don't know. See, Jesus was born in Bethlehem and grew up in Nazareth."

I must have looked as blank as I did at my last pre-algebra pop quiz.

"Those were little nowhere towns, like Magdeline, which God chose for his purpose, so there must be a reason the armor of God ended up here." She leaned back and closed her eyes, but not in a sleepy way. *"Soterion. Koinonia,"* she said softly, and got this smile that's hard to describe. It's sort of like when you smell brownies baking, or the first time in spring when you can roll the windows down in the car and stick your head out and feel the sun and wind—that kind of smile.

I think she was praying.

CHAPTER 22

I put one last log on, drew the fire screen closed so no sparks could escape, and listened to Robbie snore until Reece woke up, or whatever you call it when you're done praying.

We have a bird clock at the lodge, which chirps a different birdcall every hour. The robin chirped, which meant it was 2:00 in the morning.

"A body detached from its head will die," she said plainly.

"Yeah…" I said back, grasping the obvious.

"Well, Jesus is the head of the church. The Bible says so. If the church separates from Jesus, it will die too."

Skid's eyes popped open and he practically yelped, "Whoa! Reece, I think you have it!"

I jumped. She sat up and leaned forward, curious and excited. "Elijah, didn't Mr. Dowland talk a lot about dinners and fancy programs at the church?"

"Yeah."

"But did he ever say anything about helping poor people or doing mission work or Bible study—anything like that?"

"No, nothing like that."

"Well, that doesn't necessarily mean the important stuff didn't happen, but if the minister was focused only on the partying, then the church wouldn't be a real church for long. It would turn into a club or a block party."

I wasn't really following her. "What about the arm piece? What does that mean?"

"Severed *koinonia*," Skid said, turning his head toward us. "Somewhere along the way the church broke its connection with God."

"And with each other," Reece added. She must have seen the blank disappointment in my eyes. This didn't seem like much of a quest. "I know it sounds like no big deal, Elijah, but look what we've been through, some pretty heavy *koinonia* trouble ourselves. And it was just awful."

I remembered how my heart caught a bad case of the flu when I lost my friends. How would it be if a whole church full of people felt that way, all angry and sad, worse and worse for years? Pretty yuck. And a once-nice preacher turning into sour, crazy old Stan Dowland—the human face of Telanoo. Whoa…

"Skid, do you have the Quella?" Reece asked.

"Yup."

"Cross reference *koinonia*."

"Sure." He pulled that little gold gizmo out of his jacket and punched in some letters. It took a few minutes, but then he said, "How about this one? 'What fellowship can light have with darkness?' That's 2 Corinthians 6:14. He punched some more. "Or…'If we claim to have fellowship with him yet walk in the darkness, we lie and do not live by the truth.' That's 1 John 1:6. I'll have to do more research, but it seems like when fellowship is broken people fall into darkness."

"Just look what happened to us," Reece said.

"Because of the armor?" I offered.

"No, because we were all wanting what we wanted. If we had found any kind of treasure, the same thing would have happened. Our problems weren't because of the armor, but be-cause of how we treated each other in a crisis."

"Not so good," I admitted. "I thought we'd never be friends again. How did it get so messed up?"

"One bad apple spoils the whole bunch," said Skid. I was about to take offense when he added, "What if the bad apple in Old Pilgrim was the preacher himself? What if he started it all, but didn't turn things back around and make it right, like Elijah did with us?" He paused and turned to me. "Hey, I'm sorry if I made it hard on you."

"No prob."

Reece said, "We all did things without considering each other's feelings. I called in Skid because I knew he could be trusted. But no one else knew that."

"So the mystery of Old Pilgrim Church is solved, anyway. We know why it died. Basically it was beheaded," I said. "Hey, let me see that Quella thing? What's that mean? What is it?"

Eyes closed, Skid tossed it in my general direction. "The name's a take-off of a German word for source. The Quella's a combination Bible, concordance, lexicon, and encyclopedia. It's a prototype. I can't be hauling a ton of books around."

I fiddled with it.

"Cool, huh?" Reece said. "Facts from the most important ancient scrolls ever, high-tech access."

I punched keys. "But…why?"

"Answers," she said.

"Answers to what?"

"Oh, not much really," she teased. "Just life and death and eternity and supernatural powers—little piddly things like that."

· · · · ·

The others drifted into sleep. I was the only one awake when the bird clock chirped 3:00 a.m. I turned my face to the dying embers, and bedded down. The door creaked. Wisps of cold air swept across the floor. The dark red coals flared. "Night, Bo," I whispered into the dark. He didn't answer.

I woke a couple of times later, when the cold wisps swept around me again.

· · · · ·

Gray light came through the high windows of the lodge. One by one we roused.

We'd already decided that we would see where the other path in Telanoo led, but I didn't know how to break it to Reece that she couldn't make the trip, and she hadn't said anything either. I was sweating over how to handle the situation.

She sat up and stretched and said, "Off to Telanoo. What's the weather?"

She must have read shock on my face, though I was straining to hide it. I guess that's why Robbie's the actor and I haul props.

"I'm going," she said.

"Sure, okay," I said in a fake cheery tone. "No prob."

"It will be a problem, Elijah, a big problem. You may have to carry me the whole way. But there's no way I'm not going."

"Yeah, that's fine. But, um, do you think you should call your mom or something, to make sure?"

"I already told her we might be going on a long hike, that you and Skid would take care of me. She said okay."

It wasn't that I was afraid of a little hard work. I just didn't want to be responsible for tripping across Telanoo with Reece riding piggyback and breaking every bone in her body. It was an established fact that I'm not the most graceful thing.

Dad came by and asked how we were.

Fine, I told him, and that Bo had looked in on us regularly all night.

"All night?" Dad said curiously.

"Yeah. He was in the office some, and the door kept opening and closing all night."

Dad grinned, "You must have dreamt it. When Bo saw you had settled down and drawn the fire screen, he left for the night."

He pulled a note out of his pocket, small and crumpled, and tossed it to me. It read: *3:00 a.m. The kids are down. All secured. I'm turning in. Bo.*

"Oh. I guess I was dreaming," I said casually, but I could have sworn the door had opened at least once more, right after the northern oriole on the bird clock chirped 6:00, and footsteps came over to where we slept, then back out with a rush of cold air. My face had been turned to the fire, my back to the door, and the sleeping bag pulled up high around my head, but still I would have sworn it.

"We're going on a hike. Is that okay?" I asked him.

Dad was halfway to the stairs. "Sure." Then he turned. "Just be on the lookout. Some dog got loose in Newpoint and bit a child. They haven't found it yet."

The five of us looked at each other. I hardly dared to ask, "What kind of dog?"

"A big black malamute, and not the best disposition, from what the neighbors said. It'll probably turn up in Newpoint, but just as a caution."

Robbie's eyes got big as saucers as he breathed the word, "Salem."

CHAPTER 23

Aunt Grace and Uncle Dorian were into antiquing, combing old properties for buried lockboxes and such. They weren't the least bit suspicious when Robbie asked his mom to drop off their metal detector. He told her we were hiking around, looking for ancient buried treasure, and she said, "Sure. If you find anything, I get ten percent."

Reece prayed for a clear, warm morning and we got one. I asked her why didn't she pray for that kind of day every day. She rolled those sky blue eyes at me and said, "It doesn't work that way, Elijah. God helps his children. He doesn't spoil them rotten. And can you imagine the earth with all sunny days and no rain? You know better than that."

She went on to explain that prayers aren't all about getting what we want either. They should have the idea of "thy will be done." It seems prayers work best if that part is added in somewhere.

We took the golf cart as far as we could. Then we separated out our gear: detector, shovel, walkie-talkies, binoculars, canteen and sandwiches, and my bow and arrows thrown in as an afterthought.

Reece could make it okay on the smoother parts. And we had plenty of rest stops along the way. None of us could shake the idea that the old man's riddle meant separate secrets were buried with each piece, and that each piece might be along the path through Telanoo. That's when Skid remembered a letter from Dr. Stallard. He pulled a folded envelope out of his jeans pocket and tore into it. "I wanted to open this when we were together. I totally forgot last night."

He read: *"Dear Marcus and other children, I have discovered a bit of interesting news you should know. A few of the links in the fragment of chain mail you gave me are pure gold."*

"Pure gold?" Robbie wheezed.

"Twenty-four carat," Skid read on. *"This is quite remarkable. From a defensive standpoint, this makes no sense, of course. Gold is a soft metal. Other alloys can be added to strengthen it. Sometimes pure gold is used with ornaments or overlays, say, on a ceremonial breastplate or sword hilt. But solid gold mesh in battle armor is unheard of. The weight—and therefore the value—of these links is insignificant. Also, from the small sampling we have, it's impossible to say whether the gold links are random or if they make a pattern, perhaps a symbol. Time will tell when the pieces come together. Destroy this note, and tell no one. Stay the course. Dr. Stallard."*

"We have to find it!" Robbie burst out, skipping ahead and acting like he had ants in his pants.

Conversation slacked off. We needed all our breath to walk. We'd crossed what I guessed was a third of Telanoo when we found the forked path and headed in a northeast direction. *Get it.* The words I'd told myself that night at Great Oak came back to me strong and clear.

"We'll get it, no prob," I said confidently.

"But no more lying," Reece huffed and puffed. "How can we keep it a secret, if we don't—?"

"No lying, no matter what. That's my final word."

I didn't see how that was possible, but kept my opinion to myself.

When the way got jagged and rough, Skid and I took turns carrying Reece piggyback. It was exhausting, but I didn't let on.

A couple of times she whispered thanks and "You're really great to do this" and "This is the most fun I've had," even though she had to be in a lot of pain and really tired.

The whole time I kept my ear perked for bloodthirsty barking. I just couldn't get the idea of Salem on the loose out of my mind. So I stayed close to Mei, who carried my bow.

We came to a strangely slanted hill and slowly made our way up. From the top, the view stretched out on three sides. The girls oohed and aahed. In the distance smooth hills rolled between valleys thick with trees. A few tiny white farmhouses with red or black barns could be seen. In the center of the far panorama was a heavy woods stretching to the east as far as the eye could see.

"That's Council Cliffs State Park," I pointed.

Mei had never been there, so I described it: "It has water-carved gorges, a natural rock bridge, waterfalls, box canyons, and shallow caves where some believe Indian councils were held."

"We'll have to go there sometime," Reece said enthusiastically. Her cheeks were pink, though she was pale around the mouth. She'd never ever walked this far all at one time.

Everyone agreed that we'd hike the rim of a canyon next spring.

The trail went cold on that hill of rocks and hard-packed dirt. We wandered the hilltop for clues and came up with zip. Mei, who'd brought binoculars, scanned the wide meadow below us and the thickets beyond. Robbie suggested that he and I scout ahead while the others rested.

Half a dozen crows flew over and landed in the smooth, bleached branches of a lone sycamore at the highest point of the hill. Robbie called our attention to it and named it the Bone Tree. The crows screeched at us. According to some

Indian beliefs, birds are the Great Spirit's way of acknowledging our presence. *If that's so,* I wondered, *are they saying hello, or warning us to go back?* I began to see why Indians read nature like a book.

The hill we stood on looked like no other in the whole area. It started down as a gentle curve, but it just kept curving—like a giant boulder—until it was almost straight down by the time it reached the meadow below. It was covered with thorns and decaying stumps, with cracks and crevices in the worst places for rock climbing. I worried how we'd all get down and if this even was the way. But this hilltop was where the path had led. I scouted around the hill a little, and was looking for a path down when Mei called out, "I see…a broken…house."

"A what?" I scrambled back up the hill and borrowed the binoculars.

If it hadn't been a sunny, leafless day, and if Mei hadn't been looking very hard, we'd never have found it. At the far end of the vast meadow, poking up just above a dark tangle of gnarly trees and bushes were the remains of a chimney and a wall. "It's a ruin!" I cried.

"Maybe that's it!" Robbie said. "Maybe the next grave is there! Let's go!"

I couldn't leave Reece behind, even though she knew how excited we were to get there quickly. She kept saying, "You guys go on. You can describe it through the walkie-talkies. I can watch from here. Please, I want you to go ahead."

But it was so strong in my heart to bring her along that the extra half hour it would take wasn't important. That brave smile and sad slant in her eyes nailed it for me. If I was going, she was going. When I said so, her whole face lit up.

We all were scared going down the hill, an unnatural curve compared to the rest of the landscape, shaped like the back of a crusty old skull. Robbie came up with the name Devil's Cranium. Mei pretty much scooted down on her backside from rock to rock with our gear tucked under her arm or hanging from her neck. Even easygoing Skid clamped his jaw shut and didn't relax the whole way down. We formed a kind of box around Reece: Robbie went in front, with Skid and me on either side, inch by inch. Most of what we said on the way down was, "easy, easy, step here, yeah, good, okay, take it easy, good," and so on.

Reece was white as a sheet when we got to the bottom, but her smile was ear to ear. "Made it," she said, breathing hard. "Made it."

All of a sudden we were in a huddle, hugging and laughing, like we'd just won the World Series.

We didn't dare think how we were going to get back up that ripped and ragged place where nothing new grew. Nothing died there either, but just sort of hung on to life half-heartedly. Maybe the devil himself *was* buried up to his neck in Telanoo.

It was a ruin, all right, burned, decayed, overgrown. Only part of a charred creek stone chimney remained, with so much other stone scattered around the base we wondered if it had been a two-story house with an upstairs fireplace. Thickets of thorns swallowed the one upright corner of foot-thick logs. Strips of rusty metal and broken or melted glass crunched under our feet.

Quietly, we picked our way around the ruin, looking here and there for clues, wondering who had lived at the literal edge of nowhere, and why. We steered clear of the chimney, which was ready to topple any second. Beyond my surprise that someone had actually lived in Telanoo, I kept wondering if this location tied in to the armor.

Robbie showed Mei how to use the metal detector, and they found a few more metal strips buried under the dirt.

We took a break. I built a fire on the old concrete stoop and made hot drinks for everyone from our canteen water. We had peanut butter sandwiches too. I went and sat by Reece on the corner logs, still finding it hard to believe that she was speaking to me again, much less was still my friend, still part of my clan. Forgiveness had to be the coolest thing ever, especially for people like me.

"Maybe the treasure's not here," she said tiredly. "Maybe it's back at Devil's Cranium, where the trail ended."

I hadn't thought of that. "Now that you mention it, Stan Dowland couldn't have made that cliff, do you think? He's seventy-eight."

She told the others what we were thinking.

Robbie said, "You mean to tell me…we climbed down that suicide hill, nearly broke our necks, for nothing?!"

I expected Reece to blow a fuse, to zing one of her sarcasms at me. Instead she started to smile, then broke into giggles. I started laughing too, and in a minute we were all cracking up…until I heard over our giggles what I'd listened for with dreaded anticipation all day. Echoing across the meadow came a fierce, raspy barking that chilled me right to the bone.

My head shot around. There on top of Devil's Cranium was an angry, jittery, black speck. "Salem," I breathed. "It's him!"

We watched the beast pace back and forth across the top of the hill, barking like mad, looking for a way down.

No, I said inside. *No. No!*

The black dot stopped pacing and raving across the top of Devil's Cranium and started in a fever to work its way down the pale gray slope. From such a great distance, Salem looked as harmless as a marble bouncing its way down through a pinball machine. But I'd seen those blazing eyes and dripping fangs bared and hungry for flesh. Everyone looked at me, and saw pure fear.

"Mei!" I yelled. "Where's my bow?!"

"I put it down!" she cried, and started running. "Oh, where is it? Where is it!?"

It seemed like hours, but a few seconds later she shoved the bow into my hand.

"The arrows! The arrows!" I yelled, my eyes still locked onto that dark spot. Salem had made it to the bottom of Devil's Cranium in precious little time. He disappeared in the tall, bleached grass of the meadow, but his fierce bark kept getting louder. We watched in horror as the tall grass quivered. It was like standing on the bow of a ship, watching a torpedo cut through water, aimed dead on for its target.

Salem had my scent.

I'd done a lot of target practice, but never at a swift moving thing. Never a thing coming at me at top speed. In a flash Mei thrust the quiver in my hand. I slung it over my shoulder.

"Get a weapon!" I yelled. "Everyone! Girls, get back!" Robbie had the metal detector. He ran and stood on the porch slab and held it like a bat. Mei helped Reece up on a rock, then handed her a couple of small stones. She got stones too, and they stood together, their eyes wide with terror.

Skid came up to my side with the shovel, held like a spear. He shot me a look. "How's your aim?"

I drew the bow up and aimed at the approaching snake of quivering prairie grass. "Not bad."

I could see Salem's head now, hear him cutting through the dry grass, thrusting forward with power in every stride like a racehorse in the final stretch. I was his finish line. He was coming after me first, and then the others who carried my scent because they were my friends. My arms trembled under the tension of the bow.

Steady! Steady!

. . . . .

I had one chance, maybe two. The black malamute's loping head fully appeared in the thinning winter grass. I shot. I heard a yelp, but the face kept coming. I pulled another arrow, drew back, aimed, shot.

Missed.

"One more!" yelled Skid.

Salem, the guardian of the curse of Old Pilgrim Church, was in full view now, his wild glowing eyes fixed, fangs bared. I'd broken into his house and he was coming to settle the score.

For the first time in my life, time stretched itself out. Sound stopped. I couldn't hear him ripping through the grass any longer, his vicious barks faded. I saw no hill or meadow or sky, nothing but a gaping, fanged mouth coming at me, dead in my sight.

Aim…aim…

We locked eyes. He came off the ground in slow motion.

Shoot!

I released. The arrow cut through the air and penetrated his mouth. He yelped, a black bulk writhing in mid-air, still hurling himself at me. I jumped back, but his body caught me on the shins. I stumbled backward. Skid attacked the thrashing, howling creature, jabbing the blade of the shovel into its neck and side. I recovered my balance, drew another arrow and released it into the creature's spine. He went berserk, clawing and gnawing at the arrow shaft sticking out of his mouth.

"Turn him over!" I yelled to Skid, drawing another arrow. "I need a shot at his belly!"

"Can't!" he yelled back. But gathering courage he took aim, rushed forward, and thrust the shovel into the beast's side, sending him sprawling. Swiftly I moved in, crouched, positioned the point of my arrow inches from his heart, drew back the bow, and released. A howl, then a whimper escaped through the stream of blood spewing from his mouth.

It was gruesome, what my arrows and Skid's shovel did to that beast of a dog.

• • • • •

Time resumed. I looked around to the others. They had been screaming and crying, I guessed, but I hadn't heard it.

Now the sounds came rushing back. My head spun dizzily. I breathed. "It's okay," I said. "We got him."

Mei had the hiccups from crying. Robbie stayed frozen in place with the metal detector held over his shoulder like a bat, until I went over and pried his fingers loose. Reece was a terrible shade of white.

"You okay?" I asked her.

She smiled at me, trembling. "I'm good."

When Salem was altogether dead and finished twitching, we approached him in a clump, all moving together like we had in the church basement—only this time with *five* heads and *ten* feet—until we stood over his bludgeoned remains.

No one said anything for a long time. We all seemed to realize that this wasn't just about a mean dog getting loose in the neighborhood.

"Dowland let him loose on us," Skid said quietly.

As one, our heads went up, our eyes on the far crest of Devil's Cranium. We scanned the edge of the cliff for the old man. But he wasn't there.

"We need to get out of here," I said. "Gather your things."

Reece stood staring at the hill for a long time, while the rest of us hurried to leave. She came up to me, her eyes full of tears. "Elijah, it just occurred to me, just this second: what if you hadn't brought me down with you, what if I'd stayed…" she turned to the hill, "up there?"

The others overheard. It struck us all, the grief of what might have happened…the four of us watching helplessly from the meadow while far away, up on that hill, all alone and defenseless, Reece…I can't even say what would have happened, it's so horrible.

But I couldn't take credit for saving her. "I felt it strong that you should come, Reece. Something told me not to leave you there."

I think I grew up a whole year in that one minute.

CHAPTER 24

We left Salem's body draining blood onto the hard, cold ground of the ruin.

On the way back across the long meadow, I asked Reece what *maranatha* meant.

"It means 'our Lord comes.' It's a word of victory and encouragement."

I rolled it around on my tongue. "Sounds Indian."

"Aramaic," Skid murmured.

"The language Jesus spoke two thousand years ago," Reece explained.

"No one speaks Aramaic anymore?" I assumed.

"Not around here," said Skid with a sly smile.

"Do you?" I asked him.

"*Talitha koum.*"

"Show-off," I said tiredly.

He laughed. "I only know that one phrase because it's in the Bible. It means 'little girl, get up.' Jesus said it to a dead girl when he brought her back to life."

I laughed. "A dead girl made alive?"

"Yeah," said Skid.

"You say it like it's no big deal."

He shot me a direct look. "It isn't, not to him."

The climb back up Devil's Cranium was a piece of cake compared to what we'd just been through. Robbie reminded us of the old movie. With crows crying above our heads on that curved gray stone cliff, a screaming skull wasn't much off the mark.

When we'd made it up to the Bone Tree and had caught our breaths, I asked if anyone had heard footsteps or felt a draft in the lodge after 3:00 the night before. No, they said, but they knew where this was heading.

Skid looked out over the meadow. "If it wasn't Bo, and it wasn't your dad…"

"Dowland was in the room?!" Reece cried. "While we were sleeping?" Mei added.

Robbie looked at me wildly. "Hold on! Did you ever find my cap, the one I lost at the fence?"

"No, and…I have to confess here and now. The night we saw Dowland in the graveyard I never said anything, Robbie, but Dowland probably did see us. He may have found your cap, taken it—"

"—to give Salem my scent!"

We were creeped out at the possibility that Dowland had been plotting against us from the very first. But at the same time, we were more determined than ever to follow our instincts and see where they led us.

The trail did seem to end at the top of the hill. All around was rock and scrub grass. Even the five of us tromping around the entire cusp of the hill hadn't left a print. So now what?

Remembering the medicine ways of the Indians, I wondered out loud if the crows were a sign, and I got ready to hear a sermon about what a silly idea it was. But Reece surprised me.

"'Ask the animals, and they will teach you, or the birds of the air, and they will tell you; or speak to the earth, and it will teach you.' That's in the book of Job. See, everything belongs to God, Elijah. He created everything; breathed life into it. He can use what he likes, when he likes, to teach us about himself."

I hopped to attention like a soldier. "Okay, then, we'll take a clue from the crows and start at the Bone Tree, where they landed and where the trail ended. Let's get the metal detector going. We'll start at the trunk and move out in a systematic way."

While Mei and Robbie worked, Skid and I kept our senses tuned for any sign of life approaching the hill. Skid found a stick to use as a club. I was armed and ready with my bow.

Reece rested and told me how God used a dove and a raven after the great flood, and how Jesus used sparrows in a sermon on how God cares for people. A faraway look came over her face. "I've never told anyone but Mom, but the week before my dad left, a pair of doves built a nest right outside my window. They sat on the branch and just stared at the house. A month later they kicked the nest apart and flew away." Her eyes got misty and she turned to me and smiled. "My mom said maybe God was teaching us lessons: that homes could be easily made and easily broken, and that God knew our home was being broken. He was there watching."

I wanted to ask why didn't he do something if he was really God, but I could tell it was hard for her to say even that much.

"So that stuff about learning from the animals—that's in the Bible?" I asked.

"You might be surprised what's in there," she said with a flirty kind of smile, wiping her eyes. She took a deep breath.

While Reece talked about the Bible, I kept an eye on Robbie and Mei using the metal detector, to make sure they didn't miss a spot. They circled the tree, working their way out in bigger and bigger circles. The ground was lumpy with rocks scattered and in piles here and there, as if it could have been recently disturbed. On a bare hill exposed to the weather, a spot of freshly dug earth would have settled soon enough.

I went picking around the tree ahead of Robbie, when I noticed a cluster of moldy rocks. The odd thing was that some had mold on top, while some were bare on top with mold growing on the underside.

"Somebody turned these stones over. Fairly recently. Hey, guys, I think I found something." The others gathered around. The sunny morning was long gone by that time. A cold front had moved in. I shivered.

Mei pointed the metal detector and began scanning. "Here!" she said excitedly.

Without a word, Robbie and I kicked aside stray stones and made a bare spot. I grabbed the shovel and jammed the blade into the ground. Setting my shoe on the head of the blade, I actually wanted to say some kind of prayer. Reece had said "thy will be done" works good, so I said it under my breath and put my weight into the shovel.

We took turns being lookouts and diggers. The dirt was rocky and coarse; it was painstaking work. Each time that shovel hit dry grit and stone, I hoped for the resistance of burlap. But nothing. Down two feet and counting, shovel after shovel…nothing…more nothing…then…

"Hit something!" I said, tossing the shovel aside and dropping to my knees. Robbie and Skid joined me and we dug with our hands. When Robbie's hand swept across burlap, we let out a whoop. It was as good as gold to us.

"Let Mei get it," Reece said quietly.

We stopped. She was telling us nicely to back off and let Mei get a piece of the action. And she was right. Mei was shy and always took a back seat to whatever the rest of the group wanted to do.

"Sure," Skid said. "Mei, you get it out."

"No, go ahead," Mei said.

"No, you can," Reece said. "I want you to be part of it too."

She nodded and smiled. Ever so carefully she lifted it out.

At first we thought the bag was empty. There was no bulk or weight to it.

"It's empty," Robbie whined, then his eyes lit up and he said, "No, wait! It's just like Dowland did before. Remember, he buried the pieces deep and threw the bag on top. We're going to have to dig more."

Mei lifted the sack out by two fingers of each hand. "Something is in here. Reece?"

With a gasp of pain, Reece got down on her knees and reached out for the sack. Mei put it in her hands. Carefully she ran her hand under the burlap to feel the shape of its contents. She didn't tear into the sack, like I expected. She looked up knowingly and smiled. "Of course."

"What is it?" I asked.

"It's the belt of truth. I know it, even before looking."

My shoulders slumped. I'd hoped it was the helmet and arm piece.

"Oh, don't be discouraged, Elijah," she said. "It's the first one."

"What do you mean?"

"The first one listed in the Bible. We were supposed to start with this piece, after all," she beamed. "See, it makes perfect sense. If we had found the belt first, we might not have thought anything of it. Just an old belt in a sack. But finding the helmet first, having it for a while, was like a hint. The helmet was to spur us on to search for the rest."

"When do we find the helmet again?" I asked impatiently. "Which number is it?"

She thought back. "It's the fifth piece, right before the sword." She looked around at all of us. "Don't you see? We will find it all. We have to!"

Every emotion in the world swept through me. I'd hoped we had rediscovered the helmet and arm piece, for sure. I wanted to redeem the pieces I'd lost. But when she said this was the first piece mentioned in the Bible, it did seem to me as if our feet were set on a definite course, an honest-to-goodness quest.

I knelt beside her. "The belt of truth…so, what's that mean?"

Her answer—when she finally said it—sent a thrill and a chill right through me.

She pierced into me with those sky-blue eyes, with the wind blowing her hair back from her face, her expression holding all sorts of kindness, but ruthlessness and courage too.

Reece said, "It means, Elijah Creek, that whatever plans you had for your life…well, that's all about to change."

THE ANCIENT OMEN

BOOK 2

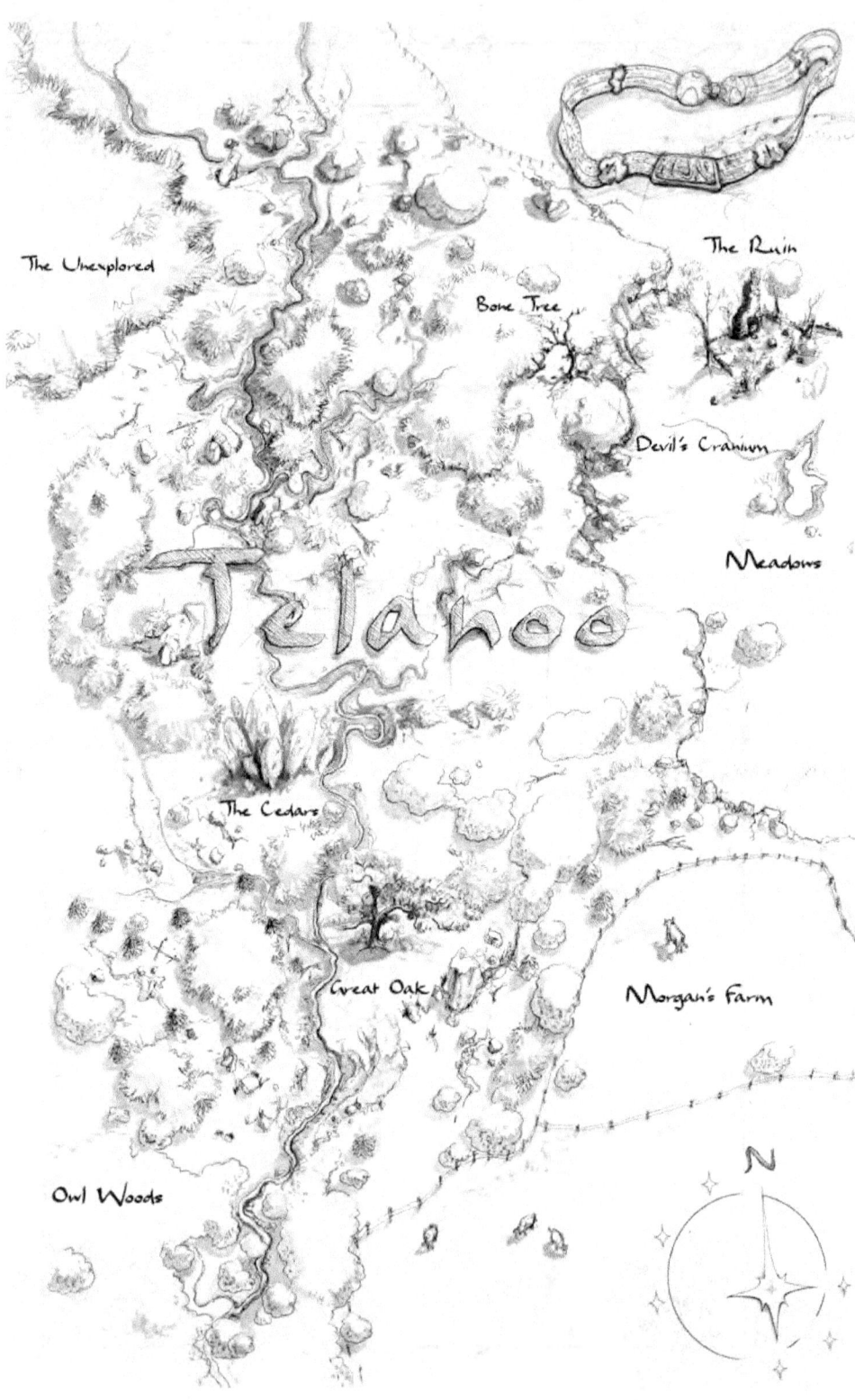

The Unexplored

The Ruin

Bone Tree

Devil's Cranium

Meadows

Telahee

The Cedars

Great Oak

Morgan's Farm

Owl Woods

N

CHAPTER 1

There we were under the Bone Tree with a muddy sack we'd just dug out of Devil's Cranium. The sunny day Reece had prayed for suddenly turned blustery and cold. Wind cut like razors across that hill and right through our jackets. We kept low to the ground on our hands and knees around the spot where the metal detector had beeped.

Mei put on plastic gloves—like we'd decided to do when handling the artifacts—as if we were investigating a crime. We held our breaths as Mei slowly reached into the sack. Something small and round fell out. It was a broken compass.

Weeks before, we'd found the helmet and right arm of the armor of God, which had long ago been buried in the basement of Old Pilgrim Church, and which old Stan Dowland had dug up and re-buried near the cemetery. The rest of it was still at large. We had ourselves a mystery involving two ancient relics, maybe worth a fortune. But thanks to my stupidity we had lost them, with little hope of ever finding them again. Only a thousand-year-old scrap of chain mail remained, and it was now in the hands of a scientist in Chicago by the name of Stallard.

It was clear that this was a quest, and that all of us—but especially me, Elijah Creek—had been chosen for it. Reece came to that conclusion after I told her about my night alone in The Cedars when a Bible verse came ringing inside my head: *Put on the full armor of God.* That kind of thing had never happened to me before.

So I became head of this operation.

The rest of the group on the quest were Reece and her Japanese friend Mei, my cousin Robbie, and Skid. I don't mind saying I wasn't thrilled about letting Skid into our group. But he was useful. He found Stanford Dowland, the key to our quest; and Skid made connections with Dr. Stallard, who advised us to keep quiet about the armor until further notice. Skid was convinced the scientist could be trusted.

Mei laid the compass in her palm and we all leaned in. It was rusty and the glass was shattered and mostly gone.

"Is that it?" Skid asked. "That's no relic."

"I thought you said you felt a belt in there," Robbie snipped.

Reece was still holding the sack. "It's in here. Has to be. Get it out, Mei."

Mei laid the compass down and looked in the sack again. "It is a belt!" she said.

The wind swept over us, building as it blew across the dead meadows of Telanoo. We braced ourselves against it and studied the belt. It didn't look ancient, but it wasn't modern either. It was a leather strip about the width of your hand. The buckle was strange: a metal plate with rough lumps and lines, like it had been hammered into shape. On either side of the buckle was faded tapestry material.

"Those designs, do they look Indian to you?" I asked.

"Maybe African," said Mei, "or from the Middle East." Odd-shaped pieces of metal were strung around the back of the belt on leather laces.

"Yes!" Reece looked at it lovingly. Her breathing was uneven. I thought she might faint.

"You okay?" I asked.

"We will find all of it," she said with conviction. "It may take a while, but we will find the whole armor of God."

For a long time she knelt over the belt, easing the dust and dirt off. "*Aletheia,*" she whispered excitedly.

Skid repeated it, and they looked at each other across the dig, their eyes all glittery. *Skid and Reece and their blasted secret bond!*

"What?" I asked, scooting over beside her. "You see something?"

"Truth." Reece smiled at me. "The belt should say *aletheia,* which is 'truth' in Greek."

"How do you know that?" I asked.

"The other two pieces had Greek engravings, so I looked up all the words from Ephesians chapter six that describe the armor."

Reece's leg was killing her and she needed to stand. She handed the belt back to Mei, and I helped her up. We all examined the belt, hoping to see the same kind of letters we'd seen on the other pieces: the helmet of *soterion,* or "salvation," and the right arm piece engraved with the word *koinonia,* "fellowship."

Mei picked away the mud caked on the buckle. "Is this a word…or a symbol?"

"It has to be the belt of truth!" Reece cried.

Skid tried to be encouraging. "Does it have to have the word on it?"

Reece said, "It should. Truth doesn't hide."

Huge gusts of wind slammed into the hill, stronger with each slam. The last one almost knocked us over. Mother Nature had taken up bowling and we were the pins.

"We gotta get out of here!" I yelled over the wind. "C'mon!" Getting Reece over the rocks and across the rutted terrain of Telanoo was going to take a while.

Time and time again I'd asked about who owned this land northeast of the camp. Once Dad said, "Oh, it's probably part of the Morgan farm." Another time he said, "Maybe Old Pilgrim Church owns it." Then another time, "Could be part of Council Cliffs State Park. I'm not sure, Elijah."

I'd asked others and gotten the same runaround. Bo, the camp activities and security director said, "There's nothing back there."

Mrs. Horstley who does office work at camp said, "Well, I don't really know, hon, but it couldn't be near as pretty and nice as the campgrounds. If you see 'No Trespassing' signs back there, you should stay out." Never a real answer. There were no signs, nothing to keep me out or fight against my crazy curiosity to prowl about whenever I had the chance.

The five of us made the long hike back to the golf cart in good time. Reece walked much better on the way out than she had on the way in. Maybe it was the excitement of finding another piece of the armor. We loaded ourselves and our gear into the golf cart. As we zipped along the paved path through Owl Woods, we talked about where to take our treasure for a closer look. Once in plain sight of the camp buildings, it hit me: the camp was busy on all fronts today. I yelled above the roar of the wind and the cart's motor, "We've got to find another place! Camp's busting at the seams. High school retreat in the front cabins, historical meeting at the lodge, Pioneer Days for middle schoolers at the shelter house. And...oh no..."

A dead serious look must have washed over my face.

"Elijah, what's wrong?" Reece asked.

"The Mad River Boys are coming later on. I just remembered."

"Mad River Boys?" Reece asked.

"From the boys' ranch upstate. A reform school. Big trouble! Dad has to put them in the back cabins!"

We burst out of the shelter of the woods into the wintry blast again. Skid tucked the sack into his black suede jacket, buttoning it up to his neck.

Reece and Mei were shivering but not complaining. The smell of snow was in the air. I went full throttle around the lake trail toward home. "I'll let you out at my house. You guys scope out the situation there while I drop off the cart."

We unloaded the metal detector and canteens at the front porch. "Keep the belt hidden, Skid," I reminded. "My sisters are around. And don't lose that compass. It may be a clue."

I sped to the maintenance building and slammed on the brakes, skidding to a stop. Tossing the keys onto the wall hook by the sign-out board, I dashed back to the house. While the others stood in the entryway, I cased the place. Straight ahead in the kitchen, Mom was glued to the phone while unloading groceries. The twins, Nori and Stacy, were acting like typical four-year-olds—not a good thing since they were almost seven. They'd built a fort with blankets and couch cushions in the living room, dragging every last baby doll and piece of toy furniture downstairs from their room. In about three minutes they'd be tired of it and on to something else, with the house a wreck and Mom saying, "Elijah, honey, can you give me a hand? The girls have over-extended themselves."

There'd be no privacy with them bored and on the loose—not even in my room with the door locked. Call me crazy, but I wouldn't be shocked if it turned out the twins had surveillance equipment in my room. Maybe they crawl through the heat ducts and spy on me. I swear, I can tiptoe down to get a snack in the kitchen, and in the three-fourths of a minute it takes me to throw a slice of ham on bread and get back to my room, they've sacked it, or have flattened themselves under my bed pillows or behind my camping gear in the closet. I swear they can hide out in my room for days without food or water. When I complain, Mom always pats my face and says, "It's because they admire you, Elijah," to which I usually say, "Why can't they admire me from afar…like Siberia?"

"This won't work," I said to Robbie. "What about your place—in the attic?"

We sat around the table in our log kitchen, acting casual and drinking hot chocolate while Robbie called his mom to come pick us up. I didn't get roped into cleaning up the twins' mess, but only because I had company.

"She'll be here in twenty minutes," said Robbie.

Mom said, "Then why don't you take off your coats and get comfortable?"

We said we were still cold.

CHAPTER 2

We rode along, listening to classical music playing on the radio under Aunt Grace's small talk. She asked in a real mommy voice, "Did you kids find any buried treasure with the metal detector?" (I should say here that if you're ever on a quest for ancient treasure, there's no need to hide it from your parents. They'll think you're playing a kid game and go right along.)

Robbie said, "Yeah, we found a broken compass." (I should also say that he didn't tell her about the belt of truth because the five of us had made a pact of secrecy. What I mean is, talking about plain old priceless buried treasure is one thing; spilling the beans about the armor of God is another.)

Aunt Grace said, "Better luck next time." We grinned at each other secretly.

Reece and Mei had never been to The Castle, as it's called around town. It's an 1800s Victorian-style home, on some historical register because it's the twenty-first oldest house in the state. A world-traveling politician built it, with imported Italian marble for the fireplace and entry floor, and teakwood paneling from India for the dining room. I never did understand the big deal about having all that fancy-schmancy stone and wood. Our log house is every bit as nice. And nothing is more awesome than the huge creek-stone fireplace at the Camp Mudj lodge. Aunt Grace and Uncle Dorian were constantly telling Mom and Dad all about the future "Wingate Bed and Breakfast and Tea Room."

To be honest, they hadn't made much progress. The white clapboard siding was all chipped, the little round window in the tower was cracked and boarded up, and the left side of the porch sagged like an old mattress.

Mei flipped over the house. "This is so beautiful. And so big!"

"It was one of the very first houses in Magdeline," Aunt Grace said proudly. "We rescued it from destruction." She dragged us around to every room, showing Reece and Mei her antiques and paintings. I'd heard it all before. Mei seemed interested, but she was always so polite, you couldn't tell what she really felt. Reece was polite too, but she was like me: in a big rush to get to the attic.

"Anyone feel like lasagna?" asked Aunt Grace. "I can have some warmed up in half an hour."

"That'd be great! We'll be in the attic," I said, pulling Reece toward the stairs.

Aunt Grace snickered. "Secret club? Private meeting?"

"We're too old for secret clubs," I said.

I led the way to the second floor, past Robbie's room, to a set of narrow steps going straight up to the attic. We closed the door behind us and turned on the one lone lightbulb overhead. It was creepy all right, but Robbie had cleared a place for hanging out in the middle of all the clutter. His parents were always going nuts antique shopping and talking with historians and decorators, so we were usually left alone.

There are clawing noises in the attic wall sometimes—not skittery mouse scratches you might hear in your own house— but big sounds. And the *thunk*ing noises on the roof at night! Robbie and I figured it was probably raccoons jumping onto the roof from a big tree behind the house. But if you're trying to sleep up there, it sounds more like Kodiak bears dropping from aircraft.

The attic had an old velvet couch waiting to be reupholstered. There was an oriental screen and an antique kitchen cabinet where we kept books and a radio. Mannequins—left over from Aunt Grace's short career at Mitts Bros. Department Store, right before it went out of business—reached out from the dark corners with stiff arms and blank stares. A rocking chair faced the one window. A couple of years ago, I'd joked to Robbie, "One of these days you're going to come up here at midnight, whip that chair around, and there'll be *Psycho*'s old Mrs. Bates herself, all dried up and gaping at you."

Robbie always said that watching so many old, scary movies was going to warp me. To prove his point, he fixed up a skinny dummy with a shabby brown dress and beige shawl. She had a bleach bottle head, a wig, and some hands from one of the mannequins. A magazine picture of Eleanor Roosevelt with the eyes blacked out was her face. Robbie went to a ridiculous amount of work for it not to scare me, so I pretended it did.

Movies weren't the problem. To be honest, I hadn't been the same since meeting Stan Dowland. After the old church burned down, and after his demon dog Salem came after us, it preyed on my mind what kind of revenge Dowland might be planning next. People tend not to like you after you hack up their pets, even though it was a clear case of self-defense, and I'd say that in a court of law.

The girls sat on the velvet couch with the burlap sack in their laps. We guys gathered around on the floor. Mei put on the plastic gloves again, took out the compass, placed it on her palm, and studied it. "It is not so old, I think. Maybe this is glue." Moving it in front of our eyes, she showed us the clear hard stuff which stuck the needle to its face. We each examined the compass without touching it.

"It looks like someone broke the glass and glued down the needle to keep it pointing in one direction," Robbie said.

"You think Dowland did it?" Skid asked.

"Who else?" I said. "He buried the armor."

"But why?" Mei asked, examining the back of the compass.

"Maybe it points to where the next piece is buried," Reece said excitedly. Suddenly her face dropped. "Oh no…"

"Oh no!" Mei repeated. "When I opened the sack, the compass fell out! We don't know the way it pointed when it was in the ground!"

"Rats!" Robbie said. "Another clue lost!"

Mei's small eyes got wide. "I made the mistake?"

"Mei, it's okay." Reece smiled. "*Daijoubu.*"

"Yeah," I said. "Anyone pulling the bag out would have flipped the compass. That can't be the answer."

Mei looked closely at the compass. "The needle is glued to ENE."

"That's east-northeast."

Skid turned to me. "From there at the Bone Tree, where we were standing, which way was east-northeast?"

"I don't know," I admitted. I tried to reason it out. "Wind usually comes from the west…but it was crazy up there, whipping at us from everywhere. Dad's map of the camp doesn't show Telanoo either.…Man, I should have paid attention to the sun," I said, angry at myself.

Skid said, "We'll figure this out."

He and I cracked fists in a friendly way. I wasn't totally convinced that Skid was as cool as everyone gave him credit for, but it was getting easier to be around him.

"The library!" chirped Robbie. "We can find land plats there."

"Land plats?" I asked.

"Maps showing where the borders are, record of ownership, and topography: hills and creeks and roads."

"*Record of ownership?* You mean we can find out who owns Telanoo from the library?" I thumped him. "Why didn't you tell me before? I've been wanting to know that forever!"

He frowned. "Sorry!"

"Hey, Wingate, pretty smart about the land plats," Skid said. "How'd you know that?"

"When my parents were looking to buy The Castle, they dragged me all over creation: real estate offices and libraries and—hey, wait a minute!" Robbie interrupted himself and shot me a look. "Why'd you thump me? You *never* asked me who owned Telanoo!"

"I didn't?"

"No!" Robbie punched my arm.

"Ouch!" I said, as if he'd really hurt me.

"Wimp!" he got up and ran behind the couch to escape the punch he knew was coming.

All of a sudden we were seven years old again. "Coming through!" I leaped over the couch. The girls squealed and ducked. I got Robbie in a headlock and knuckled his fuzzy scalp. "Dork!" I let go, dodged his next punch, knocking Mrs. Bates out of the rocker and onto her face.

"Toad!" He threw a hatbox at me and caught me on the shoulder. I caught it before it fell, lobbed it back, and followed with a wad of artificial flowers. We could have gone on another hour, but Reece and Mei were giving us superior girl looks.

CHAPTER 3

By the time we'd finished off Aunt Grace's leftover lasagna and took off for the library, a few blocks from The Castle, it was dark and spitting snow. I walked ahead of the others, thinking. The whole armor of God idea still puzzled me. *If there is a God, why would he hide his armor in the first place? I can't speak for him personally, but I wouldn't stash it here of all places.*

Magdeline was Nowheresville, U.S.A. It had only one main street, with a library, two banks, an antique mall, a courthouse, a drugstore with an old-fashioned soda fountain, and a few other places, like law offices. A little side street in the business district had a few more shops and the news office; that was about it. Mom said it had "charm" and "a ton of potential." Frankly, the town wasn't much without Camp Mudjokivi.

Skid and Mei found us a table next to the magazine rack and waited for Robbie to get the book. He ran up to the counter, trying to make his short neck longer, to look official. Reece and I stood on either side of him. Mrs. Otto's big eyes had landed on us the moment we came bursting in from the cold. She came tromping out from behind her desk in the back room. "Ten minutes to closing!"

Magdeline's head librarian was a squat lady with gray-brown hair and a flat face. Thick glasses made her eyes un-human and large. Think lemur, and you'd be close.

"Current land plats around Camp Mudjokivi, please," Robbie said.

She peered at us suspiciously, glancing over at Skid and Mei to get a head count. I could hear her alarm bells going off. Here it was closing time and five eighth-graders come racing in for no good reason, right before Thanksgiving when everyone else was out Christmas shopping. I personally never came into the library, except once or twice to get books on Indians and weapons. Skid—wearing his usual black gang-type getup—looked like he'd never cracked a book in his life. She thought we were up to no good. "That will be a reference book, which means you can't take it out of the library."

"It's for a school project," I explained to put her at ease.

Reece shot me a look, then leaned in and went eye-to-lemur-eye with Mrs. Otto. "Actually, that's a big lie, ma'am. The truth is," she whispered dramatically, "we're trying to find ancient secret treasures in the forbidden land behind the camp."

Reece got uptight about always telling people the exact truth, even though we were sworn to secrecy. It was a problem—for me anyway—knowing what to say and not say.

Mrs. Otto smiled sweetly at Reece and said, "I see. Just a minute." She scowled at me, pivoted, and tromped into the back room again.

I nudged Robbie and whispered, "I'm impressed. You are king of the nerds."

"And you're a primitive savage Indian," he teased back. He knows it gets my goat, calling the Indians primitive, because Creeks were one of the Five Civilized Tribes, and I may be part Creek.

I was ready to punch him again when Reece turned to me and practically snarled, "Elijah! You don't *lie* when you're trying to find out about the belt of *truth,* for Heaven's sake!" She heaved a sigh and shuddered like I had no clue about anything.

Then she actually said it: "You have no idea how the universe works, do you?"

How do you answer a question like that?

Mrs. Otto came back with a book the size of a football field. "You may sit at this table." She pointed at one closest to the desk. "Eight minutes!"

"But our friends are over there." I thumbed in the direction of Mei and Skid.

Reece ignored me and said, "Yes ma'am, we'll sit here. Thank you very much." They swapped smiles again.

You might think that people are nice to Reece just because they feel sorry for her. But the truth is—and I'm thinking this right after she insulted me, so you know I'm being objective— how can you not like her? She's got guts and she's pretty, and she doesn't jabber on and giggle all the time. I like to compare people to animals, but Reece is hard to nail down. She's kind of like a little yellow canary with a sharp beak.

After all the wondering and asking, I was antsy to find out who owned Telanoo. Each page of the big book was nothing but curvy lines showing creeks and roads, straight dotted lines showing boundaries, numbers like S50W 700p, and little paragraphs like: Edmund Blanchet to Cadwallader Young D 046, 27 June, 1939—to show who owned what and when.

Camp Mudj and the surrounding areas were on page 21. I figured Owl Woods and Devil's Cranium would be easy to spot, but they weren't.

We hovered over the map while Robbie's busy finger traced across it. He's great with maps. The type was so small only he could read it. "Okay, here's the camp lake."

"Elijah, you know the land best," Skid said. "Where's Devil's Cranium from there?"

"I want to know who owns Telanoo first," I said.

"I can't make anything out," said Robbie. "Look at all these paragraphs. It'll take an hour to read every one, and we only have eight minutes."

"Six minutes!" snipped Mrs. Otto from behind her big desk.

His finger stopped. "Hold on! Remember that *S*-shaped creek where you hid the helmet and arm piece, and where Mr. Dowland stole them back? This looks like it!"

"Shhh!" hissed Mrs. Otto, even though we were the only ones in the library.

"Sorry," whispered Reece, and smiled.

"Yeah, but there were lots of curves, remember?" I said quietly.

He studied it a little more. "No, I think this is the one. We've found the first landmark."

We cheered in a whispery way.

"Hurry!" Reece said.

Robbie dug his finger into the page excitedly. "So…go a little north, away from the camp…there…I think that's Devil's Cranium."

Out of the blue Reece said, "The truth will set you free." We all looked at her.

"'You will know the truth, and the truth will set you free.'" She grinned at me, but she was using that serious tone she uses when she quotes the Bible.

"Why'd you say that?" I asked.

She shrugged. "I don't know. It just popped into my mind." I went back to looking at the map. I never know how to take Reece when she talks Bible.

Robbie drew a straight line with his finger. "There's Council Cliffs State Park."

"Looks like the line points toward Hermits' Cave," I said, surprised.

We argued over which was more east or northeast until the librarian shushed us again. "Two minutes!"

"We should have brought the compass and laid it right on the map," said Skid.

"Let's make a copy and take it back," Robbie suggested.

Mei quietly asked, "Where is the old broken house?"

"Oh yeah, the ruin," said Reece.

"But we didn't find anything there," I reminded her.

Robbie's finger moved in a straight line back toward Devil's Cranium. "It was at the far end of that big meadow. The ruin would be in a wide place with no landmarks."

Sure enough, the meadow lay directly east-northeast, between Devil's Cranium and the park.

"You mean the compass would have led us back to the ruin?" Reece asked.

This was bad news. "We've already been over that place," I said.

"Maybe there's something we missed," Skid said, keeping an eye on Mrs. Otto's whereabouts.

"Maybe it's not metal," said Robbie, with a look of disappointment. "Remember from ancient history: battle gear sometimes was made from leather or wood. It wouldn't set off a metal detector."

We all sighed.

Skid suggested, "Before we do any more digging, let's give Dr. Stallard a look at the belt."

"Yeah," Robbie said, and closed the book.

"Wait, wait!" I cried. "Who owns Telanoo? I have to know!"

"Shhh!" Mrs. Otto came tromping over. "Are you kids finished with that book?" She reached for it. "It's time."

I wanted to say that I'd quit talking if she'd quit tromping, but she would have tossed us out for sure. I'd been needing this information forever. "I'm sorry, Mrs. Otto," I said. "We have to find one more thing. Just one more minute. Please." I was glad to grovel.

"One minute!" she announced to the world.

"Hurry," I told Robbie. He riffled through the book until he came to page 21 again and found a tiny paragraph in the corner of Telanoo. "Here it is, here it is!" He read: "Alfred Theobald to—"

His head popped up. He looked creeped out. "It's been blotted out! The name's been blotted out!"

We were all in deep thought while Mrs. Otto—with a lemur scowl of disapproval—made a copy of the map.

CHAPTER 4

Snow came down heavy on our way back to The Castle. We talked about where to meet with Dr. Stallard to show him the belt. I had my reservations about his coming, but everyone else seemed to think it was a good idea.

The attic of The Castle was a weird place to take a big-city scientist. Camp was out: too busy. The coffee shop was out: everyone's a regular customer. Dr. Stallard would stick out like a sore thumb, and we needed to keep a low profile.

"Oh no, I just thought of something," I said to Skid. "What about your parents? Won't Dr. Stallard tell them he's coming?"

Skid said, "Don't panic, Creek. I handled it before. I can handle it now."

That's all he was going to say.

"I'd like details," I said. As the leader of the group, it was my right.

He shoved his hands in his pockets and faced me, nose to nose, with huge flakes of snow falling between us. "Here it is, all laid out," he said. "Dad and I went up to Chicago last month. I asked Dad if we could see Dr. Stallard, that I was getting interested in archaeology. We tracked him down to a museum. I asked for a tour. Stallard obliged. When I got him alone, I slipped him the piece of chain mail and said I'd be in touch. Couple days later he called, asked where we got it; I said the other pieces were in good hands. Later he wrote us about the gold links in the chain mail. The end. You got a problem with that?"

"Just make sure to check with me—with the group—first."

He saluted casually. "Yes, sir. Am I court-martialed, sir?"

I shot a glance at Reece. She was watching me, not him.

"At ease, Private," I said, smiling.

Skid said, "What do you say I send Mei's sketches to Dr. Stallard, as a preview for our top secret meeting? But only on your orders, sir!"

I looked at the others. "What do you think?"

Mei said, "That is a good idea."

Robbie and Reece agreed.

While Aunt Grace pulled the car around to take us all home, we waited in the front hall.

"We have to decide fast," I said. "Where should we meet?"

Mei said, "We can come to my house!"

"Good idea," Reece said.

We guys were leery. Mei was so quiet, we didn't know much about her or her family. Could they be trusted?

"Not sure…" I said.

Mei piled up reasons. "My mother would like visitors, and to meet my friends. My brother and sister are in college, and she is lonely. My father works very late every night. He will not be there. It will be private."

"How will we explain the meeting?" I asked.

"With the truth,…" Reece said in a preachy tone, "that a professor is here to talk to Mei and her friends about local ar-chaeology."

"My mother can make dinner for us. She will enjoy it." Mei gave us a pleading look. "I will be so happy to help my friends."

We guys still doubted this was the best idea, but no one wanted to tell her no and make her cry.

Reece looked at me. "*Daijoubu?*"

How could I say no? "That settles it. *Daijoubu.*"

A few days later, Skid was waiting at my locker. "Dr. Stallard called the minute he got the sketches. He wants to meet with us tomorrow."

When Mei got the news her mouth dropped open. "My mother must shop *today!*"

· · · · ·

Mei lived on a nice street in a plain, one-story brick house. She didn't warn us ahead of time that we'd have to take off our shoes at the door. I yanked mine off and grimaced. Hanging off my feet were the gray, holey remains of last Christmas's traditional big bag o' socks. Pathetic. Mei offered me slippers, but my heels hung over the backs and looked goofy.

She'd already described her house, I guess so we wouldn't make jokes about it. "My parents didn't buy too much furniture. We are in America for two years. And Japan is very crowded, so we like a big empty house."

She showed us around. Her room was purple and pink with just a bed and a desk. The other bedrooms were bare and plain too, with only a bed and dresser each. The den was empty except for a table holding a fancy Japanese box about two feet square. It was dark wood with gold-trimmed doors open on the front. Inside sat a black-and-white picture of an old Japanese woman. The picture was surrounded by candlesticks, flowers, and signs in Japanese.

"That's Mei's grandmother," Reece said.

"This is where we pray," said Mei.

"You pray to your grandmother?" I asked.

Mei nodded. "It's our tradition."

I thought Reece would get on her case, like she does me when I say something about religion she doesn't like. She and

Skid exchanged secret looks. Then she said, "Mei misses her grandma. I think they have the same smile, don't you?"

* * * * *

The doorbell rang at the stroke of 5:00.

Dr. Stallard, as it turned out, was two people.

A skinny couple showed up wearing khaki outfits and hiking boots—like they were heading out on safari. They introduced themselves as Dr. Eloise and Dr. Dale, doctors of science. They were gaunt like Mr. Dowland, but energetic and talkative with bright eyes and pink cheeks. They looked sixty maybe but acted much younger. He carried a battered briefcase. She had a camera.

Mei let them in and showed them to the bathroom where they could freshen up. Skid leaned over at me in the hallway and said between his teeth. "I didn't know she was coming, I swear!"

My eyebrows went up, resigned. "Too late now. We have to go with it."

"I've met her only once before. I didn't know she was a scientist too. I didn't invite her."

"Forget it." I should have been miffed, this being top-secret business, but Skid was feeling bad enough. I asked, "You told them we don't have the helmet and arm piece anymore, didn't you? That we just have the belt?"

"Was I supposed to?"

My heart sank. "Well, yeah!"

"Listen," he said, "I sent the sketches like you said. He called to set up a time. That's it."

"You should have told them!"

He glared at me. "I didn't have high-level clearance."

Mrs. Aizawa, Mei's mom, bowed and waved everyone into the dining room and served tea. Reece and Robbie were good at chitchat, so I let them have at it. I kept thinking about that bombshell I had to drop: the Stallard's had come all this way to see two pieces of God's armor, and I'd lost them—a big deal any way you slice it.

The first course was soup: a little boiled quail egg and a couple of weeds swimming around by themselves in broth. Then the main course: steak and vegetables and rice, which was really good. Mei showed us how to use chopsticks. Reece and Skid already knew how, Reece being Mei's best friend, and Skid being an army brat from all over the world. Robbie and I did pretty well, though I'll always think a spoon and fork make better sense. It was as good as a fancy restaurant, with lots of dishes and the best service.

Nothing was said about the armor while we ate. Instead the Stallards talked a lot about the history of the Hopewell and Adena Indians, ancient mounds in the area and things like that, for the benefit of Mrs. Aizawa. We were saving the important stuff for the private meeting.

After the meal Mei's mom led us to a living room that had just a couch and a coffee table, a lamp, a bookcase, and a stack of cushions to sit on. She bowed and backed out of the room. The scientists and Reece sat on the couch; the rest of us sat around the coffee table on cushions. Skid got his coat from the closet and joined us. He broke the news to the Stallards. I appreciated how he did it, not mentioning me by name.

"We have good news and we have bad news," he said, laying his coat on the coffee table. He unfolded it carefully, saying, "The bad news is that the helmet and arm piece have been stolen from us by the man who buried them in the first place." Before the Stallards could react, he said, "But I sent you the sketches Mei made, so you know what they look like. And the good news is—"

Mei handed plastic gloves to Skid. He put them on quickly and unveiled the belt, spreading it out on the coffee table.

The Stallards moved like they were surgically joined at the shoulder, leaning way over until their chins almost touched their knees. They made mouth noises and muttered to each other, phrases like "interesting workmanship" and about "confounding certain skeptics," at which point they chuckled low. They commented on the condition of the leather and judged it fair and relatively new. They bickered some over whether the leather was original, and what might be considered "original."

"Debatable," Dr. Dale said. He adjusted his bifocals to examine different parts of the belt, finally fixing his eyes on the buckle. "Ah, there it is, yes, Eloise. Hebrew is it not? Primitive, but there. Do you see it?"

"Yes, yes…" she nodded. Closing her eyes, she whispered, "It is the omen belt."

"Omen?" I asked.

Her eyes popped open and jumped to my face. "The Ancient Omen!" she chirped, with a strangely excited smile. Her gray eyes sparkled.

I don't mind saying I was a little uneasy about all these eyes glittering around me in recent days—first Reece and Skid, now the two Dr. Stallards.

People often remind me of animals, like I said. Mrs. Stallard looked at that moment like a wild turkey, skinny neck and jerky head, in a nervous thrill over her pile of corn.

After some time the Stallards sat up and gave each other a high five, which seemed pretty silly to me: two high-fiving senior citizens on safari in a bare Japanese living room, all over a dirty belt. It was weird. Not freak-show weird, but not your typical evening either. And besides that, I wondered why they were smiling. I'd always thought an omen was *bad* news.

CHAPTER 5

The Stallards said they would need to take the belt back to Chicago for scientific tests. They promised to keep everything under wraps. I was about to get bummed out about letting another piece of the armor out of my sight, but since I was the one to lose the other pieces in the first place, I had no room to talk. Skid trusted them; Reece did too, which meant Mei probably did, and Robbie too, I guess.

We told them everything we knew: that Stanford Dowland was a preacher who brought the armor over from a castle in Ireland; that after he preached some sermons on it, his little congregation fell apart and closed down; that he buried the armor, but when we found it, he dug it up and buried it someplace else.

"What about the possibility of meeting Mr. Dowland? Could such a thing be arranged, I wonder?" Dr. Eloise asked.

I told them how determined he was to keep the armor a secret, how strange he'd acted, and how his vicious dog had come after us.

Robbie added, "And it would have killed us if Elijah hadn't shot it with arrows and if Skid hadn't hacked it to death with a shovel!"

They got quiet and blinked at each other. Dr. Dale said, "For now we should pursue every other option without involving adults."

We agreed.

The coolest thing was what they had discovered about the little piece of chain mail. Dr. Dale opened his raggedy briefcase and brought it out, unwrapping it very carefully from the old rag. He placed it in his wife's hand. I felt silly being so excited about a scrap of mesh wrapped in a rag, but there you have it. "The mail is very, very fine," said Dr. Stallard. He went into lecture mode, but it wasn't boring. "Historically armor was used for battle and for ceremonies, as in royal processions. These links are so very fine, most assuredly the piece this came from was not used in a real battle."

We guys were naturally disappointed to get the official word, but not Reece. "You mean a *military* battle," she corrected. "There are many kinds of battles."

"Yes, of course," he said, looking at her curiously. "But here's the surprising discovery I wrote you about. See these links right here? See how they are a different color?"

We closed in around Dr. Eloise's hand.

"They are gold," said Mei.

"Pure gold," she corrected.

"But not a treasure?" Robbie asked, disappointed.

"Hardly," she answered. "A mere fragment. But very interesting, especially what is engraved on it."

"Engraved?" Reece gasped.

"You gotta be kidding," I said.

Robbie said, "No way! Where?"

Dr. Dale pulled a little velvet bag out of his pocket and emptied into his hand a lens mounted in black metal, about an inch and a half square.

"This is a linen tester," he said. "It's used to count the number of threads in fabric for quality control. Not as good as a microscope, of course, but much more portable. And," he laughed, "I dare not bring anything of value on long trips.

I tend to lose things. Sadly, all that rot about absent-minded professors is true."

I was already worrying that he'd lose God's belt on the way back to Chicago, when his wife giggled, "Once he left a piece of Etruscan pottery in a hotel room. I was livid, as you might imagine. But since I had once lost our daughter at Tel el-Amarna, and got halfway to Cairo before realizing it, I had no room to talk!"

"You lost…your daughter?" Reece asked.

"Just once or twice," she said with a wave of her hand.

"Wasn't she scared?" Mei asked.

"Heavens no! She was ten years old, perfectly capable, knew a bit of the language. A nice family took her in. She watered camels and played video games—had the time of her life. She was fine…on *that* trip anyway."

Dr. Dale said, "I suppose we think differently about children than most people do. We don't worry."

All of a sudden those two senior safari scientists seemed pretty cool.

"Here! Have a look," Dr. Eloise said. "Let's move under the lamp for the best light." She unfolded the linen tester and offered it to me. "Now look for the gold links. It will take some wiggling of those little rascals to see the engraving."

I wiggled those little rascals for a good minute. Finally I found numbers etched into each gold ring. "I see it! It says…22…and…25." I looked up confused. "22, 25? What's that mean?"

"You see? Isn't this such a fascinating mystery!" Dr. Eloise said happily, and I could hardly wait for her answer. "On modern jewelry the weight of the gold is stamped somewhere, on the back of the piece or perhaps the clasp. It might say 10 carat or 14 carat. That was our first idea about the meaning of the numbers. But pure gold—with no alloys added—is 24 carat, not more. So that can't be it!"

Either this lady was a glutton for bad news or she had something up her sleeve.

"So…what is it?" Reece asked.

"We don't know!" she chirped. "But we have ingested untold gallons of hot tea day and night to get to the bottom of it."

Her glazed eyes made sense now: caffeine rush.

Dr. Dale took over. "In ancient times gold was not just a precious metal; some believed it had magical powers. An armorer might put a few links of gold into a weapon or armor piece, to insure good luck on the battlefield. But the fine quality of these links suggests that the armor was used for ceremony. Do the gold links make a kind of decorative design, we asked ourselves? Are the numbers a mark to identify the soldier it was issued to?"

"Both!" Robbie made a stab at it.

"Neither!" I tried.

"Both of you might be right," Dr. Eloise said. "Except,…" she said cryptically, "except for this…"

I wiped sweat from my forehead. She was wearing me out with suspense.

She curled her finger at her husband. He handed over the sketches of the arm piece from his briefcase. "Except for this," she said again, pointing to the engraved *koinonia*.

"We've *seen* that already," said Robbie, whose patience was wearing thin.

"What armorer would engrave the word *fellowship* on battle armor, or even on ceremonial armor?" she asked. "Wouldn't he engrave *victory*? Or the name of the king? But *fellowship*? Ridiiiiculous!"

She was going to string us along into the next decade.

"22, 25?" Mei said thoughtfully.

"Do you have *any* leads?" I asked the Stallards.

"Could it be a numerical code for another Bible word?" Skid asked.

Dr. Eloise bubbled over. "Brilliant, Marcus! Children, I believe Marcus is correct in his deduction!"

Robbie asked, "Deduction? What deduction?"

Ignoring him she opened her hand, palm up. Dr. Dale pulled a Bible out of his briefcase and put it in her hand like he was giving her a surgical tool. She held it out to us dramatically, "The Book is a living thing, children, a living thing. I anticipate the wonderful messages we'll find."

I slumped. "Okay, I'm totally lost."

Reece was smiling, like it was all clear as a bell to her.

Dr. Dale chimed in. "Who knows what secrets we will discover…that is, *if* all the pieces can be retrieved!"

"Yeah," Robbie sneered at me, "if *Elijah* can keep from losing them."

I wanted to strangle him. The professors shot me a look. My face turned hot. They turned away quickly, acting as if they hadn't heard what Robbie said. Everyone stood in that bare room looking around for something to stare at instead of me, the irresponsible chowderhead.

Then Reece looked at me with pure happiness. "What's over is over. Elijah found the pieces in the first place, and he'll find them again!"

"To the task!" said Dr. Dale.

"Precisely," said his wife.

"The plot thickens," piped in Robbie dramatically.

"Ready, aim, fire," said the army brat, Skid.

"*Ganbatte!*" chimed in Mei.

"Yeah," was all I could think to say.

We showed them the glued compass, explained how it pointed back to the old ruin of a house, and that we were going back there to see what we could find.

Before they left, the Stallards made us get in a circle and hold hands. They asked if anyone wanted to pray. Right away, Reece said, "Yes, please." I bowed my head and closed my eyes like I'd seen people do. Once I peeked at Reece. Her face was raised to the ceiling. She went on about how wonderful and great God was. She thanked him for the quest and the Stallards and each one of us by name—which felt awkward, but good. She even prayed for Mr. Dowland, that whatever happened to him years ago might be put to rest. Finally she asked if she could please have the strength to go into Telanoo with the rest of us for the next part of the search—but that if she couldn't, that was okay. She ended with, "Your will be done."

Let her go, I thought to myself. *Please let her go with us.* A feeling of peace washed over me.

How could I know that the next leg of our search would lead us into things we didn't *want* to know, throwing the whole town of Magdeline into chaos and anger, with all fingers pointing at me.

CHAPTER 6

After the Stallards left Mei's house, I suggested we keep searching land plat records, in the courthouse or wherever, for the owner of Telanoo. Reece and Skid thought that snooping through court files would arouse suspicion. "Okay then," I said, "I'll go to a real estate office and pretend I'm on an errand from my dad."

Reece rolled her eyes and said it would get back to him for sure.

I skulked out to the hallway to put my shoes back on. *I don't know what's up with her sometimes*, I thought. *They were good ideas and they might have worked.*

· · · · ·

Reece was always telling me I should go to church. For some odd reason, the recent experience in the rat-infested emptiness of Old Pilgrim Church had left me curious. But I agreed to go to the community Thanksgiving service with her mostly because she said the minister was going to preach about the Indians. To tell the truth, it was also because if I said no, it would be just Skid and her there together. Robbie and Mei would be out of town.

Skid still liked Miranda Varner, or so he said. But he hadn't worked up the nerve to ask her out, which kept me on edge about him and Reece. I couldn't figure why someone who'd been all over the world, and who was so cool that the rest of us were gutter slush by comparison…I didn't get why he was so shy.

Reece's church was fifteen miles west of Magdeline, on a smooth ridge of grass with a basketball court at one end of the parking lot. It was big and bright outside and in. There were some pretty amazing windows with stained glass scenes of Jesus sitting on a rock talking to people, Jesus praying on a rock, and Jesus standing in front of a rock with his arms out and a glow all around him. With all those rocks around, it looked like he lived in Telanoo. I pointed this out to Reece and joked: "I hope that isn't the same rock in all three windows, because that would mean he was stuck in the same spot forever, just talking, praying, and glowing."

She jabbed me in the ribs and told me to shut up. I said, "You shouldn't say 'shut up' in church."

"*You* just did," she snipped back.

There was another window of Jesus out in a field with sheep, which was nice.

The place was packed with chattering people. Then the music started. Without Skid on one side and Reece on the other, I'd have felt supremely dumb. It's hard to explain why. I figured there were rules to follow, but nobody told me what they were.

If I got bored, I was going to imagine myself at an awards show, with my bodyguard and press agent at my sides. I'd be called up to that impressive stage to say something, and everyone would cheer.

(Before you criticize me for mentally drifting off in church, remember that I didn't know the songs. Even if I did, I can't carry a tune in a bucket. And I'm a man of action more than a man of words.)

Just like Reece said, the minister had dug up stuff about what Native Americans believed. He said many worshiped the creator and called him the One Above. He read Bible ideas that matched what the Indians believed. I agreed with a lot of it. The minister said that we should take time to be alone and read the Word and hear the creator's voice.

"That sounds like your vision quest," Reece whispered.

"Yeah," I whispered. I drifted back to that night again, when it felt like my whole universe went silent. The memory of it hadn't dimmed at all but had gotten stronger every time I recalled it.

The preacher said that the One Above had many names in Indian thought: Master of Breath, Creator, Moneto, God, and Ruler of All That Is, Was, or Ever Can Be. Then he spewed a whole list of names from the Bible, like light and vine and Redeemer. He ended with Jesus.

I had figured out a long time ago that Jesus was a great teacher, but no one ever had told me Jesus was the same as God. It was kind of a jolt. My eyes settled on the stained glass Jesus, glowing in front of the rock, as the preacher talked on about Indian ideas. The creator doesn't spoil the created with too many gifts or easy answers, he said, but that everything, even every struggle, has purpose. And we should seek our purpose and give thanks for it.

The preacher ended by telling the whole crowd we should be thankful for a country that was not originally ours, but which we are blessed to live in. And to ask forgiveness for how our forefathers and their native brothers cruelly mistreated each other, and may it never happen again, and so on and so on. He ended with a prayer.

If Indians get talked about every week, I thought, *I might not mind church.*

A big song from the organ blasted everyone to the back of the church and out into the cold.

· · · · ·

Grandma wasn't coming up until Christmas, so my family had Thanksgiving dinner by ourselves. I spent the afternoon in my room, digesting turkey and studying the map we'd copied from the library book. The ruin wasn't too far from the west end of Council Cliffs State Park, which gave me a new angle on getting there without having to go through Telanoo. Getting someone to drop us off in the park would save a lot of legwork. Problem was, the map didn't show what kind of terrain lay between the park and the ruin. *Probably no worse than Telanoo*. It would make no difference to me, being an outdoorsman. But I had to think about Reece.

I sat on my bed, propped against the log wall, planning our next move....

Next to Owl Woods, my room was my favorite place. When we moved here six years ago, my room was crawling with stenciled bears and puppies. Aunt Grace wanted to help me with decorating, but I begged Mom in private not to let her force her frills on me. Mom said I could have a guy-type room if, and only if (this was blackmail pure and simple) I kept it clean. Otherwise, Aunt Grace would have free reign.

My bed sat against the log wall, under the window where I could see the sky as I fell asleep. My bow and arrows hung on the opposite wall next to a genuine Indian rug Mom and Dad bought me in Gatlinburg. I had started an arrowhead collection, which was on a shelf, but I only had five so far. My room was the smallest because the twins needed lots of toy space. I didn't mind; I spent more time outdoors than in.

From my second-floor window I could see our backyard, the side of the lodge, and the camp pool. While I sat staring at the burned and blackened hole that once was Old Pilgrim Church, the phone rang. It was Reece. She sounded excited and upset.

"My dad's in town," she said. "He just popped in. He'll be here for only a couple of days. So if you were going back to the ruin…"

"We'll wait," I said.

Long pause. "I don't think you should."

"A couple of days won't matter."

"It could matter. The temperature's dropping every day. If the ground freezes, you can't dig. You guys should go on. Mei's still out of town."

"But you prayed to go," I said.

"And the answer I'm hearing is no." She didn't sound disappointed.

"If you're sure."

"Positive. Just be very, very careful."

Hesitantly, I told her about the possibility of getting to the ruin through the park, that I didn't know how rough a hike it would be.

"See? It all works out. That settles it."

The hint of relief in her voice told me how hard the last hike through Telanoo had been.

We hung on the line a minute, saying nothing. "Have a nice time with your dad," I said.

"Thanks. Did you like the church service?"

"Yeah."

"I hoped you would."

"I didn't like the organ music though."

"That's okay. Well, you be careful. Take your bow and arrows."

"Dowland doesn't have any more demon dogs," I joked.

She laughed, and said in a sinister way, "Not that we know of."

"Oh, thanks. I feel better now."

"The walkie-talkies don't reach that far, huh?"

"Not from camp. We'll be on our own."

Out of the blue, I remembered the old movie *Gorgo* and a scene when people capture this giant flesh-eating reptile that's terrorizing the coast. They think all their troubles are over, that they have this great scientific find. What they don't know is that he's the baby. When their backs are turned, up pops the parent out of a crack in the ocean floor and swallows them whole.

But that was science fiction.

CHAPTER 7

None of the moms would have dropped us off in Council Cliffs without asking questions. Could you imagine me saying, "Hey, Mom, how about putting me out in a state park in the dead of winter, and don't come back?"

Yeah, that'd go over big.

Robbie was due back in the morning, and Skid was free all weekend. I called Justin Brill, because his big brother Jeremy had his own car and could probably be bought off cheap. Eighteen years old and two sizes bigger than his kid brother, Jeremy got on the phone and said he'd drive us for a few bucks. I set up a time and place.

"It'll be one way, Jeremy," I made clear. "You won't have to hang around or come back and pick us up."

"Fine by me. You going hunting, Nature Boy?"

"Yeah. Hunting."

· · · · ·

The day was calm, with a few big puffy clouds. I wore a tan jacket and jeans to blend in with the landscape. Skid showed up in his usual head-to-toe black. Robbie wore a bright red jacket so he wouldn't be shot by hunters.

"It's bow season for deer hunting," I explained. "Half the time we'll be in the park where hunting's not allowed. Don't go paranoid on us."

We took the usual gear: canteen, knife, bandana, snacks, binoculars; and what we needed for the search: map, metal detector, shovel, my bow with hundred grain broadhead arrows—big enough to bring down a bear—and a real working compass. I hardly ever used a compass, but we needed precision here.

· · · · ·

Following the winding road through the park, we pointed Jeremy Brill to the spot nearest Telanoo and had him drop us off. We started unloading our equipment.

"Hey, jerks, how about my money?"

"Give us a minute!" I said.

He eyed our gear. "What are you guys up to with that shovel, anyhow?" he asked.

"Exploring," I answered, and slammed the car door.

He rolled down his window. "Exploring what? I thought you were hunting."

We looked at each other. I was ready to blurt out the truth like Reece always did, that we were looking for an ancient treasure. Skid beat me to it in his own way. He sauntered around to Jeremy's window, tossed in a couple of bills, and said, "None of your business, Brill."

Jeremy snorted, "Well, good luck, you kiddies. Hope you don't get lost and start crying for your mommies to come find you." He tore out and was gone.

I thought for sure Skid would be miffed. He just laughed and gave us a mission-accomplished nod.

We set off due west. The woods were old and tall and scraggly, the undergrowth dense. We kept a straight course into the cold wind, except when we had to swing around big, tall clumps of brambles. I had an uneasy feeling heading toward Telanoo. That place rattled me.

Huffing and puffing, Robbie said, "I don't know what more we can find at the ruin."

"We missed something important," I said, plowing ahead. "The compass pointed there. The next piece of armor has to be there."

"Maybe not," Robbie pouted. "I did a good job before with the metal detector."

"I know, but we have to look again," I replied. "I didn't mean anything by it. Don't be so touchy."

"I'm not!" Robbie barked.

"Maybe Dowland hasn't buried anything there *yet*," Skid threw out his idea.

I stopped. "You think we jumped the gun on him?" I hadn't thought of that.

Robbie stopped too. "Maybe we shouldn't go. What if he's there burying it right now? What if he sees us coming?"

The last thing I wanted was another face-to-face with Stan Dowland.

Skid spoke up: "I say we go, but carefully; and look ahead. Don't leave tracks. Wherever we dig, we cover it over."

"Oh, pickle!" said Robbie. "You know what just hit me again? Ancient history."

"You're weird," I said.

"I mean what I said at the library before, that some ancient battle gear had no metal. Shoes might be all leather, a shield might be wood overlaid with leather."

"*Could* be metal," Skid said optimistically.

"Or not," Robbie went on. "How will we find—"

"Fresh dirt," I said and started walking again. "We'll spot it. I'm good at this kind of thing." It was cold, but I'd worked up a sweat; and Robbie's doubts were working on me. *It could be a dead end.* "I've said this before, but I don't think Dowland could make it to the ruin, even this way. He's so old and frail."

"Someone buried something there," Skid said. "The compass says so."

"What if he has an accomplice?" was Robbie's next theory.

I hadn't thought of that either.

Skid sneered, "Don't make it worse than it is, kid."

"Don't call me kid. I'm older than you."

"You don't look it."

"I'm ignoring that." Robbie stopped for a drink from the canteen. "Remember the old man said, 'Piece by piece they will rest in peace. Like the ones in the ground.' If the ground's frozen, we might have to wait until spring."

Doubts or not, I wasn't about to have the search derailed. I wanted to find the full armor and put it on, like I'd been told by…by God. Or whoever. "We're talking in circles. I say we shut up and keep our eyes and ears open."

"When we get there, let's treat it like a crime scene," Skid suggested. "Measure it off into a grid and search square by square."

We came out of the woods of Council Cliffs State Park onto a wide meadow with tall grass the color of my jacket. The long, flat field was surrounded by the hills of the park wrapping around behind us, the rolling ridges of Ohio farm country to our right, and the strange cliff ahead that we called Devil's Cranium. We plowed on across the field.

"There!" said Robbie. "There it is!"

We were a few hundred yards off course to the north. We'd overshot our mark, but not by much. The ruin stood just as we'd left it—a crumbling stone chimney and the last remains of a house hunkered down in a thicket.

We kept low, watching and listening for signs of life. There was nothing alive in that pale field but us. We moved with stealth, circling wide around the ruin to make sure the coast was clear. Hooking up with the path we'd made before, we traced along the very route where vicious Salem had pursued us in dead earnest.

We smelled him before we saw him. "Peeeyoooo!" Robbie said.

The elements already had been working on the big black malamute's carcass. His eyes were dried and sunk in, his shriveled mouth frozen in a snarl and crawling with bugs. My arrows were still sticking out of him.

We pulled the necks of our shirts up over our noses. Robbie turned to Skid. "Garosss! Leave no footprints, you said? We left a lot more than footprints!"

Skid said to me, "Yank out those arrows, Elijah. They're a dead giveaway as to how he died."

I sucked in air, yanked one out, backed away, and dragged it through the grass to wipe off the decay. I went back for the second one but couldn't do it. I needed fresh air.

"What if Dowland's already seen this?" Robbie asked.

"He hasn't," I tried to sound confident. "There's no easy way to get here. I'm telling you he couldn't make it."

"He stalked you all night, remember?" Robbie said. "He could be on his way right now."

Skid snapped, "You're a bundle of optimism, Wingate." He turned to me. "We won't be able to stand it, working here with that stench. We have to bury him." He nodded to the right. "I'll dig a hole over there in the bushes, way past the house. We'll drop Salem in and cover him over good."

I probably could've handled the smell a little better than the other guys. I'd cleaned out a boa constrictor cage at the nature center, after it...you know. That stink will bring tears to your eyes. But a rotting malamute was no bouquet of flowers either. I was grateful for Skid's offer.

"Thanks," I said and grabbed the sleeve of Robbie's jacket. "Let's start on the other side of the ruin. We'll make long straight passes, like mowing the yard. Side by side, so we don't miss anything."

Robbie and I dug our toes here and there looking for soft spots. In the back of my mind, I kept stewing over what Dowland would do when he discovered I'd killed his precious Salem. As if he weren't already mad enough at me for breaking into his garage and refusing to give up on the search for The Armor of God. Not to mention I'd threatened to tell all his neighbors if he didn't spill the story of Old Pilgrim Church. He had a bucket load of reasons not to like me.

"Find a place to bury that dog yet?" I called to Skid after a few minutes.

"I'm looking, I'm looking," he called back, heading farther into the weeds.

It was a dry, desolate feeling, the lonely sounds of our feet crunching hard ground, Skid's shovel testing the rocky soil: *tch...tch...tch.*

No wonder this farm failed, I said to myself. *They probably starved to death.*

"The treasure can't be here, the ground's too hard," Robbie said.

"It has to be here," I insisted.

"Maybe it's farther back toward the park," he said. "Or *in* the park."

I scanned the place we'd come from: Council Cliffs State Park, a thousand acres of woods and cliffs, caves and waterfalls.

Robbie followed my gaze. "Dowland could get there easy, Elijah. All he'd have to do is drive in after dark and find a spot where there are no trails or picnic areas."

I didn't want to buy the idea, mostly because of the hope-less, sinking feeling it gave me. We could spend years searching the park and never find a thing.

Skid was still milling around on the other side of the ruin, poking here and there with the point of his shovel.

"Hurry it up, Skid. We're dying from the smell over here."

I turned back to Robbie. He was working the metal detec-tor, muttering about a needle in a haystack.

"Keep going," I said.

"I went over this area last time," he complained. "There's nothing—"

The sound of splintering wood came from Skid's direction. I heard him yell. When I looked up he was gone.

Robbie dropped his metal detector. "What happened? What was that?"

"Skid!" I hightailed it over stone and bramble toward where I'd seen him last. "Skid!" I tore across the field, hearing noth-ing, seeing nobody. Robbie cried out something from where he was. "Stay there!" I yelled back at him.

I heard a groan and followed it through the high dead grass. What I saw threw me back in shock.

There was Skid, flat on his back, grimacing in pain, and missing a leg from the knee down.

CHAPTER 8

"I'm okay," he said. "I stepped on a board and it fell through. There's a hole under here."

I breathed a huge sigh of relief. But when he tried to sit up, the wood beneath him cracked and sagged. Fear shot through me. "Don't move!" I yelled. "You're sitting on rotten wood!" I ran around by his head, testing every dry, grassy step. Quick but careful, I scooped my arms under his armpits, in case the wood should let go.

He tried to raise his leg out, but something caught it. Blood seeped through his black jeans.

"Don't yank!" he yelled. "Something's got the back of my knee!"

I planted one knee on hard soil. "Stay calm, man. Hold on."

Robbie came running.

"Watch your step!" I warned him back. "Bring the canteen and the bandana." I turned back to Skid. "I'm going to ease you this way. See if you can pull free from the broken end of that plank."

He worked himself out easy-does-it as I dragged him away from the hole. He had a long gash behind the knee. I flushed it with water and wrapped it with the bandana. He winced and got to his feet. "Thanks. I'm good to go."

The three of us yanked the old boards off the hole, which was two-and-a-half feet across. We leaned over it.

"It's deep!" Robbie said.

"Looks like an abandoned well," I said.

Skid said, "Then I got a lucky break on the grave digging. Let's dump old Salem in that hole and get on with it."

Robbie leaned farther in. "I think it's dry."

"Careful," I said again. I looked at the sky. "Give that cloud a minute. When it passes, we should have some light down there."

Slowly the cloud passed. Sunlight beamed down on us and into the well. We peered in. There in a puddle of black water at the bottom were big splinters of rotted boards, some old rags… and what looked like a human skeleton.

CHAPTER 9

Robbie screamed and fell back. His hands flew to his face. "A body!"

The sun cast bright rays on the well's stone sides and lit the murky bottom. There was no mistake. They were most definitely human remains.

Skid's voice was flat and serious. "That's what it is. We have to tell the police."

Our heads met over the hole. We stared silently at the bones and a skull and what was left of the clothes.

The first thing out of my mouth was, "Dad will know I've been here."

"All our parents will know," said Skid, thinking on the same track. He glanced at me and said aloud what flashed into all our minds: "They'll know everything."

Everything. It didn't take long to sink in.

I said, "We'll have to tell them about the armor."

"And about the Stallards," Skid said, shaking his head. "Man, I never told my parents they were in town. The whole story will come out."

Robbie backed away from the hole, his hands still clamped over his jaws. In spite of our predicament, relief suddenly rushed over me. I was glad Reece and Mei hadn't come along. This was too gruesome for girls.

Anxiously I ran my hand through my hair, coaching myself to calm down, to stop and think. Skid shoved his hands into his pockets and kicked at the dirt.

"Dowland will know too!" Robbie suddenly burst out. "This will be in the papers, and he'll know we killed Salem!" He whirled to me. "He'll know how *you* killed him, Elijah, with your bow and arrows, and *you* with a shovel, Skid!"

"Salem attacked us, Robbie!" I yelled back. "It was self-defense. But thanks for sharing the blame!"

Skid checked to see if his leg had stopped bleeding. "Stay cool, guys. We can't bow out now. This is a crime scene. We shouldn't touch anything else."

I stared off toward Devil's Cranium. *We're in deep as it is, out here with a shovel at the scene of a murder, and no good reason for it.*

The sun went behind a cloud, throwing the well and the ruin and the three of us into shadow. Then out it came again, back and forth, light and shadow, like a searchlight, and we were criminals caught in the act.

"You may need stitches," I said. "We should get going."

Skid didn't answer. Again and again our eyes were drawn down into the hole.

Robbie said: "We shouldn't have been here in the first place. We were trespassing."

"But no one owns it," I said. "The name was blotted off the map."

"Someone has to own it," Skid said, being logical, "even if he died. Even if that person in the well is the owner himself."

I started pacing, just to use up some adrenaline, thinking out loud, "This is where the compass pointed. Not to the next piece of armor, like we hoped, but to a body."

"My mom and dad will kill me!" Robbie said. "They think I'm at your house right now!"

"Okay, so we didn't tell the exact truth the whole time," I said. "We haven't done anything wrong. We found old relics, followed the clues, killed a dog who attacked us, and found a dead body. We're in the clear."

Skid sat and squeezed the pain out of his wound. "I don't know, man," he said doubtfully, "we're not really in the clear."

"Okay, then," I said, "we can explain about finding the armor in the basement of Old Pilgrim Church, and—"

"We can't!" Robbie came to his feet. "They'll think we set the fire and burned the church down! You saw how the fire-fighters looked at us that night. No one else was around. They already suspect us."

"No, they don't. It was ruled inconclusive," I said. "And besides, nobody cares. Everyone's glad to be rid of the old building."

"We're going to jail!" Robbie wailed.

"Dowland set the fire," I said firmly. "If anyone will get into trouble, it will be him. We know that."

Skid shook his head, got up, and strolled over to peer into the well again. "We *don't* know that. Actually, there's very little we do know about anything. We're in the dark, just like that poor guy down there."

Robbie said, "We don't have to tell them we were even in Old Pilgrim Church."

"Dad knows we were, remember?" I said. "I told him, at least the first time. But no one will make the connection between the old church and this. Will they?"

Robbie's quick brain drilled right through that idea. "Yes, they will! Because how else do we explain being here, unless we backtrack all the way to the armor which we discovered in the church, and dug up from the cemetery, and which was lost in Telanoo, which led us to the forked path, which led us to Devil's Cranium, where we dug up the compass, which led us here—to a body?"

Swirling through my mind came a dozen explanations I could offer to get us off the hook. I could say we were working on a school project, or that Jeremy Brill had known a body was out here and paid us money to find it. I could blame Skid, saying it was all his insane idea for a secret club, or that we'd followed Dowland here. Most of the explanations even made pretty good sense, but none of them was actually true. When I realized this, something rose up in my chest—a hard question that would nag at me for a long time: *how'd I get so good at lying?*

My stomach felt heavy. Suddenly Salem's stench filled my nose, even my mouth. Nausea rolled up into my throat. I swallowed in disgust. Looking in the hole made me dizzy. I felt as if I were falling in. I reeled back to save myself the same fate as that guy.

"The police will ask us why we were digging here," Skid said rather calmly, as if from far away. "They'll want to know what we were looking for."

"We could just leave," Robbie answered, in a panic. "Not say a word. Forget the treasure hunt, forget Salem. Everything! Just go back to being our normal, innocent selves!"

While I forced myself to get a grip, Skid went on, thinking in a straight line, "Someone will find it, eventually…Jeremy Brill knows we were here; he brought us. They will ask us why we had a shovel out here at the scene of a murder…Guys, this looks really, really bad."

I braced myself for one last glance into the well, just to prove to myself that I could. The lonely white skull lay facedown at an angle, strangely calm, as if he'd nodded off to sleep. "Maybe it was an accident," I said weakly.

"Maybe," said Skid, but his gloomy voice said otherwise.

I said, "Let's get our things together. Take care where you step, just in case."

Robbie said, "I've got to get out of here. I'm going to throw up!" He grabbed his stuff and headed across the meadow toward Devil's Cranium. Skid and I stood there just looking at each other.

"Got any brilliant ideas?" he asked me dryly.

The cool Marcus Skidmore is asking my advice, looking to me for answers. What should we do?

Reece's voice floated into my ear. With knots of dread and determination in my throat, I said, "Here's what we do: we tell the truth. The whole truth."

CHAPTER 10

I couldn't find Dad.

Safely through Telanoo and back at Camp Mudj, I sent Robbie and Skid home. No reason they should take the heat from my parents.

Dad wasn't at the house, in his office, or in the maintenance building. I checked the dining hall. The Mad River Boys had arrived, a different brood than last year, but still sour-faced and smelling like tobacco. They were finishing a meal. I walked past without making eye contact. Bo was organizing their next project with the counselors. I caught his eye and mouthed the words, "Where's Dad?" He pointed toward the Tree House Village.

Two men hammered away at big panels of drywall. I breathed in the welcome smell of new wood and tried to look calm. When I saw him in the central meeting room overseeing the construction, I became a bundle of nerves.

"Hey, Dad."

He was checking blueprints and glanced up. When he caught the look on my face—try as I did to be casual—his face went slack.

"Elijah, what's wrong?"

"I have to talk to you."

"Sure, what is it? Are you sick?"

"No, I…have to talk to you, in private."

"Give me just a minute." He went over to the men and said he'd be back in a few. He came back to me. "Okay. Let's go to my office."

I'd planned to start from the beginning, but once he sat down behind his desk, I sort of exploded, "We found a dead body."

He pitched forward in his chair. "A what?"

"A body."

"Where?"

"In a well."

"What well?"

"At some old farm."

"What old farm? Talk to me, son!"

I pointed northeast. "That way. Out behind the camp."

"What were you doing off the grounds, Elijah?"

I didn't answer.

Slowly he stood. "Did Mom know where you were?"

"No." I sort of crumpled in the chair in front of his desk. "I'm sorry, Dad, I'm sorry!"

He came around and squeezed my shoulder, patted me on the back, and talked soft: "It's okay, son. Just tell me. Start at the beginning."

"I can't start at the beginning. Can I start in the middle?"

"Start anywhere, Elijah, just tell me what you found. You're sure it was a body?"

I nodded. "A skeleton. At the bottom of a well, Dad. We weren't trespassing. We went to the library to see who owned the land, and no one did, there was no name! It was blotted out!"

He pulled up a chair and sat facing me. "Okay, slow down and make sense. Where?"

"This old farm, between here and Council Cliffs."

"What were you doing there in the first place? How did you get there?"

"We got a ride."

"You…sneaked away without telling us?"

He read guilt all over my face. His forehead wrinkled. In the silence that followed, he was obviously thinking back over the past months. "You've been acting different lately…those secret campfires, having those girls over…Elijah, what are you hiding?"

I couldn't answer. Suddenly my whole life flashed before me like they say happens right before you die. I saw all the sneaky things I'd done the last few months: lying about what we'd found in the church; lying that I knew nothing about the grave robbers; sneaking off to Newpoint without permission; lying to Mom and Robbie so I could go on my vision quest; the dozen other times I would have lied if Reece handn't stopped me.

And why did I have to lie? I asked myself. *Didn't Mom and Dad trust me, give me free reign? Didn't they count on me—with baby-sitting Nori and Stacy, and with setting up campfires and finding little campers who wander off—because I'm the best fire maker, the best tracker? And couldn't I get free snacks and the golf cart anytime I wanted? Didn't everyone at school think I'm the luckiest dog because I live at Camp Mudj?*

From the beginning I wanted no adults in on our search for the armor of God, but why? I'd wanted it all for myself. I'd been a jerk to Reece a few weeks before. Now I was about to be a humongous disappointment to my dad. For all my telling myself I'd been straight up about the quest, I had lied and lied and lied.

I looked into Dad's hurt eyes. He seemed to see right into my mind. "Elijah, what's going on here?"

"Nothing." I couldn't help lying just one more time—and hated myself as soon as I said it. He saw right through me.

He reached for the phone. "I have to call the police, Elijah. Do you know how to get back to the place where you found this...body?" He punched numbers.

"Yeah."

"Officer Taylor, please." He covered the mouthpiece with his hand and said to me, "They will be asking you questions, like they did on the night Old Pilgrim Church burned."

I looked up at him. His expression turned dark with suspicion and disbelief. He leaned in, nailing me with his gaze. "Elijah, did you have anything to do with *that*?"

"No, Dad."

"You know *nothing* about it?"

There I went mute, because I did have suspicions about Mr. Dowland. I gulped.

"Elijah, look me in the eye and tell me you know nothing about that fire."

"It wasn't me!"

Dad was back to the phone. "Yes, Darrell? This is Russell Creek, at the camp. Can you swing by at your earliest convenience? My son has made a discovery, and we're going to need your help. We'll be in my office." He paused. "Well, according to Elijah, it's a human skeleton."

He hung up the phone slowly, considering it for a minute. His eyes slid to me. His voice was stern. "Start at the beginning, Elijah. And I mean the *very* beginning."

CHAPTER 11

My story to Dad was a pretty confusing mess. I explained about us going to the library and how no one owned the land, and that we were looking for buried treasure and found a broken compass. I threw in a few more facts here and there, how two pieces of the treasure had Greek words on them, which meant a big mystery. And that those were stolen, but we weren't giving up the search.

I knew it sounded idiotic. Who could cover three months of adventure in three minutes? As I said before, I'm more a man of action than a man of words.

As the cruiser pulled up, I rushed to the part where Skid almost fell in the well. I mentioned about scientists coming to Mei's house and taking an old belt to have it tested.

"So Mei's parents know about this…but you didn't tell *your mother and me?*"

I shook my head. "They don't know anything. The scientists only talked about it with us. Mei's mom didn't see the belt or hear anything about our quest."

"And these…these scientists were aware that none of your parents knew what you were doing?"

"They told us to keep it secret."

He got all ruffled. "Oh, I don't like the sound of this!" Officer Taylor was coming up the steps.

"Dad, you can't tell the police about the treasure. They wouldn't understand. What if news got out and everybody in the county went combing the countryside and digging around camp here for priceless artifacts?!"

"Let me handle it, son."

Dad let me call Skid and Robbie while he talked to Officer Taylor outside. I explained that the police were here, that we were going back to the ruin. I told them to lay low and not say anything to anyone about the skeleton or the armor until they heard from me.

Dad and I drove to Council Cliffs State Park behind the cruiser. As we pulled in at the entrance, Dad said, "Here's what I told Officer Taylor: that you boys had been treasure hunting and had dug up a broken compass which pointed in the direction of the ruin. That one of you accidentally had stepped on the hole, which was covered by rotten wood, and discovered the remains. Is that the truth?"

"Yes."

We parked near a picnic area. My feelings were all mixed up. I was glad I wasn't keeping anything from Dad anymore, glad he was dealing with the police. But the secret of the armor had now spread to one more person. By the time news got out about the body in the well, questions would be flying all over town.

Reece and Mei had to be told. If I knew my parents at all, they'd be setting up a meeting with the other moms and dads to hash things out.

I could feel the belt of truth slipping through my fingers.

I cut through the woods the same way as before, with Officer Taylor and Dad following. In about an hour, we were at the edge of the meadow. I showed Officer Taylor the dog remains first because it was still stinking to high Heaven and hard to ignore. I admitted that the arrows lodged in his body were mine, and I showed them the hole where I'd pulled out the one.

I don't mind saying that both Dad and Officer Taylor were very impressed with my marksmanship.

"It happened on our first trip. He came from up there," I pointed to Devil's Cranium. "He saw us and came tearing down across the meadow. If I hadn't decided at the last minute to take my bow, we'd have had no way to protect ourselves. Skid had the shovel, but it wouldn't have been enough."

With the back of his hand across his nose, Dad studied the bug-eaten body. He frowned, heaved a couple of big sighs, turned me toward himself, and gave me a hug. Then he looked over my head toward the hills and frowned and blinked and squeezed my shoulder.

"The well's over there," I said, and led them to it.

Officer Taylor shone his flashlight down into the hole a long while. He shook his head and groaned. I guess no matter how much crime you see—though in Magdeline there isn't much murder and gore—if you're a good solid person like Officer Taylor, it still gets to you.

He started writing in a little notebook. He and Dad decided that the deceased had been dead a long time, years maybe. They exchanged guesses about the depth of the well. Officer Taylor remembered some fuel company coming into town a long time ago to dig for natural gas, though only a few pockets were ever found. He wondered if this was a drilling site. But they both thought the walls of the hole looked more like stonework than bedrock. The location next to a farmhouse seemed logical for a well. He studied the old wood planks awhile, asked me how Skid happened to fall through. The department would have to bring in special equipment to get the remains out, he said.

We walked around the ruin, Officer Taylor asking more questions, me answering every one with the absolute truth.

"You were here looking for treasure, you said?" asked Officer Taylor.

"Yes, sir. We had a metal detector, but all we found were some metal pieces that had fallen off the house."

"Do you know anything about this?" He nodded to a pile of ashes on the front stoop.

"Yes, sir. Our first time here, I built a fire to heat water for hot chocolate."

"So you were here twice."

"Yes, sir. We didn't find anything the first time. But the compass pointed here, so we thought we'd missed a clue and came back for one more look."

"You're quite the outdoorsman, aren't you?" he asked with a smile.

"I learned a lot from my dad." I smiled back and felt a little easier.

"And where is this compass you found?"

"I think Robbie has it. I can get it for you—and whatever else you need, as soon as we get back."

"Good. Did you boys camp out here?"

"No, sir. Both times we were here for just a couple of hours." I paused at this point, because I figured this next bit of information would complicate things, but I'd promised myself to tell the whole truth, as much as I could. (I should say here that if you are ever questioned by the police, always tell the truth. They have ways of getting it out of you, one way or the other. They're trained to tell if you're lying.) "By the way, there were five of us the first time, not three."

"Five of you?" asked Officer Taylor.

"Five?" Dad repeated.

"Yeah. Mei and Reece came with us." I prepared for an explosion and it came.

"Reece?!" Dad's voice cut through me. "You brought Reece all the way out here!" He explained to Officer Taylor, "That's Reece Elliston, a classmate of his. Little blond girl who walks with a limp." He scowled at me. "Elijah, I can't believe you'd—" he broke off, scanning the meadow and surrounding hills.

"She really wanted to come, Dad. I was worried too. I wanted to back out of it, but she never gets to have adventures."

"Which way did you come?" he asked, perplexed.

The truth was getting pricklier and pricklier. I felt my face going hot.

"Elijah, how did the five of you get here?" Dad persisted.

My words came in a rush. "We took the golf cart through Owl Woods and walked the rest of the way. She really wanted to be on the treasure hunt, Dad. And her mom said she could go hiking. Reece promised her mom that I could take care of her—me and Skid and Robbie. And we did."

Officer Taylor headed back toward the well, radioing headquarters with the news. But Dad wasn't through with me yet. Getting his bearings between the spot where we stood and where the camp was, he fixed his eyes on Devil's Cranium with an expression of disbelief and anger. "You didn't bring her down that cliff?"

"It was the only way."

"Son, do you realize how risky that was? If she had fallen…"

"Us guys were there all around her, every single step."

"Her mother would be furious if she knew you brought her down a cliff! Elijah, you know better than that!"

"It was the only way we knew to get down! We couldn't go through the Morgan farm. That would be trespassing, not to mention their Black Angus bulls! And actually, Dad, it turned out for the best because, if we'd left her up there, Salem would have got her for sure."

"Salem?" Dad's eyes turned suspicious again. "Who's Salem?"

I nodded to the carcass, my heart sinking. "That was his name."

CHAPTER 12

Reece might believe that the truth will set you free, but all I got was grounded.

When Officer Taylor had finished questioning me, we hiked back through the park. He said he'd be in touch. Dad and I went back to his office for more privacy. I explained about Salem and Mr. Dowland: how I suspected that the old ex-preacher and alleged arsonist was crazy and had set fire to Old Pilgrim Church and then set his vicious dog loose on me while my scent was still fresh in his nose.

Dad sat there, leaning back in his chair, one arm crossed in front of him, the other hand gripping his chin for dear life, all kinds of worries and scoldings working around in his head, though he never said a thing until I was done.

I said again that I was really, truly sorry, but we kids had promised each other to keep the treasure hunt a secret, never having any idea it would come to all this. He asked about the scientists again, and I admitted that, yes, the Stallards did know the whole story. But they were the only adults who knew, and they had agreed to keep it to themselves.

Dad didn't trust them. "Elijah, responsible adults don't tell children to keep secrets from their parents. Did you think about that at all?"

"It was Skid's idea," I continued. Suddenly I felt sick about giving them the belt of truth—them in their safari outfits, probably off to Tanzania or Morocco, where we'd never hear from them again. Who from Chicago wears clothes like that anyway?

"His parents know them," I defended. "That's why I thought it was okay."

"Well, I'm having a talk with all involved. And you—" he stood and heaved a sigh, "are staying home. This grounding will be until further notice. It's as much for your safety as anything. You'll come home right after school and help me at the camp."

"Okay," I said cautiously, waiting for the other shoe to drop. He studied me a long moment, gave a dry chuckle, and softened a little. "Actually, the timing's pretty good. I'm going to need your help with those high school guys from Mad River Boys Ranch."

"Help?" My stomach felt uneasy again.

He shoved his hands in his pockets, looking like Skid in the way he carried himself. "I feel sorry for those boys. Their families have given up on them, labeled them incorrigible. We have to watch them like hawks." He looked at the calendar on his desk. "It'll be a good lesson for you, Elijah, to see what happens when you break faith with your parents." He came from behind his desk and wrapped his arms around me. I hugged him back and felt tons better.

We headed out the door. He turned back to lock it. "Elijah, you have made some risky choices, bad choices perhaps—the biggest one being hiding the truth from me. But I understand why you did most of it. Promises are important." He considered me with an expression that looked like admiration. "The way you protected your friends from that dog, Elijah, was quite—" his voice kind of cracked, "quite heroic."

"I didn't have a choice, Dad. I had to do something."

· · · · ·

Mom and Dad were worried about my safety. They made it clear I wouldn't know a whole lot of what was going on with the investigation. But Dad would stay in contact with Officer Taylor and promised to keep me informed.

Dad said Mr. Dowland had been questioned about his dog. He'd claimed it accidentally got loose one day and never came back. I had my doubts about the "accidentally" part.

Three dark clouds were now hovering over my life: the investigation, the Mad River Boys, and the twins.

Mom had babysitting dibs on me. Every year she and her friends organize the school's annual Christmas Village and Breakfast with Santa. They buy up a ton of cheap presents: key rings and picture frames, coffee mugs and doilies. Then they throw together a pretend village in the band room for a day of shopping frenzy where kids can buy Christmas presents for their friends and families. There's always caroling and a pancake breakfast going on the whole time, after which the kids' choir performs out in the commons. Somewhere in there—surprise, surprise—Santa pops in with bags of candy.

As Mom rushed out of the house on Saturday, she said, "By the way, Elijah, I volunteered you as stage manager for the choir performance. Miss Flewharty likes your work."

For the next three hours, the twins had their own personal monkey bars: me. It was fun for a while. But to save my skin from being rubbed off, I said, "Okay, let's play grapevine." I tied a rope from the railing of our loft for them to swing on. Mom says swinging over furniture on a rope is a bad idea and can only lead to broken bones or lamps. But it hasn't yet.

The twins were due to turn seven on Friday the thirteenth. They bugged me about getting them presents.

I said. "Your birthday is bad luck! And get this: some Indian tribes say twins are a bad omen, and they're taken into the woods and smothered with moss!" (Most Indian stuff is really cool, but not all of it is rational.)

"Nuh-uh!" said Nori, the darker, strong-willed one.

"I'm telling Mom you scared me," whimpered Stacy, her little face all eyes surrounded by brown fluff.

"Tell on me and you get no more grapevines," I threatened.

Nori snickered. "Then we'll lingle you!"

I'd only been able to decode a few words of the twins' secret language over the years: rinken-rascal meant "bully," for one. And I knew about their imaginary pets, the lobbies, because the twins were always leaving bowls of weeds around the camp as food for them. You'd think they'd catch on when the food never disappears that lobbies don't exist, but it never mattered to them.

Lingle, I pondered. *Whatever that means, it can't be good.*

CHAPTER 13

The newspaper story about the investigation was sketchy, saying only that remains were found "in a remote spot west of Council Cliffs State Park." It didn't say who found them, which was fine with me. I figured my dad had a hand in keeping my name out of it. The less everyone knew, the better.

But little good that did. That very Monday, Justin Brill shot off his big fat mouth in the school hallway. "Hey, Creek, you were out there where they found the body, weren't you?" He followed me to my locker. "My brother said he drove you and Skid and Robbie to the park and you headed west with a shovel."

"So?" I said.

"So did you guys find it?"

I shrugged. "What if we did?"

"Cool! Hey guys, Nature Boy found the dead guy! Hey, what did it look like?"

I shoved books into the locker and pulled books out, not thinking about which ones I needed for the next class. I just wanted to get out of there. Half a dozen of Brill's buddies surrounded me, firing questions like, "How did you know it was there?" "Who clued you in?" "Was it gross?" "Who is it?"

They were thinking and acting exactly how I would have, if I hadn't seen it myself. But after that first horror of discovery, a quiet, creeping isolation had settled in around me. I couldn't imagine dying like that. To be honest, I couldn't imagine dying at all, although my little run-in with Salem had given me a glimpse into the possibility.

I'd been viewing my life differently since finding the skeleton in the well.

Slamming my locker, I turned to face them. "Look, somebody died, and nobody knew about it for years. It's not funny, guys."

"Well, woo-hoo," said Justin, backing off a little. "Hey, we just want to know what it looked like. Was it all bones, or was there rotting flesh, or what?"

I pushed past them and headed down the hall. Justin and his gang sauntered after me, saying stuff about how I was "in good" with the cops now. And how they'd need to watch out when I was around. I turned the corner in a rush and almost ran right into Reece.

"Hey," I said.

"How've you been?" she asked.

"I've got to get to class," I muttered and hurried on.

. . . . .

I felt bad about pushing her off like that, so I spent second lunch choking down cold mushroom pizza and writing her a note.

She came over to my desk in pre-algebra. I couldn't tell if she was hurt or mad. "What's going on with you?" she whispered. "Why won't you talk to me?"

"I can't." I handed the note to her. "This explains everything."

She took it to her desk and started reading:

Reece,

Sorry. I was getting away from Brill and his gang. I guess it's all over school about how Skid, Robbie, and I found the dead body at

the ruin. I'm grounded. I can't talk about it even over the phone
because of the investigation. But I need to ask you other stuff. Has
my dad or mom called your mom yet? Things are pretty strange at
home. Be sure to volunteer for Christmas Village. You'd make a
good elf. We can talk there.

  E—

She flashed me a smile.

· · · · ·

After school I babysat, and at night I helped with the Mad
River Boys.

I wouldn't generally be uneasy about hanging out with high
school guys, even ones who go by names like Blade and D-Day.
To each his own. But they had criminal records. They'd been
hauled off to the ranch because their parents couldn't handle
them or didn't want them anymore. They were in the care—if
you could call it that—of Lafe, a burly red-haired guy always
flexing his fingers, like he was working up to strangling somebody.

Dad had bribed the boys with a promise of winter kayaking
at the end—if they behaved. I was warned I'd have to help
chaperone. In the meantime I did night duty, 8:00 to 11:00.
The Mad River Boys had already torn up a couple of bunks
the first night. They'd snuck out to smoke, thrown hot coals on
each other, filled the foosball table with pop to make a "lake,"
and tried to run some raggedy undershorts up the flagpole—
with the kid still in them. If I could catch them in the act of
tearing up one more thing, Dad might send them home, and I
wouldn't have to risk my life on the icy waters of Deer Creek.

Night watch also gave me time to ponder all sorts of unan-
swered questions. From the upstairs office in the lodge, with
the lights off and using high-powered binoculars, I could see

the open areas of the camp. The moon was full, the trees bare. I could even see through Owl Woods almost to Great Oak.

Camp Mudjokivi was beautiful at night in late fall—like a charcoal drawing on dark paper, with streams of chalk-white moonlight on the lake, and a dark purple sky dotted with stars. The cabin lights on the far hillside made little squares of gold on the dark landscape.

I edged open the window, letting in a stream of cold air. It was the only way I'd hear any goings-on. Compared to summer days when trees are thick and green, when lawn mowers buzz and swimmers squeal and team whistles blow, camp on a winter night is lonely and delicate, silent and fine.

I checked in with Bo on the walkie-talkies every so often, focused my binoculars on the far cabins where the Mad River Boys were staying, and watched.

My dad had gone to a lot of trouble to make Camp Mudj a safe place for kids. For that reason he always scheduled the Boys' meals and activities apart from the rest of the campers. They hounded the counselors all the time about riding the golf carts, and eyed me like a pack of hungry coyotes when I drove around the lake to haul paint to the Tree House Village. Dad dreaded this week all year, but we needed the business if we were going to expand.

The bird clock sounded the coo of a mourning dove—10:00. Night watch worked a spell on me; minutes ticked by slowly. I thought dark, random thoughts. *What would people think of Camp Mudj if news got out about dead bodies near the property, about criminal boys in the back cabins, about man-eating dogs running loose, about Russ Creek's own son prowling the countryside looking for buried treasure?*

Why did the compass point to the well, and not to the next piece of armor? If the compass was our last clue, how can our quest go on? Where is the broken compass anyway? Last time I saw it, it was in Robbie's hand at Mei's house. I need to turn it over to Officer Taylor.

Where are the Stallards, and what are they doing with our belt of truth?

Who is that person at the bottom of the well; and did he have anything to do with Old Pilgrim Church?

I stuck on that last question, chewing it over. Dowland had said that things happened right before the church died all those years ago. As he put it, "Another terrible thing swept through the church, a thing that can't be explained by common sense, *a thing no family should ever have to go through.*" Maybe that person at the bottom of the well was a member of his church. Could Dowland have wanted someone to find the body, so it could be put in a grave and finally rest in peace? I needed to call Reece and ask her opinion, but I couldn't leave my post. I wasn't supposed to talk to anyone about the case except Mom and Dad, Robbie and Skid until further notice. I sat there in the cold and dark, thinking about questions with no answers.

A chill ran through me, not from the cold draft. *Was Dowland lying about Salem, lying to protect the armor...lying...just like me?*

CHAPTER 14

Things were looking up. I was only ninety-five percent grounded. My previous work on *The Adventures of Tom Sawyer* had scored points with Miss Flewharty and Mrs. Coyle, so I was officially a Christmas Village stagehand. It was as good an excuse as any to get out of the house. I asked Mei if she wanted to use her talent painting the village backdrop. Robbie and Reece signed up to be elves. They'd be selling junk in the village and passing out candy for Santa.

And one of my dark clouds was passing: it was the last day of camp for the Mad River Boys. They didn't deserve the winter kayak trip, after chalking up $612 in damages. But Dad felt sorry for them. He knew that when they got on the bus to leave, a few of them would bawl like babies.

I had to go along. Dad and Bo and Lafe were big strong men, but the Boys outnumbered them four to one. Counting me it was three to one, not much better. There was no way of telling how it would go. Either they had learned something about good sportsmanship from camp, or they'd see the kayak trip down Deer Creek as one last chance to go hog-wild.

The afternoon was cold with a white fog still heavy in the valleys. Mom made me wear layers and pack a change of clothes in a plastic bag…"just in case."

I figured my fate was sealed as tight as that bag.

On the half-hour bus ride to Deer Creek, the Boys made it clear they were never going to like me. Maybe they were jealous of the cool setup I had. They'd hounded me all week about driving the golf cart. Dad had coached me to say, "Sorry, guys. Camp policy," and keep moving. But one night the lock of the maintenance garage was jimmied. The Mad River Boys didn't like taking no for an answer.

While Dad was lining up the kayaks, Leon slipped up behind me and said in a creepy, threatening voice: "I know things about nature. I know that if you catch a cicada and yank off its legs, its head pops right off too. *Pop!*"

Dad made them listen to me talk about kayak safety. They just snickered and nodded knowingly to each other. I was sure I was doomed.

We floated down Deer Creek, Bo and Dad doing their nature spiels, the Boys not paying much attention.

D-Day paddled up beside me. "Hey, kid, do you have any sisters?"

When I ignored the question, he jabbed my kayak with his oar. "What do you do for fun around here?"

They all laughed at my answer: hiking and helping with the camp. What I liked best was practicing with my bow and arrow, but I thought it best to keep weapons out of the conversation.

They wanted to know who lived in the other cabins. "Nobody," I said. "They're rentals for campers."

All afternoon they griped, one guy's temper setting off another:

"This is boring."

"You're boring, Javier. Shut up."

"Both of you shut up!"

"Who stole my water bottle? Leon?"

"C. T. did."

"You're dead, C."

"He's a lying—"

"I'll kill ya.'"

Lafe broke in. "I'll dump you all and hold you under till you're blue and bloated."

Maybe it was just their way of getting along. I don't know. But it got on Dad's nerves big time.

I'd learned years ago that when tomcats get in a fight—tearing around the neighborhood bothering people—you can sometimes shut them all up by hitting one in the gut with a big rock.

I don't mind saying it crossed my mind.

Watching for one to slip out of the pack and escape or fracture another's skull with a paddle, I kept my distance from the Mad River Boys as much as possible. I'd maneuver close to Bo, who's built like a world-class wrestler, or I'd move up behind Dad who's tall and knows how to put a commanding edge to his voice. But I steered clear of Lafe.

I actually missed having Skid around. I could have used the moral support.

We'd gotten off fairly easy with the Mad River Boys, I thought. Javier got a good enough whack with his paddle to flip C. T. into Deer Creek, but at least it wasn't me.

Building a good campfire was the last lesson, and not a moment too soon. The Boys were starving for hot dogs, and C. T.'s lips were blue. Leon went with him back to the bus to get him a change of clothes.

We should have known better.

I demonstrated how to place the tinder, the kindling, then the logs. When it was their turn, they did it all wrong on purpose, bunching up the kindling too tight, using wet wood. I tried to help but they cussed and yelled, "Lay off!"

Okay, fine! I thought. *That sickly fire will never take off.*

It was barely hot enough to roast one hot dog, much less twelve. They crowded into a circle and pushed their sticks into the measly fire, getting ashes all over their hot dogs and marshmallows, fighting for the hottest spot. The flames sputtered. Dad and Bo went looking for dry tinder. Lafe already had disappeared into the woods. The boys were carping about "raw" hot dogs, when Leon eased up beside me in the circle.

"Just taking care of business," he said wickedly. He was hiding something under his jacket. I got a whiff of gasoline. Out came a paper cup; in a flash I knew he'd siphoned gas out of the bus.

"No!!!" I yelled, but it was too late. He'd already flung fuel across the wood.

Whhhfff! A pillar of fire ten feet wide billowed out. The Boys fell back, whooping and cussing. I felt the blast of heat as flames rolled up into the sky.

For a second, they thought it was cool. But when the pillar of fire dissolved into the trees, the Boys were faced with the remains of their dinners: shriveled, black wads of char on the ends of their smoldering sticks.

They looked stunned.

I threw my head back and laughed and kept on laughing until Dad and Bo came running. "It's okay," I said. "Leon decided to help the fire along."

Dad fumed silently for a moment. Then his frown slowly changed to a grin. He turned to me with an expression of sweet revenge. "Looks like somebody's going home hungry."

We loaded them on the bus. D-Day called me a name and said something I can't repeat. As their bus drove off, he gave me the wickedest smile. But there were a few in the bunch who cried and wanted to stay. The look on Dad's face told me they'd be invited back next year.

When the bus had disappeared, Dad and Bo blew out lung-fuls of air and shook hands. Bo threw out his arms like an umpire and yelled, "Safe!" He punched me and said, "Thanks, kid."

There wasn't much to like about the Mad River Boys. But I couldn't help thinking that, if Leon had wanted to pay me back for having a better life than him, he could have given me a shove into that pillar of fire, and I'd have ended up a black wad of char.

CHAPTER 15

It was the first of December and surprises were still coming in twos. First there were two Dr. Stallards, when we thought there was only one. And as it turned out—when the police got their equipment back to the ruin—they found two skeletons in that hole: a woman and a baby.

When I came in from school, Mom was looking at the newspaper. Nori and Stacy were coloring at the kitchen table. Mom put a finger to her lips and let me look at the headline: Remains of Two Found at Site.

We weren't supposed to talk about it at dinner, but Nori brought up the subject, even before the chili was dipped. She wriggled into her chair and looked over at me.

"Tara said you found two skeletons in a well."

So much for small-town secrets.

Mom passed her a bowl. "Cheese and crackers and carrot sticks are on the table, girls. Don't take more than you'll eat. That story you heard is a matter for the police. It's nothing you need to talk about with your friends at school." She murmured to Dad, "I can't believe people discuss things like this in front of their babies."

Nori studied her bowl a minute, then looked back at me. "Did you?"

"Yeah," I said.

Mom shot me a look.

"I did. I'm not going to lie about it." Then I turned to Nori, "But that's all I'm going to say."

"Did a bad guy kill them?" Stacy asked, her voice small and squeaky.

Mom smoothed Stacy's wavy hair. "Whatever happened took place years ago, sweetheart. It's not for us to be concerned about."

It was Dad's turn. "We don't know that they *were* killed. How was your day at school, Nori?"

"Where is the deep hole?" Stacy asked.

"It's way far away," Mom said. "You don't need to worry."

"Maybe they fell in and died," Nori said to Stacy cheerfully, "and nobody killed them!"

I said, "Or…maybe they had a big brother named Elijah, and they asked him too many questions and he went berserk." I grabbed Nori, pulled her off the chair, and pretended to beat on her. Not to be left out, Stacy piled on us right there on the kitchen floor. Mom knew I was trying to distract them, so I didn't get the usual viper stare.

After dinner Dad brought me into the living room. He showed me the newspaper article, and we read it together. Dad asked me about what Dowland said when I went to his house.

I ran to my room and got my notes, hidden in my quiver hanging on the wall so the twins wouldn't find it.

Dad sat down and read it over. "This part where he talks about terrible things happening…did he go into any detail?"

"No. That's all I know. Bad things happened at the church before it closed down, was all he said."

"May I show your notes to the police?" he asked.

I tried to stay calm. "Well, it tells all about the armor, and I wanted to keep that quiet."

"I understand that, but you may have some very important information here."

I sat on the ottoman in front of him. "Can I rewrite it and leave the armor parts out?"

"The police will want to know why you went to Mr. Dowland's house."

The problem of telling the truth cropped up again. Truth ends up being so narrow sometimes. What I mean is, I could make up a zillion reasons why I went to Dowland's that day. But there's really only one *true* answer.

"Son," Dad said in an even voice, "I don't think they really will care about an old suit of armor that once stood in a church." He went on carefully, like he didn't want to hurt my feelings. "It's not a priceless artifact. Mr. Dowland said so himself; it's a trinket. And this nonsense of it being cursed—you're smarter than that, Elijah."

"I just don't want anyone else looking for it," I said. "Finding it means a lot to me...and the others."

Dad leaned back and sighed tiredly. Dark circles under his eyes told me he had clouds hanging over him too. He said, "I can't see the police taking any interest in it, since it has nothing to do with the death of this lady and her child."

"But I think it does, Dad. Why else would the belt be buried with a compass that pointed to the well?"

He was stumped and gave me long thoughtful look. "You're a smart kid, you know that?"

"Yeah, I know." We grinned.

I asked him, "Since the belt was buried with the compass, would it be evidence?"

"It could be."

"But the belt is in Chicago, you know. The Stallards would have to make a special trip to bring it down. That's a lot of trouble for a trinket."

We sat there a long time just looking out the front window at camp. He read my notes again and thoughtfully repeated Dowland's riddle, "'Piece by piece they will rest in peace.' What do you think he meant by that?"

"He's loons, is what I think."

Dad gave me a look. "To call someone loons is disrespectful."

"How about daft? That's Robbie's word."

"How about troubled? He must be a troubled man."

"Loopy?" I teased.

"Troubled!"

Dad was grinning.

"Deranged?"

He shook his head at me and laughed. A long, quiet moment passed. His eyes wandered around the room, then returned to me. "Elijah, I want you to keep this between us just for now, everything we've discussed. I need to think this through."

"Okay."

He said in a low voice, "If this turns out to be a murder, or if Mr. Dowland is involved, then we may have to consider the possibility that all the other pieces of the armor are connected to…other crimes."

A chill went down my spine. "You mean other murders?"

"If that's the case—" he bounced my notes in his hand as if to weigh them, "then we must turn this over to the police as is. We don't want to withhold evidence." He looked at the paper, then at me. "This whole affair is bizarre."

"You're telling me. You know, Robbie's real smart with the library. He could check into the history of Old Pilgrim Church and see if anyone died mysteriously after the armor came."

Dad was reading Dowland's story again. "Uh-huh. He said some people died and others moved away."

Another chill followed the first one down my spine. "Whoa…what if they didn't move away? What if everyone in town just *thought* they moved away?"

I can hardly describe all the expressions that crossed my dad's face. It started with a stare, his eyes in neutral while his mind considered my idea. Then he suddenly looked right at me—like Dowland did, but not in a scary way—reading every inch of my face, trying to figure out who I was.

I couldn't bring myself to tell him about the vision quest, and how that old "trinket" could very well be the armor of God. He might understand, or he might think I was going off the deep end like Dowland. Deranged. Daft. Loopy.

Dad was calm and quiet on the surface, but stuff was raging on the inside. I saw a little of myself in his face, deep and thoughtful in the lamplight. I let the sights and sounds of my home all soak in: the clatter of Mom doing dishes, the twins sounding all *skippity-hoppity* in the kitchen, the serious quiet of the living room. A strange feeling of warmth and strength welled up in me.

"Dad?"

"What, son?"

"I'm not giving up on finding every last piece of the armor. I'll wait until the heat dies down, or the murders are solved." I shook my head. "But I'm not giving up. I can't."

"Okay," he said, eyeing me curiously. "We'll play it by ear."

CHAPTER 16

Thanks to Jeremy Brill, people were feeding on rumors like a school of piranhas.

One grapevine claimed the guys and I had gotten lost, found an old house, and were drawing water from a well when up came a bucket of bones. Another rumor had us digging for a body after a mad dog chased us to a well. Robbie and I stayed to ourselves as much as possible, swearing on our honor we'd keep quiet. "Mum's the word," we'd say to each other. It was hard for Robbie because he's a talker. I didn't see Skid much—our class schedules are pretty opposite—but we crossed paths once and punched our fists together.

"*Daijoubu?*" he asked in Japanese.

"*Daijoubu,*" I said. "Mum's the word."

"*Ganbatte,*" he said back.

Work on the Christmas Village came as welcome relief. In the buzz and whine of woodshop, the shop teacher and I cut out the plywood buildings. Then Mei and Reece showed up to paint. Mrs. Coyle set us up with drop cloths and then left us on our own. She'd given the go-ahead on Mei's cutesy sketches, each storefront a different color. The little kids would go crazy over it. Since senior art students would be doing the detail work, our job was to slap on a coat of color. We propped the wood cutouts against the wall, grabbed brushes, and started in, me in the middle with Reece and Mei on either side, and the sketches stuck to the wall in front of us so we'd get the colors right.

We spent the next hour trying *not* to talk about the mysteries stacking up on us. But the more we tiptoed around the problems, the bigger they got.

"We can't worry about this," said Reece finally. "So here's the drill: we wait for news from the Stallards and keep our eyes open for the next clue. That's it. No panicking, no looking too far ahead. Believe me, that never works."

My guess was Reece had been fighting panic a lot in her life, not knowing whether she'd ever walk right or end up in a wheelchair. When Reece made a comment about big things in life, I tended to listen.

I asked, "So do you have any Bible words for us—" I faked a southern preacher's drawl, "to brang comfurt tew ar trubbled lahves in ar tahm uv need?"

She stopped painting and tipped her head at me, almost like Mom's viper stare. "You should always, *always* leave the acting to Robbie. You sounded like a complete idiot." She went back to painting. "I have a Bible verse for you: 'Then he went away and hanged himself. Go and do likewise.'"

"It doesn't say that in the Bible!" I said, but I was guessing.

"Does too. Both statements are in there," she grinned. "Just not together." She pointed her brush at me. "Gotcha!"

I slopped some aqua paint on her nose. She came back with pink and caught me on the ear. Mei stood there snickering until lilac ran down her arm and dripped off her elbow.

Yeah, it was welcome relief to hang out with them for a while.

· · · · ·

Mom and Dad staged a holiday get-together, as they called it. Really it was a chance to meet Skid's parents face-to-face and find out what they knew about the Stallards. The tree was up—decorated with everything from fancy angels to little scraps of sparkly paper the twins had made every year from the time they were in diapers. Some of my creations were on the tree too: a clothespin reindeer, a sled made from ice cream sticks, stuff like that. The house was fixed up as usual for the holidays, with electric candles in the windows and lots of angels and teddy bears in Christmas clothes stacked here and there in the corners.

After being at Mei's house, I wondered what foreigners think of our Christmas decorations: a tree hauled inside with sparkly ropes and things draped on it, girl dolls with wings and satin dresses hanging around with flesh-eating animals dressed in sweaters.

Where do those crazy ideas come from? Beats me.

When Skid's parents stepped into the entryway of our log house, I understood where their son got his coolness. Carlotta Skidmore was Skid's Latino half. She looked like a flamenco dancer in her red dress and red high heels. She had short, dark pixie hair, and a wide smile with lips the color of her dress.

Dominic Skidmore was your basic military man: muscles and posture, iron handshake, buzzed hair, and square jaw. He had Skid's lime green eyes and dark skin. He was half-black, half-white, the other two halves of Marcus Skidmore's three-way genetics.

Aunt Grace and Uncle Dorian came in matching Christmas sweaters. Dad was in a sweater and slacks, casual but nice. Mom looked pretty in a dark green dress, but I could tell she was a little rattled hosting the new people. She'd dropped the girls off at the babysitter's so the adults could gab in peace.

We guys didn't dress up.

It wasn't a dinner, but there was still a ton of food. The house smelled of hot cinnamon cider and sausage balls. There were cheese balls with crackers, big plates of vegetables, and Aunt Grace's homemade bread. And eggnog. And cookies.

While the parents got acquainted, we guys piled up plates and went upstairs to my room.

I'd mentioned before about suspecting the twins had surveillance equipment in my room. That night I solved the mystery. There's something about the way the heat ducts and cold air returns are situated, so that if the heat's off and the vents are open, you can hear from other rooms. In certain spots voices come through almost as clear as a bell. We figured it out when we could hear our parents talking downstairs. I shushed the guys. We stopped to listen.

"I bet they're talking about the case," Robbie whispered.

He began to move around the room to track the sound and ended up with his ear to the floor vent, his backside high in the air. I came over to listen.

It's not polite to eavesdrop, but the conversation involved us. We checked the other upstairs vents for the best reception, and ended up in the girls' room. Their vent must have joined the other vents right over the kitchen. With our ears pressed to the opening, we started piecing together the latest news. Robbie ran back to my room for pencil and paper. I'd worked on my listening skills out in nature, so I dictated what I heard.

"Young woman…and infant…remains of dress and sweater, baby blanket."

"Baby blanket?" Robbie said excitedly. "Remember that piece of rag that we found with the helmet and arm piece? That looked like a blanket. Do you think they're the same?"

"Shh! They may be able to hear us," I said, turning my ear back to the vent.

"Severe blow, suggesting…" The rest was muffled. Our heads met over the vent as they had over the well. "On impact…the baby."

The moms' voices crooned sadly for a while.

"Accident?…How can they determine?…So many years. We pieced together that the woman must have died on impact, but that the police couldn't tell if it was an accidental fall or a deliberate push. We also picked up that Mr. Dowland had been questioned and released already, then more mumbling about him, the words *danger* and *troubled.*

The conversation faded to white noise as the parents drifted back to the kitchen counter for seconds on food. I smelled coffee, which signaled dessert time.

"Want some cookies?" I asked. We headed down the steps with our empty plates.

"That coffee gives me an idea," Skid said.

"What?" Robbie asked.

Skid stopped us at the bottom of the stairs. "You know where we can *really* get the scoop?"

"Where?" I asked.

"Florence's."

Robbie's face screwed up like he'd been punched in the stomach. Florence's, where the R.O.M.E.O. (Really Old Men Eating Out) Club hangs out, the greasy spoon where no self-respecting kid would be caught dead or alive.

"Can't," I said with relief. "I'm grounded."

Skid said, "Robbie and I can still go."

Robbie's face perked up. It would be just him and Skid hanging out together. *Without me.*

"I'll try to get out of it," I said, hardly believing I'd risk getting re-grounded for a meal in Florence's.

"You shouldn't," Skid said.

"No, you shouldn't," Robbie echoed.

"Wouldn't hurt to ask," I headed for the food.

Lounging around back in my room, we discussed timing. "How about Sunday morning?"

Skid shook his head. "I do church."

"Then Saturday?" I suggested.

"It has to be early," Skid said. "Senior citizens don't sleep much."

"Yeah, when Grandma comes, she's up at the crack."

"Crack o' dawn then," Skid decided.

· · · · ·

When the company left and mom had gone to get the twins, I asked Dad, "So what's the verdict?"

"The Skidmores are really nice people," he said, and I could tell he meant it. We cleared dishes.

"What'd they say about the Stallards?" I asked.

"They really don't know the Stallards that well, and have met Dr. Eloise only a time or two. Dom and Carlotta were both in the military, serving in the Middle East, where they met Dr. Dale. He was on a dig."

I wiped the counter. "They're archaeologists."

"Your mom and I think it's best to meet them as soon as possible. They still have this belt you found?"

"Yeah."

"And are they going to bring it back?"

"They'd better."

Dad handed me a little piece of paper. "Here's their phone number. Why don't you give them a call and see what they've found out?"

"Me? Sure, well, okay. But I've only met them once. Maybe Skid should call."

I looked at the number while Dad shoved leftovers into the refrigerator.

"Dad, could I go with Skid and Robbie out to breakfast, so we can talk about it?"

He thought a little more. "Where?"

"Florence's. Tomorrow."

He laughed. "Do kids hang out there now?"

"No," I said sarcastically. "That's the point!"

He shut the refrigerator door and stood looking at me for a while. "Are kids at school giving you a hard time?" Before I could answer, he said, "I didn't think about that. You have a lot to process, don't you?"

I said, "Uh-huh," though I didn't get exactly what he meant.

"Well…if you go straight there and straight back. And clear it with Mom first."

"Thanks! You're awesome!" I popped up on a counter stool. "Dad, I know I've asked you this before, but did you ever hear who owns Telanoo?"

"The land behind the camp?"

"Yeah, and all the way to Council Cliffs, including the meadow."

"I don't know."

"I think we should find out."

"Okay. It shouldn't be too much of a problem."

Yeah, right, I thought. *That's what I used to think.*

CHAPTER 17

The whole idea of sliding into a sticky booth at Florence's and ordering a greasy breakfast was pretty mortifying. Robbie beat me there a few minutes before 7:30, and boy, did he look like a fish out of water, sitting there at a table and gripping the bottle of ketchup.

"You look like what the cat dragged in," I joked and slid in across from him.

"And what the kittens wouldn't eat," he agreed with a wimpy smile.

The waitress came over and asked what us "young 'uns" wanted. I sat up straight and said in a formal voice that we'd be waiting to order until our *third party* arrived. We sat there on ripped red vinyl chairs, looking at stained paper menus.

Robbie heaved a sigh of relief when Skid came. I sighed too, on the inside.

Skid cased the place. "Let's sit over there." We moved to a booth surrounded by old men in adjoining booths and at a table beside us. Robbie and Skid sat on one side, me on the other. Robbie whispered a joke, "Nothing like being in a geezer sandwich with an order of old men on the side."

The waitress was on her way over when Skid leaned in, "Don't order the oatmeal, whatever you do. Your best bet is scrambled eggs with grits and bacon."

She took our orders and said, "No more funny business," about our moving around on her.

Robbie kept one ear to the gossip while Skid and I made small talk.

"So," I asked, fiddling with the syrup jar, "when are you going to make your move on Miranda Varner?"

"Make my *move?*" His eyebrows went up. "Yeah."

He made an uncertain gesture with his hand. "What do you mean?"

"You know…make your *move?*"

"Like what, tackling her in the school hallway?"

"No, jerk! When are you going to let her know that you like her?"

He crossed his arms and grinned like a sly cat. "She knows."

"Yeah? Well, don't you want to make it official?"

Skid shook his head. "You Americans."

Robbie sat up. "*You're* an American…*aren't* you?"

I knew what he meant right away. An army brat like Skid was a man of the world, whereas Robbie and I were corn-fed Ohioans.

Skid shook his head. "You guys treat romance like it's the Indy 500."

We must have looked blank.

He leaned in, resting his elbow on the table, "Okay, here's the lowdown on the current guy-girl thing, as I see—"

"Shhh—" Robbie said and nodded behind him.

We got quiet. A voice behind Skid said, "…found the bones at the old Theobald place."

I couldn't believe it when Skid threw one arm across the back of his booth and piped up, "The old Theobald place, huh? Is that what it's called?" He took the Romeos by surprise. They stared. He went on. "You're talking about the recent investigation."

Three old men in different stages of hair loss and all wearing plaid shirts fixed their eyes on us. (I got the strangest feeling that we were pretty much looking at ourselves in sixty years.) The one with his back to our booth groaned and strained to get his rickety body hauled around until he had us in his sights.

"Haven't you been in here before, sonny?" he asked Skid.

"A couple of times," Skid said. "I like the grits."

They all nodded approvingly. One bared his yellow teeth.

Skid reached his hand over the booth awkwardly and shook hands.

"It was some boys who found those bones," said the one old man nearest to us.

"That would be us," Skid continued.

They reared back. "You don't say?"

"This is Elijah and this is Robbie," Skid said.

We exchanged niceties. Their names were Charlie, Obie, and Walter.

"We have to stay out of the loop because we're kids," Skid said smoothly, "in case we're talking crime here. But you gentlemen have the history; you know what there is to know. We were wondering about who owned that farm where the remains were found."

We hardly noticed when our food came.

Obie, bald as a cue ball, twisted himself into a pretzel to see us, and did most of the talking. "Years ago, boys, Old Pilgrim wanted to buy that meadow as a location for a new building— the preacher's idea—in hopes of growing."

"The preacher?" I asked innocently.

"Stan Dowland," he said.

"They planned to put a road in and everything," said Walter, the round, red-faced one with the yellow teeth.

"But the owner wouldn't sell off the meadow without selling off the scrub land with it."

Skid and Robbie looked at me. We all thought the same thing: *Telanoo.*

"Al Theobald," said Charlie, a hangdog man with a comb-over starting behind his ear.

Robbie leaned to me and whispered, "That was his name on the land plats, Alfred Theobald."

"But it was sold!" I whispered back.

Skid gave us the eye. We shut up and listened.

Obie took over the story again, "Oh, they haggled and fought, I recall. But the preacher got his way and the church went ahead."

The waitress came by to give the old men refills. We asked if we could have some coffee too, and turned our cups over.

"They paid more than it was worth," said Charlie.

"Big debt for a little church," said Walter.

They argued among themselves whether the loan was borrowed from First Federal or from Theobald himself. I didn't care.

"When church attendance fell off, the money stopped flowing," Obie went on. "Theobald called in his lawyers and the land was foreclosed."

"Foreclosed?" Robbie asked.

"They canceled the deal. Theobald threatened to sue the church if he didn't get his money," said Obie.

"You can sue a church?" I asked. All this church stuff was new to me.

"Things weren't so cut-and-dried back then, boys. A little country church like that didn't bother to get incorporated as a lot of 'em do nowadays. There was an uproar all over town.

Theobald didn't want that land. He'd tried to unload it for years. He wanted the money. Anyhow, the church lost it all."

"So who owns it?" I asked, hardly believing I finally was going to find out!

They scratched their heads. They swilled coffee and mopped up gravy. They frowned at each other.

Obie said, "Well, a board of trustees would have to sign for the deed. But they didn't have trustees at Old Pilgrim. Harking back to the old days, I recall a couple of the head men passing away during the fracas."

Charlie turned to Walter. "Wasn't that when Harry Goodman passed? Does that ring a bell with you?"

Walter shook his head and chuckled, "I don't have much of a bell to ring."

Obie went on. "When it came right down to it…I'm thinking the preacher was left holding the bag."

"So Stan Dowland owns Tela—I mean, that old farm?"

More head scratching. Charlie said, "If memory serves me, he begged Theobald and First Federal to hold off retaking it."

"Oh, Dowland begged all right. He groveled, but they wouldn't budge," said Obie.

"A messy turn of events," Charlie said. "So let this be a lesson, boys: always get it in writing."

"Wasn't that banker's son sweet on Dowland's girl for a while?" Obie asked. "Wasn't that part of the whole ugly business, Walter?"

"It was Theobald's son," corrected Charlie.

After an exchange of words, they agreed. My neck got tight, waiting for the answer. We all were feeling the strain, but I took cues from Skid and kept listening with interest.

Obie said, "Dowland put a stop to that romance, don't you know? She left town, and soon after that, her mother followed suit. Then Dowland left. When the wife died, he moved back, but not into Magdeline. He got a little place over in New-point."

"Who put a stop to what?" Robbie asked.

"The preacher put a stop to his daughter marrying Theo-bald's boy," Obie said before sloshing down the rest of his cup. "A sad thing it was to see the church fold."

Charlie rumbled. His jowls quivered. "Dowland pushed. He soured 'em all. You don't push people around here. They have to go their own pace."

"It's still called the Theobald place?" I asked.

"That's what it was called *before*: the Theobald place," Obie said.

"What's it called now?" Skid asked.

He reared back and gaped at us like we didn't have the sense God gave a duck. He barked, "Why, the *old* Theobald place!"

"But…but after all that died down, who ended up with it?" I asked once more.

"I don't know who'd want it anyhow, that hard, clay dirt," Charlie said. "The Morgan farm, now that's good land, and he's kept it up."

"But who bought that land after Old Pilgrim Church?" I asked. "Who owns it now?"

They shrugged. Obie said, "Don't know. Dowland got stuck with it, I suppose."

"First Federal took it back, I think," suggested Charlie.

"That's right," said Walter. "But that bank closed."

"Then nobody, I guess."

A silence fell.

Skid said, "Thanks, men. We appreciate your time."

Obie turned back to his breakfast.

Robbie's wide eyes fell on me in pure awe. "It *really is* the land no one owns."

"It really is *Telanoo*," I said mysteriously.

Skid took a casual sip of coffee. "Whatever. I guess we're in the clear about trespassing."

I left that morning full of cold grits and bacon, with an old question answered, several new ones sprouting, and a sudden, uncontrollable urge to call on Mr. Dowland once more. But only with Dad's permission. And a bodyguard—maybe Skid. We could go together, and on the way he could finish explaining about the current guy-girl situation and what he planned to do, Miranda-wise.

CHAPTER 18

I cornered Reece at the water fountain before first class period. I was a bundle of excited nerves.

"I have to get the group together. I think we're onto something."

"What?"

"I may have figured it out."

"What figured out?"

"Who it was…out there at the ruin."

She grabbed my wrist. "Elijah! You're kidding!" She smiled at me. "I knew you could solve it. If anyone could…"

I pulled her around the corner to a little niche between rows of lockers, out of the flow of traffic. "I couldn't sleep all night, thinking about it. Here it is: Old Pilgrim Church tried to buy that place—the Theobald place, it's called—around the time the church started going under, the same time the armor came. Dowland's church couldn't pay for the land and there was this legal problem between them and Theobald and the bank. Dowland ended up stuck with the problem. Somewhere in there Theobald's son and Dowland's daughter started…dating, I guess you could say. Dowland put a stop to it, and his daughter left town and never came back." I paused.

"Okay…" she said, waiting for more.

"Do you see what I'm getting at, Reece? *She never came back!*"

It took only a few seconds for it to sink in. Her eyes got wide.

"The one they found in the well…was her? And her baby?"

"It makes sense, doesn't it? If Dowland was embarrassed and didn't want the church to know; and if he was fighting over the land; and if his job was in trouble and everybody was jumping ship, what would make him angrier than his daughter and Theobald's son being together?"

Reece went all soft and sad. "Poor Mr. Dowland! Everyone standing back watching to see what the minister would do… no one offering to help. Him losing everything."

(I don't know any girl who wouldn't get some kind of sick thrill out of all the romance and death, and a girl being in that kind of trouble. But there was not one glimmer in Reece's expression that this would be fun, juicy stuff to gossip about and roll your eyes over. She's something.)

"How did you figure all this out?" she asked, amazed.

"It was Skid's idea to start with. He made us go to Florence's restaurant for breakfast." I laughed.

"You're kidding!"

"They do have good grits and bacon."

"What're grits?"

"Who knows? Some sort of southern food. But anyhow, the Romeos knew all about the town history, and *we* knew about Dowland's story. We put two and two together."

"You mean to tell me, no one in Magdeline ever put the two stories together, for thirty years?"

"From what we could tell, no one knew where Dowland's daughter went. He kept her whereabouts a secret."

"He was hiding her away there? Or—" her face went pale. "Elijah, do you think he killed her?"

"He's mean, that's for sure. But in that speech to me he said a thing happened that should never happen. That sounds like a freak accident."

"With her baby," Reece whispered. "What if he told everyone she'd left town, but he actually killed her, his *own daughter*, just to hide his shame?"

I checked the hall clock: one minute until the bell. When I turned back, Reece was crying. I stammered and cleared my throat. "Hey, if you need a drink of water or something—" I thumbed at the water fountain, like I was hitching a ride to nowhere. "Dowland's gone off the deep end keeping secrets and lies to himself all these years. He may have forced her into hiding, and she got depressed. Maybe she was running from someone who discovered her, and she fell in."

"No one ever knew..." she said, getting sadder by the minute.

"But someone *did* know, Reece. They put boards over the well to hide it."

She glanced down the hall cautiously. "Elijah, if it wasn't an accident, and you're the one who brings it to light, you could be in danger. Real danger! Don't go anywhere by yourself."

I shrugged. "I'll be fine."

With determination she said, "We have to find out what happened to her. We have to uncover the truth."

"That's exactly what I was thinking. The truth."

A feeling washed over me, as if suddenly I wasn't a kid wedged in a hallway at school, but in a much larger place, a place getting bigger and bigger all the time. I saw the belt of truth in my mind's eye: The Ancient Omen. I understood that it was given to me to figure out that finding and keeping the truth is a battle, especially if it's been buried for years. The truth is as hard as granite and tough as nails. The truth can be dangerous. Sometimes getting to it hurts you; you have to brace for it. The proof of that was in Reece's face. But how the truth could set you free—I didn't have the brain space to hold what that could possibly mean.

The clock ticked off another minute. The hallway was nearly empty. "The bell's going to ring," I said. "We've got to get the gang together. But first—first let's me and you go see Dowland."

She sniffed and blinked. "What? Are you crazy!"

"I already told him about you, that the armor means a whole lot to you." A cloud of worry passed over her face, as I backed down the hall toward my class. "One of our parents can take us," I said. "Skid could go as bodyguard."

"I don't know, Elijah. I—"

"Five minutes, that's all we'd need, to see if he'd give us another clue." I called out, getting louder as I went. "Salem's gone and our parents will be right there, so actually we wouldn't need a bodyguard. Actually Skid would intimidate Dowland. Mei wouldn't go. Robbie'd freak out at the very idea, so that leaves you and me." I kept going, sprinting backward. "One or two questions, that's all, then we'd leave. See if your mom will let you, okay?"

"I'll…try," she said in a small voice.

The hall had emptied out. I turned to dash the last few yards and leap up the familiar steps to the south wing hall, but I miscalculated; the steps were already under me. I stumbled back, trying to catch a step with my heel, but my backpack was weighing me down. I spun to face the steps. The weight of the pack shifted as my feet tried to claim a foothold. I slipped down a step. Another try, another miss. I pitched forward, sprawled the length of the steps. My backpack went flying over my head, pulling my face down. My forehead hit tile with a *thunk*.

Spread-eagle on the stairs, like a facedown, half-baked gingerbread man, I hoped for all I was worth that Reece had gone on to her class. I wouldn't have cared if half the school spilled into the hallway for the pleasure of seeing me fall, as long as Reece hadn't seen it.

Crumpled, forehead bruised, and wearing my backpack practically on my head, I slithered back down the hard metal edges, turning as I went until I was back where I'd started. I looked down the hall and there she stood, all by herself at the other end, clutching at her waist, giggling until her shoulders shook.

"Hey, Elijah Creek—" she paused to gasp air, "hey (more giggles), I have a pair of crutches you can rent. Cheap."

· · · · ·

The twins were in bed. I was supposed to be. I crept downstairs past the Christmas tree and the button-eyed bears in the living room. My purpose was to beg Mom and Dad to ease off just a teeny bit more on my grounding so I could visit Dowland one last time. If I pulled if off, I'd try to weasel another un-grounding for a powwow. Then I'd never ask for another favor as long as I lived.

"Mom? Dad?" I padded barefoot into the kitchen. "There's something I want to ask…Mr. Dowland about."

Mom looked up from a pile of coupons. "The police are questioning him, hon. You don't need to."

"They did already, Mom. He claims he knows nothing. But he knows." I sat at the table with them.

"What does he know, dear?" She went back to sorting and clipping.

"Who the victims were. And I think I know too."

Dad's eyes came off the paper and landed on me. "Who do you think it is?" he asked warily.

"I'm not positive, but I think I know how to get it out of him."

"How?" Dad asked. He put the paper down.

"Can I talk to him first and give you an answer when I know for sure?"

"He's unstable, Elijah. You said so yourself. After what happened with that dog…no, Elijah, I won't have you taking that risk." He went back to his paper, as if that settled it.

"Then you come with me, Dad."

Mom looked up. "Why not let the police—"

"Because this involves the armor!" I pleaded.

He gave me a weary look. "Elijah…"

"You've got to trust me on this, Dad."

"No, son, *you* need to trust *me*."

"Reece is asking her mom right now. Either you or Mrs. Elliston could take us there." The more I pictured it in my mind, the clearer it got. "See, you can wait in the car where he can see you, so he doesn't try anything. Simple and safe!"

I knew he didn't understand. How do you explain to your dad that maybe, just maybe, God has called you to put on his belt of truth and then go do something, like fight some kind of war, but you don't know yet what kind of war?

"I know you're worried," I said. "I'm not all that keen on going to his house either. But—" I got up to raid the cookie jar. "I have to."

They studied me. I shrugged. "That's all, I just do. I have to know the truth. I uncovered this mystery, and I want a part in solving it."

"We love you, Elijah," Mom said. "We don't want you hurt."

"I know." I went to the fridge to get some chocolate milk.

Dad said, "His dog is gone, but the danger is not over."

"Don't think I haven't worried about it," I said.

The room got quiet. Mom frowned at her coupons, like she wasn't listening.

I asked a question, knowing it had no sure answer. "See, because I've been wondering…when a good man goes bad, just *how* bad does he go?"

Mom and Dad looked at each other.

"For reasons unknown I've been dragged into a death I had nothing to do with. And if Reece and I are the only ones who can get to the bottom of it, shouldn't we try?"

Mom shook her head and stuffed the coupons in an envelope. "It's between you two men. You'll have to call Reece's mother, Russ. Whatever you decide." She kept shaking her head and blinking and making a frustrated sound in her throat, like she was going to short-circuit.

It was the first time she'd ever called me a man.

CHAPTER 19

Dad stopped the car across the street from 26 Jewett Avenue in Newpoint and turned to me, worried. "I think I should go in with you." He glanced at Reece in the back seat.

I felt like we'd get more out of Mr. Dowland if it were just Reece and me and told Dad as much.

"No more than five minutes," he said, "or I'll be coming in."

We walked cautiously up to the door, Reece wincing with each step. She'd been doing well since finding the belt, but today was too much. When we got to the door, I turned and gave Dad the thumbs-up.

Reece looked at me. "Ready?"

"As I'll ever be."

She smiled bravely at me and knocked on the door. "Who starts?"

"I will."

She set her chin, clamped her eyes shut for a second, and breathed in slowly.

"Praying?" I asked.

"Yep. The truth will set you free."

The window curtain moved.

"He sees us," I said.

Nothing happened. She knocked again. After a long moment, we heard locks and bolts moving. The door opened. I'd warned Reece ahead of time that Dowland was scary in a pitiful way. She was ready for him with a beaming smile.

"Hi, Mr. Dowland," I said. "This is Reece. She's the one I told you about before."

His eyes shifted between the two of us.

She kept her smile. "It's nice to meet you, Mr. Dowland. May we talk with you for a minute?"

"Not the best time," he said flatly.

"We won't stay long. We just wanted to know if we were able to do what you wanted us to?"

He kept sizing us up, as if we were kids selling vacuum cleaners door-to-door. "What'd that be?" he finally asked.

She leaned in. "I wish we could have kept the whole thing quieter. We didn't understand that part until it was too late. We'll do better next time."

His eyes narrowed. "I don't know what you're talking about."

"We want to help, piece by piece, so they can all rest in peace."

Her words registered.

"Come in," he said grudgingly, "but you can't stay long." The living room was painted an icy blue and was cramped with fifty-year-old furniture and dusty stacks of magazines and newspapers. It seemed to me Dowland's whole world was stuck in the past while his body had skipped ahead a couple of decades. I noted the familiar green-gray flannel shirt and dry, cracked face—the face of Telanoo. I wondered if that's what happens to a person or a piece of land that belongs to no one: it just dries up and dies.

Dowland closed the door behind us and looked around as if he'd lost something. Reece and I sat on a couch covered in a faded navy blanket. There were no family pictures. I noticed the stale smell of dog.

"The clue was excellent, sir," Reece said. "We found her for you. We found them both. Now they can rest in peace." She gulped back her nerves. "It was a very good thing you did."

"Why'd you come?" He was already drifting toward outer space.

She said, "We thought you might tell us more, so...so, um...we could help you again."

"I don't need help."

Reece was at a loss. She shot a look at me.

I threw out a cheerful, "Well, we know about Theobald— and the baby."

Mistake number one.

Whatever was caged in his mind broke loose. His face went chalky, his thin lips lost all color. He brought up bony fists. "Why, you little meddling brats!"

I knew he was no Mr. Personality, but that was way out of line.

I sat tall. "Excuse me, but don't say that about my friend."

"Get out!"

I'd heard that before. "Reece, let's go." I helped her up. We headed for the door. I wanted more information, but his reaction showed that we'd hit on the truth. I turned. "Sir, I thought I should explain about your dog. I'm sorry about killing him, but he attacked us. I had no choice."

On the one hand I wasn't sorry at all. Then I remembered how Reece had cried in the hallway over the mess Mr. Dowland had gotten himself into. From the look of things, he might never get out. I felt bad for him, trapped in a cold, smelly house.

He looked around for Salem, then back at us as if trying to make the connection. A word slipped out of his mouth that I didn't catch.

I decided to give it one more try. "Mr. Dowland, if your daughter's death was an accident, why didn't you tell someone?"

"They should have helped you," Reece jumped in. He tried to focus.

"The church should have helped you," she repeated.

His face went into a kind of landslide. His head drooped. "No one stood by me. No one." He croaked in an evil voice, "They owed me for all I did. They *owed me!* Shame on them all!"

We eased open the door. In spite of how he'd acted, Reece turned to him kindly one last time, "'Piece by piece they *will* rest in peace.' It will be all right, Mr. Dowland. I'll pray for that."

His head turned mechanically in our direction. In a hateful tone he sneered, "Hell and damnation to all who bring trouble on the house of God!"

I took Reece's hand. "Well, thank you. If you have any more pieces we can help you with, just feel free to let us know, anytime—"

She elbowed me hard in the ribs.

Big mistake number two. I was so antsy about getting the next piece of armor, I'd spewed out an open invitation for Dowland to just show up at my door. Night or day.

We stepped outside. I turned back, "But call first, okay? Call *first*."

He slammed the door.

We got in the car and punched the locks down. "You okay, kids?" Dad asked.

"That was strange," Reece said calmly.

I turned toward the back seat. "Hey, Reece, what did he mumble when I mentioned his dog?"

Her face was full of sadness. "He said, 'Jerusalem.' I think it was his dog's real name, Elijah. Maybe he didn't name his dog for a witch town after all. *Jerusalem* means 'city of peace.'"

I was speechless. A dog like that named City of Peace? We thought about it as Dad fired up the engine. Telanoo and Dowland and Salem all may have started out good, but somehow had turned evil. *Why?*

Dad headed out of Newpoint without a word, glancing sideways at me, then at Reece in the rearview mirror. Halfway to Magdeline, he said, "You have to tell the police how Mr. Dowland acted and what he said. Let's stop by the city building."

. . . . .

Officer Taylor was called in from patrol. He took us to a small, plain room to hear us out. It was intimidating to sit there and tell the strange unvarnished truth as best I knew it, but I told him what I believed. Some thirty-odd years ago Stan Dowland and the Theobalds had gone for each other's jugulars over a land dispute, and that we believed Dowland had hidden his daughter away from the younger Theobald and the rest of the town to hide his embarrassment about a baby.

Officer Taylor watched me like a hawk.

Reece gave her ideas, that maybe the girl didn't know the well was there and fell in accidentally. Or maybe her boyfriend found out she was hiding and went to the old house. Maybe she tried to run and hide to save her dad's reputation. Reece and I didn't want to think that girl had killed herself. And as much as we didn't trust Dowland, we couldn't believe he'd push his own daughter down a well.

It was almost dark when we headed home. On the way to Reece's apartment, I turned to the back seat to tell her thanks for coming. She looked especially small all by herself back there. Her eyes were closed and she was smiling.

"You look like the canary who just ate the cat," I joked.

Her eyes drifted open and fixed on me. In an eerie, other-worldly voice she said, "Piece by piece."

Chills went down my spine. I didn't know what to make of it. But that night I dreamed she was the ghost of Dowland's daughter, coming back to settle the score.

CHAPTER 20

While setting up the stage for the Christmas Village program, I saw just how loopy my life had become. I was a grounded outdoorsman; a police informant by day, baby-sitter by night; the keeper of the armor of God without one lousy piece of it in my possession. And my two best friends were running around in pointy green hats and leotards. My situation had reached freak-show weird.

Elementary shoppers swarmed through a pint-size version of Magdeline's business district. Robbie and Reece stood behind tables of merchandise, making change for the little customers who couldn't add. The twins got Dad a mug that said World's Best Dad in Old English lettering and a nice pen in a velvet box. I recommended a butterfly pin for Mom. We got Grandma Creek doilies and homemade jam.

The twins made me leave while Robbie helped them pick out my gift. There wasn't much I was interested in. But to avoid getting stuck with a plastic dump truck or a bright blue death noose—formally called a youth tie—I signaled Robbie that I liked a yellow flashlight with black trim. It had two settings—wide and narrow beam—and a metal ring to attach it to a belt or backpack.

I hadn't planned on buying anything there, but Reece was admiring a silver cross necklace, so I snuck it out at the last minute and slipped the money to Robbie. I bought another type of necklace with beads for Mei so their gifts would be sort of the same. The Swiss army knives were pretty nice. I bought one each for Robbie and Skid. All in all, I didn't do half bad.

Things were winding down by lunchtime. Mom had recruited Mrs. Aizawa to bring refreshments. When Mei came in carrying trays of goodies, I saw a chance for the five of us to squeeze in a quick powwow. I ran out to the pay phone in the hall and called Skid.

"Hey, we're at school. We'll be closing down the Christmas Village soon. I'm still grounded, but right now I'm on neutral turf. Could you get here for a powwow?" I glanced out the side door. The day was cold, sunny, and dry: good conditions for a skateboarder. "You could be here in a few minutes on your board."

"Be there pronto, Tonto," he said, and hung up.

I wandered to the window of the band room. In less than five, Skid swooped in like a hawk, smooth as silk, his eyes focused on the blacktop and nothing else, hair blowing like feathers. In one liquid motion he came to a stop at the bottom of the steps, flipping the board precisely into his outstretched hand.

Down to a science, I said to myself, jealous and awed.

Skid helped us disassemble the village storefronts, haul them to the commons, and stash them backstage. I told Mom I'd be hanging with my friends until she was ready to go. With the cleanup ruckus going on in the main area, we were able to dissolve into the background. We found chairs and made a tight circle behind the rear curtains at the back of the stage.

Reece and I updated everyone about our meetings with Dowland and Officer Taylor.

Mei could hardly believe any of it. "You went to Mr. Dowland!? *Baka mitai!*"

"*Baka* what?" Robbie asked.

"That seems crazy!" she said. "Your father took you to the police station to tell the story? *Sugoi!* This is strange to me."

"*Sugoi* ditto!" Robbie said, throwing his head back and scrunching his eyes shut. "Dowland *and* Taylor!"

Skid updated us on his news: "I called the Stallards like you wanted, Creek. I told them about the trouble down here. They're willing to meet with our parents to smooth things out, but they'll need to squeeze us in before they head to Bethlehem for Christmas."

Reece gasped. "Bethlehem? As in the *real* Bethlehem? The birthplace of Jesus?"

Skid nodded.

"Wow…how awesome is that?!" she breathed.

"Are they bringing the belt of truth?" I asked.

"I guess so. They didn't say," Skid answered.

"But it's *ours!*" Eight eyes glared at me. I didn't mean to bark, but that's how it came out. "Well, it *is*, and I say we get it back. Skid, if you wouldn't mind, remind them just so there's no mess up."

"Sure," he said.

"Okay, that's taken care of. On to new business: we should be looking for the next piece of the treasure," I said. "I'm working on a map of the camp. If we talk through all the clues, we may come up with something. One thing's for sure, we're not going to get any more information out of Dowland about the treasure or the murder or anything else."

At that very moment my Indian senses kicked in. Someone was standing on the other side of the curtain. I put my finger to my lips. Quickly I stood and walked cat-quiet toward the curtain. With one arm I swept it back.

"Nori! Stacy!" I lashed out. "What are you doing sneaking around like that? We're having a private conversation."

"Mommy said it's time to go," announced Stacy, her mischievous smile an exact copy of her sister's. They'd been listening in.

· · · · ·

The next Monday the gym filled up as Robbie and I made our way in for the school Christmas concert. Skid waved us up to the top bleacher.

There he was, cool as a cucumber, one foot propped on the bleacher in front of him, his chin resting on his fist. His eyes roamed over the crowd. I hoped he was keeping a lookout for Miranda.

"I've been back to Florence's," he said after a minute.

"By yourself?" Robbie asked.

Skid's head rotated toward us. "I sat with the Romeos this time, the same three as before: Obie, Walter, and Charlie. Turns out Walter, the quiet one, is related to the Theobalds. That day we talked to them, he was just taking it all in."

"And?"

"Brace yourself, boys. The whole thing's blown open around town and Bruce Theobald's fighting mad."

"Mad at who?" I asked.

He eyed me with an air of mystery, giving me a minute to figure it out.

I gulped. "Walter told him about *us?*"

Skid nodded. "Said he didn't mean any harm, but felt 'beholden to the family.' When Theobald had to fess up to his family why the police questioned him, his wife pitched a fit and moved out."

"That's just great!" I griped. "Now both suspects in the murder hate us!"

The band started tuning up.

Looking on the bright side for a change, Robbie said, "What are you getting in a lather over? Theobald doesn't know us."

"He has our first names," I said. "How many Elijahs are there in Magdeline? How many teenage boys eating grits and bacon at Florence's at the crack of dawn?"

"There's another Robbie," my cousin said hopefully. "Robbie *Cardosi!*"

I yelled. "He's seven years old, for crying out loud!" I'd just about had it with him weaseling out of responsibility, thinking he could be part of a quest with no risk involved. I went off like a siren, "But there's only *one Robbie WINGATE!*"

People turned and stared. Robbie slumped down. I'd made my point.

When I cooled off, I said to Skid, "So Bruce Theobald's mad, so what? No skin off my nose."

The choir made its way to risers set up on the floor. Mei and Reece came into the gym. I waved. Reece waved back, but took a seat with some friends down front so she wouldn't have to climb the steps.

I lowered my voice, "Skid, did you learn anything about Theobald from the Romeos?" As if I had to ask. Skid probably had everything from his genealogy to his shirt size.

"The bad news keeps coming," he said calmly. "He's a bull-dozer operator."

Robbie groaned, "Heavy machinery! He's going to squash us like bugs."

Skid went on. "Theobald lives on High Street. He's married, has four kids, all grown; but two boys still live at home."

"High Street, huh?" I thought out loud. "I know where that is."

Skid leaned over and lowered his voice. "This'll interest you. The Romeos didn't seem all that surprised about the discovery of the remains, or that it might be Dowland's daughter."

I stared at him.

"Odd, isn't it?" he said. "Another thing, when Kate Dowland left town all those years ago, people suspected that her family was lying about the reason. Dowland told people she was going to Ireland as an exchange student. Dowland even had people write letters to her, which he supposedly mailed to Ireland. And get this: Theobald was a big name around town back then. You see what I'm saying? The family had money, influence."

I thought about that. "Behind Dowland's back the church was siding with people high on the social ladder?"

Robbie looked puzzled. "Wow. I didn't know Magdeline *had* a social ladder.

Skid said, "According to the Romeos, the church let him sink like a rock."

Robbie replied, "But *he* lied to everyone about his daughter, and he was a minister! They're not supposed to lie."

"No one is *supposed* to lie," Skid said.

CHAPTER 21

With the Christmas Village behind us and Mom back on the home front, I got un-grounded. First thing, I took my bike out for a spin down Main Street. People smiled and waved, but after what Skid had said, I wasn't sure I trusted them. On the way home I made a side trip to High Street. I wanted a peek at the place where the old boyfriend lived.

You'd think High Street would be high, but it wasn't. Sure, the High Street bridge arched up over the railroad tracks. But from there it was downhill all the way. The paved street broke down into potholes and gravel, then bottomed out into a gully of rubble. High Street had only about ten small houses jammed together. *They should have named it Down-and-Out Street.* I began to wonder if nothing in Magdeline was as it seemed.

I coasted to the end of the pavement, turned around, and pumped back up the hill a few yards, stopping just shy of the bridge. There was nowhere to go without being flat-out conspicuous. I pretended to mess with the handlebars and snuck a look down the hill.

The Theobalds' driveway was a stretch of dirt crowded with old cars. The squat little house, painted white but fading to a yellowish gray, seemed way too small for a big family. To my shock, Bruce himself stepped outside. I'd counted on him being at work, but there he was, a husky man in gray work pants and a dirty undershirt. His size dwarfed the covered porch where he stood taking a smoke. As I turned my bike to make a quick escape, my right foot slipped off the pedal and went under the bike. I almost went down. I recovered quick as I could, but the mishap drew his attention.

"Hey, you, kid!" he yelled after me, but I kept going. All the way home I thought about how the mighty Theobalds had sunk all the way down to High Street. Maybe what happened those years ago had somehow tipped over Magdeline's social ladder. Or maybe it was the curse of the armor of God.

. . . . .

Because Robbie's house was, as Aunt Grace put it, "in transition," and because Reece and her mom lived in a small apartment, and because the Skidmore condo was "too vertical" for big parties, Mom arranged for the families to meet the Stallards at our house.

Everyone brought food. And Grandma Creek came.

My grandma is tall and round and healthy for an old person. Her hair is almost all white, and her face is friendly. She likes her name. "It's the most versatile of all names," she says. "I can be Elizabeth or Eliza or Betty or Beth or Betts or Liz or Lizzy. Take your pick." She gets a charge out of telling old stories of people doing embarrassing things, like their pants ripping or laughing so hard they wet themselves. And she loves it when people fall down. I know this from personal experience.

. . . . .

The Stallards showed up on the dot at 7:00. This time they came dressed like professors, wearing dark suits. Dr. Eloise had on fur-lined boots fit for a Canadian winter, though there wasn't a flake of snow outside. Dr. Dale carried his ragtag briefcase.

Mr. Aizawa was in a suit too, stiff and formal. His thick hair and bushy eyebrows made him look stern. Mrs. Aizawa brought a humongous tray of Japanese goodies, and Aunt Grace snagged her right away about recipes for the future

Wingate Bed and Breakfast and Tea Room. Mrs. Aizawa smiled
and nodded at everything Aunt Grace said, but Mei shook her
head at us—her mom wasn't catching much of it.

I'd met Mrs. Elliston a couple of times before. She was small
and blond like Reece. She gave all us kids little hugs and told
us, "Merry Christmas," and asked how we were doing. "You all
right, Elijah?" She tipped her head at me. I could tell she meant
it; her smile was a little worried.

"I'm okay," I said.

Mei and Reece ate with the twins at the breakfast table and
kept them occupied. The adults ate in the dining room. We
guys took trays into the family room and ate beside the fire.
Everybody was chitchatting and friendly through the meal, but
tension was in the air—except when Grandma told one of her
stories. Then there was lots of chuckling.

During dessert, while everyone sat around drinking coffee,
Dad finally brought up the subject of the armor. Skid, Robbie,
and I weaved our way into the corner of the dining room to be
on the fringes of the conversation. The girls were opposite us
in the other doorway, listening. Grandma brought in a rocking
chair and sat.

Dad didn't pull any punches. He was polite but "expressed
his displeasure" about the Stallards telling us kids to keep the
treasure hunt a secret from our parents.

Dr. Eloise's thin fingers came to her mouth. "Oh, dear.
We've been terrible. Oh, Dale, haven't we been just awful?"

"Mr. Creek—" Dr. Dale began.

"Please call me Russ," Dad said.

"Russ—and all of you—we do apologize. We meant no
harm or disrespect whatsoever. We simply didn't think. Our
Hester is grown now, but what an independent girl she was at
that age."

Dr. Eloise said, "How upset you must be with us! How can we redeem ourselves?" She turned to the Skidmores. "This is no excuse, of course, but your lovely Marcus was so mature when he visited Dale. My husband was terribly impressed with his interest in archaeology at the museum."

I leaned over to Skid and snickered, "You do look sooo *lovely* tonight, Marcus."

He whispered back through clenched teeth, "Just wait, Creek." He nodded. "That one's going to cost you."

Dr. Eloise went on. "*All* your children are so delightfully intelligent and resourceful."

"Maybe a little too resourceful," said Dad, glancing at me.

Dr. Dale stood and adjusted his glasses. "Let me begin by saying that we are scientists, searching for truth. In defense of our actions, we do have legitimate reasons for confiding in the children." He cleared his throat. "Many of the greatest prophets and leaders of the faith began quite young with special callings: David who slew Goliath, the boy Samuel, young Jeremiah, and Daniel. Many great prophets heard from God in their youth. 'Blessed are the pure in heart, for they will see God.'"

"I'm sorry, but I don't understand what you are saying," Mom said warily.

"Don't misunderstand us, please," Dr. Dale went on. "We are not saying that your children are going to become prophets or lamas or any such thing. No, no," he chuckled.

Robbie nudged me and moved his neck like a llama.

"Not that kind of llama," I whispered.

He made a face and whispered back, "I know!"

"The Word of God is complete. Let's be clear on that point," Dr. Dale continued. "But its messages still speak truth to us in new ways. And sometimes the clearest eye," he nodded toward me, "can see the deepest. The Scriptures are very deep."

Dr. Eloise chirped, "Deeeeep, deepdeepdeepdeep." Robbie stifled a snort and stashed himself in the corner. "And so very alive," she added.

"Alive," Dad said thoughtfully. "In what way?"

"In every way: active—working!" Her face tilted up, her arms went out like she was welcoming a crowd. "Oh, how can you fathom its depths? How can you drink an ocean?"

Dr. Dale nudged her. "One gulp at a time." They grinned at each other.

I didn't get it. By the look on the other parents' faces, they didn't either. All except Mrs. Elliston. She was smiling.

Dr. Dale went on, "Our belief is that if children are specifically called by God for a task, they must be free to obey—within the bounds of safety, of course. We adults with our agendas should not hinder their calling to suit our purposes."

Dad said, "So, if I am understanding you correctly, you're telling us that this relic they found is some kind of sign that they've been…chosen by God?"

For some reason I piped up. "Yeah, Dad. That's what they're saying."

Everyone looked at me as if I'd grown two heads.

"Well, not exactly, Elijah," Dr. Dale corrected. "If you are called, you won't need a relic to prove it. But the fact that you have found something of this nature begs the question, now doesn't it?"

"This armor is the stuff of myth," Dr. Eloise interrupted excitedly, "now brought into the realm of history."

"An artifact of great controversy," Dr. Dale said.

I spoke up again. "Mr. Dowland found the armor first. Does that mean *he* was called by God?"

"Perhaps," Dr. Eloise said.

"But terrible things happened to him," I said.

The doctors eyed each other mysteriously. Dr. Dale said, "True. But were they troubles of his own making or from outside forces? How did he respond to the armor's message?"

The whole room got quiet except for the creak of Grandma's rocker. Again I spoke up. "I think I've been chosen. Reece thinks so too."

Mom leaned over to Dad and said under her breath, "They've been brainwashed, Russ."

I picked up on that and said, "I'm fine, Mom."

She blushed. "But you've been hiding things from us, Elijah. I wouldn't call that fine—thinking you're on a secret mission, that you've uncovered this…this thing from God?!"

"Yeah, I lied to you," I said. "And it was wrong. But that was before; I get it now."

The others had been strangely quiet, like they didn't know what to ask. Mom asked, "Carlotta, what do you say about this?"

Mrs. Skidmore turned to the Stallards. "Well…if we're getting it all out on the table, I don't really know you that well. You are well-credentialed archaeologists. That's all I know."

Mr. Skidmore, who had a presence that would make anybody stand down, chuckled. "No offense, Stallards, but I had you checked out through military intelligence. You're not terrorists, kidnappers, or smugglers," he looked at the parents, "if that helps."

What a slam! I thought. *Skid's parents have put them on the spot.*

But Dr. Eloise said excitedly, "Excellent, Mr. Skidmore. If we should need to take the children overseas, we already have clearance."

"Wait a minute. Overseas?" Mom cut in.

"Not immediately, perhaps much later. There's preliminary research to be done, the other pieces to find, the question of Ireland where Mr. Dowland initially found the relic…"

"Next year, perhaps," said Dr. Dale soothingly, "or the year after. It's up to the children to find the other pieces first. And we are here only to assist."

You could have knocked me over with a feather. Me? Overseas? At first I figured they were just throwing out this crazy stuff, so whatever they *really* wanted us to do would seem tame by comparison, and our parents would be relieved and say yes. Then I snuck a look at Skid. His eyes slid to me, one eyebrow shot up, and he grinned. "Welcome to the world, Creek."

It was clear no one knew how to take the Stallards. Honestly, they were a little left of center.

Tense and red-faced, Uncle Dorian spoke up. "Dr. Stallard, you were talking about us adults having our agendas. What's in it for *you?* Let's hear *your* agenda!!"

The room got quiet again.

As if right on cue, Grandma let out the longest, juiciest, most cavernous belch you ever heard. I'm not kidding, if I hadn't heard it come from her own mouth, I would have bet a camel had snuck into the dining room and let fly.

It was hard to get everyone's reactions, I was so busy trying to control myself. But stern Mr. Aizawa's face finally cracked into a big smile, and his wife said something about the effects of onions. Grandma said, "Oh, dear me!" as she got up with a snicker and a groan and went into the kitchen. Reece's mouth was frozen in a big *O.* The adults tried to pass it off, biting their lips, pretending it hadn't happened. But Robbie curled himself into the corner again, sank to the floor, and snorted his lungs out.

CHAPTER 22

That belch was Heaven-sent. Everyone relaxed and had another round of coffee and dessert. The crowd regrouped around the kitchen counter. Dr. Dale stood at the end in lecture mode and summed up: "As I stated before, our agenda is truth. The armor of God is a spiritual reality, that much we know. But the possibility that a physical representation of that truth has worked its way through the centuries, well!…"

I was waiting for an answer that would keep the tension from building again, but the Stallards just stood there with distant, happy smiles.

Uncle Dorian said gruffly, "So all you want out of the deal is truth?"

"No small thing, Mr. Wingate. No small thing," said Dr. Dale.

Aunt Grace touched her husband's arm and said softly, "I could go along to Ireland, dear—do some shopping for the business."

"Can we see the belt?" I asked. "Certainly."

The moms cleared the dining room table. The Stallards brought out a linen packet, unwrapped it, and spread the belt on the table. To the side of it they opened up the shred of old blanket holding the piece of chain mail.

The grown-ups studied the belt.

"What we discuss here should not leave this house," said Dr. Dale seriously. "I am only trying to spare you trouble."

"What kind of trouble?" Mom asked.

"Could be anything, anytime," Dr. Eloise said. "Publicity hounds, antiquity pirates—or nothing at all. Such is the nature of our work. Now," she pressed her hands together, "we need to tell the children what we have discovered. Elijah, shall we sit here for our little discussion? Any of you parents are welcome to listen in, if you don't trust us."

"Here in the dining room will be fine," Mom said with a weak smile.

"First our little scrap of mail." Dr. Eloise flipped through her Bible. "We looked up every 22:25 in the whole Bible, and we think we have the answer. Job 22:25 says, 'Then the Almighty will be your gold, the choicest silver for you.'" She put the Bible down and smiled. "The Hebrew word for gold here is *betser* and refers to metal in a crude state, or 'dug out,' as in a treasure uncovered. What is fascinating is that the root word also carries the idea of defense. It may be translated gold, or treasure, or defense. And it looks like you children have found all three!"

"We believe this scrap of gold mail illustrates that God himself will be your treasure and your defense."

"Cool," said Skid.

Dr. Eloise added. "The engraver—whoever he was—had a deep understanding of spiritual warfare."

Some of the parents were hovering over our shoulders. Before any of them could flip out, Reece's mom said, "Let's go sit by the fire in the other room. I'll explain what she means by that."

Dr. Eloise smiled at me. "Are we correct that the mail was buried with the helmet of salvation and arm of fellowship, but is not a part of either?"

"As far as we could tell," Robbie said.

"This piece did not fit anywhere," Mei agreed.

"We're still speculating why, but perhaps its message boils down to this: fellowship with each other and with the Almighty is a powerful defense when trouble comes." She held the piece to the light. The two-inch square gleamed and glittered. "It's quite remarkable that this tiny piece was not lost."

"Mei found it stuck in the bottom of the sack," Reece said.

The Stallards congratulated her.

"Let's go on to the belt," Dr. Dale said. "The leather is relatively new, a few centuries old, the tapestry a few centuries older still. Curious, isn't it, that the tapestry is older than the leather it's applied to?"

"How can that be?" Mei asked.

"We're not sure yet. But the tapestry is Coptic, from northern Africa. The metal pieces strung along the back are decorative, but also may have some use in battle. Now, let's look at the buckle. This design here is a Hebrew word; the letters from right to left are pronounced: *awlef, mame, noon.* The word is *omen.* It means 'truth,' 'faithfulness,' and is virtually the same word as *amen.* When we say amen at the end of a prayer, we are stating, 'May it be true!'"

"So it does say truth!" Reece exclaimed. "I knew it would!"

Dr. Eloise nodded. "It was hidden in plain sight. The truth often does that."

"Now this is where it gets interesting," said Dr. Dale. "The first recorded use of the word *omen* in English, meaning 'portent of doom,' was around 1582. And the age of the metal on which the Hebrew word *omen* is engraved dates from about that time, or perhaps from the early Middle Ages. But the workmanship is quite primitive. Therefore we can't know if the word *omen* conveys truth or doom."

"Or both!" said Robbie.

"Could be," Dr. Dale said. "Our observation about the belt is that it appears quite…ageless. It can't be assigned to any single era of time. The tapestry outlasted the leather it was first sewn on, and new leather obviously was acquired to keep the belt intact. The word *omen* means two kinds of truth in two languages from two epochs of time. Quite extraordinary!"

"Quite mysterious," added his wife. "The belt is not eternal, of course, but it certainly hints at eternity, don't you think?"

We sat there, not sure what to make of it.

"Where did the armor come from in the first place?" I asked.

"To answer that we have to go back to the first century A.D. when the apostle Paul was a prisoner in Rome," said Dr. Dale. "Armored soldiers guarded him constantly. He wrote a letter to the Ephesians, a suspicious people who feared the power of gods, demons, and even stars. Paul used the illustration of armor as protection from such worthless ideas. Until Marcus handed us that first piece of mail, we'd only heard legends of an actual suit of armor which carried this message of the power of the Scriptures.

"But why is it here in sleepy old Magdeline?" said Robbie. "Why now? Why us?"

The two doctors of archaeology blinked at each other in Morse code or something.

"Shall I, my dear?" Dr. Dale asked.

"You may," she answered.

He rubbed his chin and glared into our faces. You'd have thought he was a principal, and we had just TPed the school yard.

"One of you—" he began accusingly.

Skid said, "Not me, man. I'm innocent!"

"—has been praying. Okay, which one of you was it?" Dr. Dale's eyes rested on Reece. "It was you, wasn't it?"

A shy smile spread across her face. She curled her finger at him. He leaned over, and she whispered something in his ear.

"Ah! I see, I see." He frowned thoughtfully. "Well, little lady, you may have gotten more than you bargained for."

"Fill in the rest of us," I said.

Dr. Dale smiled. "I'll let Reece tell you in her own good time. We have to consider the Day of Evil."

"Day of Evil, oh yeah," I said.

"Ephesians chapter six tells us to put on the whole armor, so when the Day of Evil comes we will be able to stand our ground. Scholars argue whether there is a specific Day of Evil coming."

"I read you that part before," Reece said to us.

"Of *course* there is a Day of Evil," Dr. Eloise said with cheery gruesomeness. "The last days are coming with untold global chaos, the likes of which never have been seen. Whether this verse refers to that time toward the end is not known. But…" her finger drilled up into the air, "the discovery of the armor at this point in time could be verrrrry significant. A signal. An omen!"

Dr. Dale calmly said, "Keep in mind, children, *always* keep in mind that this armor is *not* a magic thing that has touched a dead holy man's big hairy toe bone and has special powers, or some ridiculous thing. We are not talking about sorcery! Are we clear on that?" he asked sternly.

"We're clear," I spoke for all of us.

"The power is in the message, not the metal," I said.

The doctors beamed. "Well put, Elijah. Well put!"

"Reece said it first," I confessed.

"Look at what bright children we have here!" Dr. Eloise said.

Dr. Dale folded the belt carefully. "Press on, kids, press on."

I was glad the parents were talking in the other room. What I mean is, talking with Dr. Dale was cool. But his wife—with her Eskimo boots and business suit, grinning and drilling the air with her finger of doom—well, call me nuts, but I had flashes of Hansel and Gretel's run-in with the witch—all sweetness and candy while she's firing up the stove.

· · · · ·

While the moms wrapped their leftovers to take home, Dr. Eloise said to Aunt Grace, "We'll be in contact in the case of international travel. All of you," she raised her voice so the dads standing by the fire could hear, "please know that you are welcome to come along. The children are invited to Chicago anytime, to visit the archives!"

"Can we keep the piece of blanket?" Robbie asked. "I'm thinking it could be evidence to a crime."

We filled them in on the latest about the Dowland mystery. They were "appalled" and "intrigued."

"The police might need to see the belt too," I said. "I had to tell them we were digging for treasure."

They didn't like the idea, but they didn't give us any flak.

I called Reece in by the Christmas tree. "Hey, what did your mom tell my parents—about warfare?"

"I don't know, but here. I have something for you." She gave me a narrow box.

"Wait, let me get your present too." I ran up to my room and grabbed her gift, nearly breaking my neck on the way down the stairs. I was glad I'd gone to the trouble to buy her something.

I opened the gift from Reece. My chin dropped. "Wow, Reece, wow! Where'd you get this?"

"Do you know what it is?" she asked.

"Sure I know! It's an Indian eagle-bone whistle! With real feathers and leather and everything. This is so cool."

"Actually they're made from turkey bones now," she said sheepishly. "Eagle bones can't be used, since some eagles are endangered. It's just a replica, but it really works. Do you know what it's used for?"

"Indians use it in powwows."

She nodded. "To call the Great Spirit. When I thought about getting it for you, I wondered if it was a proper thing for playing music to God. I never heard it used in church, but I thought about it and realized that any kind of music is okay if your heart's right. It's okay not to like pipe organs."

I lifted it from its case, wrapped my fingers around it, and blew. It squeaked and hissed. But after a few tries at putting my fingers in different places, a clear sound pierced the air. Mom peeked into the room to see what the noise was.

"It's an Indian whistle, Mom. From Reece. Isn't it the coolest?"

"It's very nice." She smiled and disappeared.

"It's great," I said, quiet and reverent. "It's the best gift."

I don't mind saying Reece was crazy about the cross necklace. She said it was just what she wanted.

CHAPTER 23

Reece and I sat in the back seat of her mom's car with the belt of truth wrapped in cloth and the piece of blanket in a sack. After the Stallards left, we'd decided it all had to be turned over to the police as soon as possible. The compass was still missing. Robbie swore I put it in my pocket after the dinner at Mei's. I had a vague memory of doing that, and of having it while I worked on the map, but I couldn't find it. Officer Taylor hadn't called for it, but Reece wanted me to tell him anyway. To help me out, Mei made a sketch from memory.

"What do they do with evidence?" Reece asked her mom as we rode along.

"They study it, I suppose, and keep it until a case is solved."

"What if it's never solved?"

Mrs. Elliston was quiet a long time.

Reece asked again, "What if a case is never solved, Mom?"

"Honey, I think they have the right to keep it in storage."

"Forever?!"

"Hold on a minute," I said, a knot in my stomach. "Can we stop the car and think this over? Officer Taylor never called us back. We already know the belt has nothing to do with Kate Dowland's death. The compass might, and the blanket, but not the belt."

Reece stared straight ahead. Her mom kept driving. I knew what the answer was. "But we can't hide the truth. I guess." I unwrapped the belt and spent the last few moments of the ride looking at it: the foreign embroidery and metal decorations, the old leather, the pounded metal buckle that spelled out *truth* in an ancient language.

"The Ancient Omen," I whispered reverently.

"The oldest truth in the universe," Reece whispered back. "The truth that will set you free."

The wonder of it washed over me like a flood. It was going to kill me to let it go.

Officer Taylor showed us to a back room. "You have something for me?"

I said, "Officer Taylor, we're still looking for the compass. We can't seem to find it."

He studied me hard for a minute.

"We won't give up though. We'll keep looking. And here's a sketch of it. But we have something else."

Reece gave him the piece of blanket, and even though cops are trained to be cool, Officer Taylor was plainly shocked. "Where did this come from?"

"It was with the first piece of armor we found, which Mr. Dowland stole from us. And, by the way," I added, "if you question him and he happens to mention some old helmet, we'd really like to know."

He called over another officer who had the same reaction and took the blanket into another room right away. *Key piece of evidence*, I thought.

Reece said, "It's a piece of baby blanket, isn't it? Robbie thought it might be from that baby who died in the well."

I could tell by his look—she'd hit the nail on the head. He nodded toward the belt. "Let's see what else you have there." We opened it up. He looked it over curiously. "Hmm."

"It was with the compass, buried on Devil's—I mean, on that hill next to the meadow. It's part of set of armor that belonged to Old Pilgrim Church," I explained. "If you don't have any use for it, we'd like to keep it. I mean, you could run tests on it for whatever you need."

"We've already received a packet of sophisticated forensic data this morning from a couple from Chicago." He chuckled and shook his head. "The lab analysis even included a chemical breakdown of the type of soil it was buried in."

Reece and I exchanged amazed looks. "The Stallards?" she asked.

"That was the name," he said. "Did you tell them of the connection between these pieces and the remains found in the well?"

"Yes, sir. Was that okay?"

"Yes." He said cautiously, "They were very eager to help us move the case forward." He studied the belt. "Odd looking thing. What do you plan to do with it?"

"Keep it forever," Reece said.

I said casually, "It's just cool. So…can we have it back?"

He hesitated before measuring his words: "Kids, I appreciate this. We need to ask a few more questions around town. I'll have to keep it until then. It's procedure."

"Then we can have it back, after the questions? We don't want the blanket or the sketch," I pleaded.

"We'll see. Thanks. You've been good citizens. Tell your folks I said so. You have a good holiday now."

He wrapped the belt and stood. "And when you find that compass, I'd like to have a look at it." Taking the belt, he went down a back hallway, and just like that it was gone.

"Reece,…" I got up and walked to the glass door, staring out at a gray day, feeling as cold and empty as I ever had in my life.

"What's wrong?" she asked.

"I never put it on. I put on the helmet and arm piece that night in Telanoo…how could I be so dumb!"

She came up beside me.

"We're back to square one," I said. "And if the mystery of the well is never solved, the belt of truth will spend the next hundred years molding in an evidence box in the back room of the Magdeline City Building."

Suddenly, I wanted to forget I'd ever seen the blasted thing. I hated wanting it so much!

"Elijah, you can't doubt yourself. You did a good thing, you told the truth. Did you see how they reacted over the blanket? It's important to the case! And about the armor—just have faith." She took hold of my arm. "Maybe, just maybe, the armor is supposed to come together all at once, just in time for the Day of Evil!"

She said it in such a sweet, singsongy voice, that the Day of Evil actually didn't sound half bad. You might even say I was halfway looking forward to the Day of Evil if it meant having the whole armor of God strapped to my body.

CHAPTER 24

On Christmas Eve we had a Camp Mudjokivi staff party at the lodge, with everyone and their families, a big fire going, and tons of food. Grandma was the life of the party. "You heard about my burp the other night? Mind if I bring it up again?" she joked. But my mind was elsewhere. I bowed out after dinner to go to my room and finish the map. I wanted to find the next piece of the armor in the worst way.

I transferred all I knew to one final map. Working out from Camp Mudj toward Telanoo, I included a rough sketch of Morgan's barn and house and the main road. It wasn't nearly as cute and colorful as Mei would do, but it was pretty accurate. I included little pictures of the important details: Old Pilgrim Church, the graveyard, the Bone Tree in Telanoo, and the ruin where the skeletons were found.

Later that night, the twins padded into my room in jammies and socks while I was finishing the compass rose.

"Whatcha doing?" Nori asked.

"Drawing a map."

They climbed up on the bed beside me. "What's it of?"

"The camp and stuff." I pointed out the special places.

"What's that for?" Nori pointed to the compass rose.

"It shows the direction to important places where I've found special things."

"What things?" Stacy asked.

"The dead people," Nori answered.

"We're not talking about that, you hear?" I scolded. "This map is for finding good things."

"Can we help you find the things?" Nori asked.

I said it was too far and too cold, and they said no it wasn't. I said yes it was and if they didn't go to bed, Christmas would never come. They said a few words in their secret language, and I said, "If it's something about me, you better not!" They giggled and left.

I practiced a tune on my Indian whistle until Mom came in to hug me good night.

· · · · ·

Somehow after Christmas I got grounded again.

Dad brought me into the living room one evening like before, except the mood wasn't mellow this time.

"There's been more trouble," he said. I waited.

"I've been told that Stan Dowland and Bruce Theobald claim you've been spreading lies about them."

"Dad, I haven't talked!" I bellowed. "Me and Robbie have been telling each other every day, 'Mum's the word, mum's the word!' Doggone, it's Justin Brill and his gang and the Romeos and the town gossips, all making trouble!"

He sat there studying his hands.

"I'm not lying, Dad," I defended. "The only one I've said anything to at all is Reece, just once in the school hallway with no one else around. And I only told her because I wanted her to go with me to Dowland's!"

He took a deep breath. "Be that as it may, your mom and I think it would be best if you stay close to home for the next little while."

It sank in quick. "You're grounding me again? But I didn't do anything!"

"Just for a short while, Elijah. And it's not a grounding."

"How long is a short while?"

"We'll have to see."

"That's not fair, Dad. If people are lying about me, why should *I* be punished?"

"It's not a punishment, son. We're acting on the advice of Officer Taylor."

It was like a punch in the stomach. "Officer Taylor?" The deck was stacking against me. My own parents conspiring with the town cop, the one who had the belt of truth with no obligation to give it back, ever. "What about Robbie and Skid? What about them?"

"It's up to their parents. But apparently Bruce Theobald saw you watching his house by yourself. Is that true?"

"Yes, it's true. I went out on my bike when I got un-grounded—one lousy time! I wanted to see if he looked like a murderer. It's the oldest trick in the book, Dad. Shifting blame, that's all they're doing."

"Apparently Mr. Theobald caught Mr. Dowland poking around his house too, and there were heated words. The police were called in. Theobald claims you and Dowland are working against him. So I don't want you going over there," his voice got firm, "or anywhere unnecessarily."

I jumped to my feet, steaming mad. "That's not fair! Grounded over Christmas break!?"

"You're not listening, Elijah. It's not a grounding. You can have friends over as long as their parents agree."

"Oh, man!" I whined. "Why can't I go to *their* houses?"

"You *can* go places, Elijah, but not alone! I'm asking you to be cautious. Use those Indian skills," he tried to smile. "Keep those eyes and ears open."

He pinched the bridge of his nose and rubbed the crease between his eyebrows. I could see what a strain my troubles had put on him. I propped myself against the wall.

"I didn't mean for any of this to happen, Dad. It was a treasure hunt, that's all."

· · · · ·

Lightning and thunder rattled the ramshackle windows of The Castle. A thunderstorm rolled through Ohio, a rare thing in the dead of winter. Robbie, Skid, and I were hanging out in the attic the night before school was to start up again. Aunt Grace and Uncle Dorian had gone to Columbus to return some Christmas gifts they didn't like; we had the place to ourselves. We were down in the kitchen getting a snack when the phone rang.

"Hello?" Robbie answered. He paused for a long minute. "Hello?" His face went slack, as his round eyes drifted to us. "They hung up."

"Probably a wrong number," I said casually, piling up Christmas leftovers.

"But they didn't ask for anyone." The three of us looked at each other.

Skid shrugged. "People do that sometimes. Change their mind, forget what they called for."

"Or they call to see who's at home," Robbie said eerily. He ran to the entry and came back in ten seconds, then to the back door. "Locked!"

We took our food to the attic and locked ourselves in. Wind whipped bare branches of a big tree against the house.

"Sounds like bony fingers tapping," Robbie said.

"You have sugar on your chin from those cookies," Skid said to distract him.

"Lay off the Bates Motel garbage," I snapped. I lobbed a croquet ball at Mrs. Bates and knocked off her bleach bottle head, which lifted the mood a little.

Robbie finished his cookies and went to the window to watch the lightning. "Guys, there's a car down there!"

Skid tried to act casual getting to the window. So did I. We crowded around the pane and looked down. A big old sedan sat half hidden behind a row of untrimmed hedges. We couldn't tell the make of it.

"Just a car," Skid said, but he kept his face pressed to the window.

I was ready to suggest that Robbie's neighbors probably were having relatives in for the holidays, when I spotted the tiny fiery tip of a cigarette through the windshield.

"See that? That cigarette?"

"Yeah," Skid said, "I see it."

"Someone's in there," I whispered, and my voice was lost in a crack of thunder.

We flipped off the light and took turns watching the car until Aunt Grace and Uncle Dorian got home at 11:00. Right before they pulled in, the car pulled out.

CHAPTER 25

As if our situation wasn't tense enough, Dad got a call from Lafe over at the Mad River Boys Ranch, putting us on alert: two of the boys, D-Day and Leon, had gone home for Christmas but had skipped out on their families. They were on the run, and they might be armed.

Joy to the world.

· · · · ·

Mom picked me up after school. She said she needed my help with errands, but really it was so she could keep an eagle eye on me. I mostly tagged along. The last stop was the dry cleaners, and she made me lock the doors while she went to get Dad's suit. She looked back to check on me before she went in, and hurried back.

We had just hauled laundry in the front door when Dad came rushing to meet us.

"Are the girls out there?"

"No," Mom said.

"They didn't run out to meet you?" He looked panicked, but said evenly, "I told them to stay in the house. Mrs. Horstley had to leave early; I had business over at the lodge and said I'd be right back."

Mom flung his cleaned suit over the banister and looked up the steps. "They're probably hiding. Girls!" There was no answer. Then to Dad, "You were supposed to watch them!"

"Girls!" No answer. She and Dad locked eyes. A rush of horror went through me. I shot upstairs and swept the area: every nook and cranny of my room, the linen closet, even under the bathroom sink. (The twins are like mice. They can squeeze into places you wouldn't believe.) "Nori! Stacy! Come out. You're worrying Mom and Dad."

Mom and Dad were yelling at each other, searching and calling. I was scared. "Stacy, don't let Nori get you in trouble again," I announced. "Come out now. You're going to get it! Both of you!"

I ran back down to the kitchen. Mom and Dad had scoured the main floor, but I searched it again.

"Where could they be?" Mom asked.

"It was only ten minutes!" Dad defended. "Twenty at the most. They know to stay—" His eyes fell on a piece of paper by the phone. He snatched it up. His face went white. "It's a note from Nori. It says: 'A man called.'"

"Oh no," I muttered. They shot looks at me.

"Elijah...what is it? What have you done?!" Mom accused.

"Not me! I didn't do anything! But...the other night at Robbie's someone called and hung up, and then there was someone watching the house from a parked car."

"Call the police," Mom told Dad in a flat voice. He grabbed the phone.

I pictured my room again. Something hadn't been right. "Dad, wait a minute. Don't call yet."

I dashed upstairs. Okay...everything seemed in place—my books, a pile of clothes. What had I been doing last? The map! It was gone. Suddenly I had an inkling of what may have happened to it...and maybe to the broken compass too.

I ran downstairs. "They have my map and the broken compass we've been looking for all this time."

"What do you mean?" Dad cried.

"I made a map of places connected to the armor, and they were asking me about it. Maybe they're just out looking for treasure. Maybe nobody got them after all."

Mom clutched her face in worry. "I still think we should call the police."

"Let me go look," I said.

"You're not going anywhere!" she shot back.

"Mom, if they went into Telanoo with that broken compass, they'll get lost. They don't even know how to use a compass!"

"I'll go," Dad said, grabbing his coat.

Mom looked out the window, worried. "It's freezing out there, Russ! It's already dark!"

"Let me go," I kept on. "I know the trails. I know Telanoo. My hearing's great. I'm fast. I have my new flashlight."

Mom calmed a little and said, "I'm calling the police just for good measure. Because if they're not treasure hunting, where else could they be?"

I hated to bring it up but, "Um…well, when the Mad River Boys were here, they did ask questions about the cabins, like who lived there and what was fun to do in town. And they asked if I had sisters."

Mom gasped, and started punching numbers.

Dad said, "I'll check the buildings, Elijah, you take to the trails. If you see anything suspicious—"

"Check the remains of the old church first," I told him. "It was marked on the map. I can take the far cabins on my way into the woods."

I took off on foot down to the lake, knowing I'd make better time without the golf cart. The flashlight's long beam bounced ahead of me on the trail. I stopped and yelled into the wintry dark. "Nori! Stacy!" I listened for a response, but nothing came. I covered more ground, my feet pounding paved road.

There were enough dangers for little kids: the lake, the lagoon, cliffs. What was worse, the most dangerous spots were the very ones I had *X*ed on the map: the burned out hole that used to be Old Pilgrim Church, the sheer drop-offs of Devil's Cranium…and the deadly well. *That's too far into Telanoo. They'd never try it. Even if they went in, they'd never find it.* My eyes watered from the cold.

The well was the least of my worries.

I thought back to Theobald and Dowland. They hated my guts after the mess I'd stirred up around town. Somebody had watched The Castle. Somebody had called my house.

The Tree House Village cabins didn't have locks yet, so I peeked in each one, adjusting my eyes to less and less light. "You in there?" I called again, pausing to listen. "You're in big trouble!"

After that sweep, I zipped between the back cabins. A flicker of light caught the corner of my eye. I skidded to a stop, took a step back into darkness. All my senses went on alert. Was it a reflection of a security light in the window? Or was someone in there, smoking a cigarette?

Running for my life seemed like an excellent idea…but what if the twins were in there? *What if some scumbag has my sisters?*

I dropped down below the window and listened for talking or crying. Nothing but quiet clicking high above my head: frozen tree branches tapping in the wind. Creeping to the door, I tried the doorknob ever so slow and quiet. It was locked. But someone was in there; I felt him. I crept around to the other side of the cabin. Sure enough, a screen had been slit.

Go for a surprise attack, I told myself. Bracing myself to kick the door in, I reared back and put all my force behind my foot.

Slam! It hurt like the dickens, pain reverberating up my leg, but the door didn't budge. I tried again. *Slam!* And again.

"Okay! Okay!" came an angry voice.

The lock clicked, the door opened. I flashed my narrow beam into the disgruntled faces of D-Day and Leon.

"Are my little sisters in there!?" I raged at them.

They looked a little dazed, but not the least bit guilty at getting caught breaking and entering. "You got *sisters*?" D-Day asked innocently.

"Yeah! Are they in there?" The Boys were bigger than me, but I was hot and angry. I pushed past them and scanned the room with my light. "Okay, where are they?"

The guys were stiff as boards, shivering against the cold in thin coats. "We're just hangin', man. We ain't seen nobody."

"Well, my little sisters are lost somewhere and I have to find them…and…and…you're going with me! You've got to get some blood pumping. You want to die of hypothermia?"

They just stood there.

"Let's get moving," I barked. "When we find them, I'll take you back and we'll get warm, but not before. We're in lockdown at Camp Mudj until my sisters are found. So you can stand here and freeze, or help me."

They took off with me, slow and grumbling at first, until Leon mentioned that he had a little sister and he didn't get to see her a whole lot.

We were deep into Owl Woods with no sign of the twins, when I ordered, "We have to split up. Here, you take the flashlight. Circle around. When you get to the creek, follow it back to camp." I handed it over.

"You're going back and leaving us out here!" D-Day asked in a hostile voice.

"I'm going northeast, in there." I pointed into a dark gully that disappeared in the shadows.

His wide eyes peered into Telanoo in disbelief. "You're lying!" he said suspiciously. "You're not going in there!"

"It's okay, I can see in the dark."

"You're lying."

"I'm not. I don't lie...anymore."

He shrugged. "Way cool, man. What's up with the night vision?"

"The Indian ways," I explained. "And that flashlight was a Christmas gift from my sisters. It has two beams and a clip. Help me find them and you can have it. I mean that. But try to run off and steal it and...all I can say is, I'm working on a case with the police right now, so they know my name, and I'll have them on you like ugly on an ape. You wouldn't want jail time over a lousy flashlight."

The skinnier one, Leon, was so cold he was having trouble breathing. I took off my coat and gave it to him. "Keep moving, you hear? My sisters may be out there and I don't want them freezing."

I was ready to send them into the night, with promises of hot food and a warning about the drop-off cliffs, when I thought about Theobald. "And by the way, there's a big man, a bulldozer operator with short brown hair and a grizzly beard who might be after me. The case I'm working on involved two people he may have killed, so he could be dangerous. Oh, and there's an old guy, skinny and whacko, who's also after me. I killed his dog. If you see anyone like that, run for your life and start screaming. Got it?"

They gaped at me.

Figuring I'd better sweeten the pot all I could, I said, "And one more thing: when we find my sisters, I'll let you both drive the golf cart. Deal?"

They perked up. "Deal."

For being penny-ante criminals themselves, they weren't all that brave, at least not when it counted.

CHAPTER 26

Running through Telanoo with little more than starlight and a dusting of snow in the creek beds to light the way, I kept telling myself that the ruin and its deadly well were beyond the twins' reach. Then I remembered the straight line I'd drawn from camp, over the Morgan farm to the ruin, as the crow flies. That way would make sense to little kids who knew nothing about trespassing or Black Angus bulls. And if they should be smart enough to compare the compass rose on the map with the broken compass—its arrow glued to east-northeast—it would take them right through the Morgan farm.

Maybe an hour had passed since they'd left. It was fully dark. Pausing to catch my breath—regretting the loss of my coat—I doubled back, then switched directions to due east. I reached the Morgan fence, and I leaped it like I had wings.

Sailing across the smooth, frozen meadows of Morgan's farm, my lungs screamed from the cold air pumping through them.

Lost things floated through my mind: helmet, arm piece, belt, compass, little sisters...and all that Dowland had lost: church, daughter, grandchild, wife, everything. I thought of Magdeline losing a nice homey church because of lies and secrets.

I stopped in the middle of Morgan's pasture, wondering where his herd was. "Noriiiiiiiii! Stacyyyyy!" My voice disappeared into the brittle air. I listened for the dread sound of thundering hooves. My eyes blurred from the stinging wind, my heart pounded like a drum in my chest. The ridge was long, sweeping down in front of me toward a wooded gully. Would they have come this way, in the dark? I spun three-sixty, then spun again. *Which way, which way would cold, lost little girls go?*

Maybe they'd already wandered back, or Mom and Dad had found them poking around the old church. Maybe I was killing myself for nothing. And maybe I'd made a huge mistake, sending Leon and D-Day to look for my sisters. I'd gone with my gut, feeling like there was still some good in them.

The twins would want to go home. But home was hidden by the ridge.

If I were a kidnapper out for vengeance, if I'd lost everyone I loved and wanted someone else to pay the same horrible price, where would I go? Not the well. Too far.

Where would the police look first? Somewhere closer…

In the distance was a thin horizon of lights—Magdeline still lit up from Christmas. And between me and Magdeline…of course! If I were cold and tired and lost, I'd find a warm place, with warm, dry hay, like the stable in the Christmas story.

Morgan's barn.

I ignored the numbness in my face and limbs and the stitch in my side. Smelling cows and hay as I reached the barn, I cracked open the big door. I listened first, slipped into the blackness and stood with my back against the door. Cows breathed, their big hooves crunching frozen stall muck.

If they're not here, if they're not home, then they're not still wandering Telanoo, I thought with a sick feeling. *Too much time has passed. They've fallen asleep and frozen to death. Or someone has dragged them off, and I'll never see their little matching faces again.*

I didn't want to know the truth.

It took every effort against those feelings of doom to call out, "Nori? Stacy? Are you in here? It's me, Elijah."

Cows chewed and stomped.

"You're in big trouble," I wheezed, my eyes stinging with tears. "Don't hide. I mean it."

A scared little voice called. "'Lijah?"

"Nori?"

"Where are you?" she asked.

"I'm over here. I'll step into the doorway so you can see me. There. Can you see me?"

"Yeah."

"Is Stacy with you?"

"She's asleep."

I followed her voice. "Wake her up, Nori. Don't let her sleep!"

"We got lost," came her voice from a pile of scattered hay bales. A little head appeared.

"Stacy, wake up! Where are you?" I called.

Nori reached out her hand to me. "The compass didn't work."

"Where's Stacy?!" I knelt in the hay beside Nori, frantically feeling for a face or hand.

"Over there. She was too tired."

"Over where?!"

Desperately I felt my way through the bales until my hand found tiny, ice cold fingers, limp on the hay. I scooped her up in my arms. My heart fell. "Oh no…Stacy!"

All the ornery things I'd ever thought about my kid sisters came back in a rush. "Come on, wake up, Stace," I choked. I felt so sad and scared and guilty all at the same time, I could hardly breathe. "Gotta go…home…. Mom and Dad are waiting—"

Then she moved. Her little head turned. "Cold."

My heart leaped. I hugged her big time. "Cold, yeah. I know. Time to go home and get warm."

"'Kay," came the tiny voice.

I got them to Morgan's house and called Mom and Dad. They drove over, and cried and scolded and cried some more.

We were all safe and cozy around the kitchen table when I remembered the Mad River Boys.

"Dad! I found D-Day and Leon! I sent them into Owl Woods to find the girls an hour ago. They should have made it back by now!"

Mom yelled, "Elijah! Have you lost all sense, sending criminals—"

Dad interrupted, "Forget it, hon. We've got to find them."

"I'll get the cart!" I headed for the door.

"Where's your coat?" Mom yelled, then to Dad, "Russ, should we let him?"

"Blankets! I'll need blankets." I flew up the stairs. "And a flashlight."

Mom made that short-circuit sound, but what else could we do? I wouldn't leave my worst enemy lost in the dead of winter in Telanoo.

. . . . . .

D-Day and Leon were wandering around off the beaten path, three-fourths frozen. You have to admire their grit; they'd thought they couldn't have a turn with the golf cart if they didn't find the twins, and they weren't giving up. No sooner had I slammed the brake than they started arguing over who'd get to drive first. Leon wouldn't fork over my coat, so I wrapped up in a blanket. Once in sight of the house, I signaled to Mom; she was watching at the window.

We stopped off at our house for hot chocolate, Mom handed out hats and gloves. Then for the next half hour, D-Day,
Leon, and I took turns zipping around the frozen lake and
through the bare woods, wrapped in blankets like squaws and
whooping it up like crazy men. Considering I was a human
icicle by then and they were AWOL ex-criminals, we had the
best time. I told them if they played it straight, maybe they
could grow up to be golf caddies for rich guys at country clubs
and drive carts all day. They tried to act like it was a stupid idea,
but they were giving it some thought. Dad called Lafe and put
in a good word for D-Day and Leon, telling how they helped
in the search. I put a good word in too. We made them sound
like heroes. Sitting around in my living room, they acted nice.
D-Day even told the twins that running off wasn't a good idea.
I let them keep my flashlight like I promised.

CHAPTER 27

When I came down for breakfast the next morning, Mom and Dad were frozen in front of the TV. A reporter was standing beside Dowland's house. A Newpoint cop said Dowland had been dead a few days when his body was discovered.

I dropped down on the couch in shock. "What else? What else can happen?" I asked myself.

The reporter said that new evidence—I figured it was the scrap of baby blanket—had provided another link between Dowland and the remains in the well. They showed a clip of Theobald, who had cleaned himself up for an interview. His side of the story was that Dowland had hidden his daughter Kate and the baby at that old house in the meadow. Theobald said he found out about it—though he didn't say how—and went to see her one night. He'd found the place abandoned. When Dowland claimed he didn't know where they were, Bruce Theobald said he gave up and went on with his life.

· · · · ·

Call me nuts, but I wasn't relieved Dowland was gone. All through classes at school, I kept thinking how he'd broken ties with life and died alone during the holidays while the rest of the world was partying. No matter what he'd done, it was a rotten way to go. I kept waiting to feel okay with it, but that feeling never came. I called Reece after school, and we just hung on the phone without saying much. I knew she was thinking the same thing, but neither of us had the heart to mention it.

You probably know by now that in a crisis, my mind flashes ideas around like heat lightning. I'd already come up with a list of options: Dowland either had been so overcome by bad press and rotten memories that he'd killed himself, or he'd died from the stress, or he'd been done in by the armor of God. "But," I told Reece on the phone, "my mind keeps flickering back to big grizzly Bruce Theobald, standing in front of his shack, calling after me. If he'd loved Kate Dowland and her dad had put a stop to it, if he lost his girl and his child and went into a tailspin all those years ago…"

"We may never know," she said quietly.

Have the last clues to the armor of God died with Dowland too?

I tried to keep my mind on other things through the cold days of January, but from the way Mom and Dad talked (sometimes I listened in from the heat vent in the twins' room), they were worrying along the same lines. I wanted to know what the Romeos had to say about all this, but I no longer trusted Walter. I was starting to get why I'd been grounded twice, and why Dad had been so strict with me. This wasn't just the usual parental worry, like when they tell you that any old thing could put an eye out and that all the fun things to do in the world are death traps. They were thinking someone actually might come after me.

When Mom went on errands, she'd leave the twins with Mrs. Horstley at the camp office, and I'd have to go with her. Grandma called and asked if Mom wanted me to come down and stay with her awhile. But Mom said no.

· · · · ·

That next Saturday Officer Taylor called us in. The five of us kids went together. On the way I said to Reece, "I have a question."

"Fire away."

"Why didn't God help Mr. Dowland?"

If looks could kill, I'd have been dead meat. "You have *got* to be kidding!"

I shrunk like a turtle. "I'm just asking, since you're the expert."

"One minute I think you're getting it, then you relapse." I shrugged. I was clueless.

Then she sighed, laid her head on my shoulder, and whispered, "The truth will set you free."

I was still clueless, but suddenly I wasn't minding so much.

· · · · ·

Once at the police station, Officer Taylor came out to the front desk with a sheet of paper in his hand. He thanked us all for our cooperation. "I know this has been rough on you. The blanket you brought in corroborated a journal we found in Mr. Dowland's effects."

"A journal?" I asked.

He nodded. "The blanket gave us a piece of solid evidence. This case could have gone unsolved for months, or years. The cities of Magdeline and Newpoint thank you."

He shook our hands. Mei bowed. Reece and Robbie beamed. Skid nodded coolly, and I did the same. I gave him the broken compass, in case he needed it. "That journal…could we maybe look at it sometime?"

Officer Taylor said, "Well, this won't be in the papers, but you might want to see it. It's an excerpt."

We gathered around an old notebook filled with yellowed paper:

May 10—I confronted Bruce. He denies any knowledge. I think he's lying. There were tire tracks. His? He's taken them somewhere. Kate and Adam, where are you?

May 11—They're still missing. I called Francine. She knows nothing, is worried. Bruce calls me a liar! He accuses me of sending her away, but I think he's hiding something. I'll wait at the house tonight. Where are they??

Nothing was written for the next few days. On the next page was a sad poem. Reece read it out loud:

May 14—I called their names. I called and searched.
The late sun was blood red; I never, ever thought them dead.
But just beyond the fence, a thing beyond all common sense.
A shred of cloth, caught on a bushy thorn
From little Adam's blanket torn.
And from that spot my early shadow fell
Across the open well.
The line is ended, a loss beyond all loss,
Too great a cost, too great a cost.

Reece looked up. Our eyes locked.

I quoted that line from Dowland's story: "'…a thing that can't be explained by common sense, a thing no family should ever have to go through.'"

Officer Taylor said, "That piece of blanket was key evidence. Thank you for assisting in the investigation."

I handed over the broken compass. "No prob. So, uh… about the belt?"

Officer Taylor gave me a thin smile. "Not yet, I'm afraid. We have to officially close the case, which won't happen until we have gone through all of Mr. Dowland's effects. It may take a few weeks, depending on the case load."

"Sure," I said, "okay. But you could do us a huge favor, if you would, Officer?"

"What would that be?"

"While you're rummaging through his house, if you find anything about armor or things that look like armor, or any paper that mentions armor..."

He laughed. "I get your point. Right now, we're trying to find any remaining family members to settle the estate, but if anything turns up, I suppose there's no reason you can't have a look at it. I'll notify the detective."

"And that journal?" I asked. "We'll see."

. . . . .

Things around Camp Mudj settled back to semi-normal. As for the phone call that came to the house, we never found out who it was. It could have been Theobald; I hadn't let him off the hook yet. But a few days later an aluminum siding salesman called around dinnertime. Mom and Dad were relieved.

The man in the car turned out to be a neighbor, bored with his family, who'd gone out to listen to a game on the radio. On any other night, Skid and Robbie and I probably would have thought nothing of it. But with the storm, and Mrs. Bates sitting there gaping at us, and the Day of Evil supposedly looming ahead, we had every right to expect trouble.

Gossip about the case gradually lost steam. One dramatic newswriter summed up Dowland's tale of woe: "Mad with grief, but unable to retrieve the bodies without exposing his dark secret, Dowland may have covered the well, and simply left them there to be claimed by the earth and the elements. In a journal, he blamed the church for its shallowness, the elder Theobald for his greed, the younger Theobald for unbridled lust, the town for its blind eye. He cursed himself for the lie he'd concocted to cover up the scandal."

The paper said Stan Dowland died of an overdose of heart medication.

Mom read it and cried and hugged me and called me a hero for bringing this sad story to light at such risk. "Finally," she dabbed her eyes, "they can rest in peace."

The hairs on my neck stood up. *Piece by piece they will rest in peace.*

CHAPTER 28

The next day, Reece pressed a note into my hand and told me to read it when I was alone. That night in my room, I plopped down on my bed, faceup, unfolded the note, and read:

Dear Elijah,

I asked my mom about what she said about the warfare. She told them about Ephesians 6, like I did with you. She explained that it's not regular war, but supernatural. That it's usually safe, and anyone can do it, even a kid, if he has all the armor.

I know you've been wondering what I whispered to Dr. Dale that night at your house. I'm too shy to tell you in person. Imagine that coming from me—Miss Sarcasm! Well, here it is: I told him that I had prayed for you, starting a couple of years ago. First I just prayed that you'd come to know God better, to grow in spirit and in power, more than anyone else in Magdeline. But soon I knew that my prayer was too small. So I prayed that you'd know him better than anyone in Ohio. Then, I thought, why not the whole country? Or even the whole world?

So that's it. I think God is answering my prayer and something big is coming. I feel it, Elijah. Maybe he had you in mind for his big plan from the start, and I just saw it. If I have brought trouble on you, I'm sorry. Life may not be so easy for you in Magdeline anymore. Whatever happens with the armor, I'm proud to be a part of it.

Your Friend,
Reece

P.S. I'm sorry you got into trouble with your parents, but just think: while you were grounded, you got to talk to the police and solve a mystery, build a mini Magdeline, have breakfast at Florence's (ha), have big, important meetings with important people like the Stallards and the Skidmores, have Christmas with your friends, go on a kayak trip, have a powwow, rescue your sisters, and locate two escaped fugitives. The truth did set you free. Not too shabby!

P.S. again. The next piece is the breastplate of righteousness. So where is it? Huh? Let's get cracking!

She signed off with a smiley face.

I read her note a couple more times, then stashed it in my secret place that the twins don't know about: behind the Indian blanket on my wall. I got the idea from an old movie where they had a safe hidden behind a painting.

I hugged my sisters more, and listened more closely to their secret language, deciding that *lingle* had something to do with getting robbed. I sure didn't want them to lingle any notes from Reece. No way.

Reverently, I took the eagle-bone whistle out of the box and turned it over in my hand, thinking back to what the Stallards had said about fellowship with God being like gold.

I threw on my coat and told Mom I'd be right back. I ran to Great Oak and beyond to The Cedars where my vision quest had taken place weeks ago. I was all set to blow the whistle when I realized a cool thing. The last time I'd been here, just me and my fire and the starry sky, I didn't have to call him. He called me.

"I guess you're already here." I felt dumb saying it out loud, but I said it anyway.

The usual summer noises of crickets and campfire songs weren't there to ward off the lonely silence of Owl Woods. But something clicked, and not just frozen twigs bumping together above my head. What Reece said in her letter about my grounding made all kinds of sense. I was more free when I was grounded than when I was un-grounded. Mom had called me a man for the first time. Dad was proud of me. The police trusted me, and the Stallards were going to follow my lead about the armor of God.

All of a sudden the past few months went rushing by: from a treasure hunt exploding into a small town mystery to…to I didn't know what. A grand plan maybe.

So the truth does set you free. It can be a bumpy ride though. Maybe that's the two-sided meaning of *omen*: sometimes the truth is scary.

There even seemed to be a lesson in the broken compass: following lies will get you nowhere. I felt wise knowing that. So, was I to be the next hotshot in the archaeology world or in the crime-solving world? Since Reece had been saying big prayers for me for a long time, it was as much about her as me.

I stood there in the cold and dark with my eagle-bone whistle, just being quiet.

"You're here?" I asked, and took the wide silence to mean yes.

I looked at the whistle in my hand: "So I don't really need this?" I felt a little guilty, for Reece's sake. "Well," I said, "she gave it to me and I like it a lot. So…here's a song I've been working on, in case you want to listen."

I raised the whistle, put it to my mouth and played a melody. It was only a few notes up and down, which I repeated over and over, but I liked it. I played on, clear and high and lonely until my throat tightened up. I had to stop to breathe and work out the lump in my chest.

"That's it," I said when I finished. "Probably not the best thing you've had played for you."

I headed back. My house came into view, and as I ran, it seemed to move toward me through the trees—big and cozy, outlined against the black sky, with little squares of gold light from the windows calling me home. I felt like the luckiest person alive.

"Hey, I'm going to need your help finding the next armor piece," I said, as if he were a friend right by my side. "I have no idea where to start."

I stopped and listened. A word came into my head, deep and quiet and strong.

Signs.

"Signs?" I asked.

The word came again. *Signs.*

ANCIENT TRUTH

(page 71) "Therefore put on the full armor of God, so that when the day of evil comes, you may be able to stand your ground, and after you have done everything, to stand. Stand firm then, with the belt of truth buckled around your waist, with the breastplate of righteousness in place, and with your feet fitted with the readiness that comes from the gospel of peace. In addition to all this, take up the shield of faith, with which you can extinguish all the flaming arrows of the evil one. Take the helmet of salvation and the sword of the Spirit, which is the word of God."

Ephesians 6:13-17

(p 72) "James, Peter and John, those reputed to be pillars, gave me and Barnabas the right hand of fellowship when they recognized the grace given to me."

Galatians 2:9

(page 93) "Simply let your 'Yes' be 'Yes,' and your 'No,' 'No', anything beyond this comes from the evil one."

Matthew 5:37

(page 140) "What do righteousness and wickedness have in common? Or what fellowship can light have with darkness?"

2 Corinthians 6:14

(page 140) "If we claim to have fellowship with him yet walk in the darkness, we lie and do not live by the truth."

1 John 1:6

(page 155) "Ask the animals, and they will teach you,
or the birds of the air, and they will tell you;
or speak to the earth, and it will teach you,
or let the fish of the sea inform you."

Job 12:7, 8

(page 163) "Put on the full armor of God so that you can take your stand against the devil's schemes."

Ephesians 6:11

(page 177) "You will know the truth, and the truth will set you free."

John 8:32

(page 194) "Be still, and know that I am God;
I will be exalted among the nations,
I will be exalted in the earth."

Psalm 46:10

(page 277) "Blessed are the pure in heart, for they will see God."

Matthew 5:8

CREEK CODE

Japanese

Daijoubu—(die-jo-boo) It's all right

Mei Aizawa—(May I-zawa)

Sugoi—(soo-goy) Wow

Taihen—(tie-hen) Terrible; very, as in terribly pretty

Baka mitai—(bah-kah-mee-tie) That seems crazy

Ganbatte—(gahm-bah-tay) Hang in there

Greek

Koinonia—fellowship

Maranatha—our Lord comes

Soterion—salvation

Aletheia—truth

Aramaic

Talitha koum—little girl, get up

Hebrew

Omen, Amen (awlef mame noon)—truth, faithfulness

ABOUT THE AUTHOR

"Go far, Go light" is Lena Wood's mission. She's an author, speaker, adventurer, mom of two, and grammy of seven. Lena's been **going far** her whole life: to Asia (seven times), South Africa, Egypt, and Ireland. She climbed Mt. Fuji, slept at Everest base camp, and recently emptied her bucket list on a 5600-mile drive across the US.

Going light means traveling light, seeking simplicity, and writing books that enlighten. And Lena uses her home, The Ridge, to host friends who share a passion for taking the light of Jesus to the uttermost.

Her *Elijah Creek & The Armor of God* series sprang from a desire to prepare kids—and adults—for the dark stuff. To that end, she became an unwitting expert on occult mysticism. She speaks on the topic around the country.

www.ingramcontent.com/pod-product-compliance
Lightning Source LLC
Chambersburg PA
CBHW051331020726
47501CB00007B/2027